A MOMENT IN TIME

Deb Stover

Zebra Books
Kensington Publishing Corp.
http://www.zebrabooks.com

ZEBRA BOOKS are published by

Kensington Publishing Corp.
850 Third Avenue
New York, NY 10022

First Printing: June, 2000
10 9 8 7 6 5 4 3 2 1

Printed in the United States of America

"SASSY, SNAPPY, SEXY . . ."

—*Romantic Times* on A WILLING SPIRIT

Praise for STOLEN WISHES:

"The remarkable Deb Stover scores another winner!"

—*Affaire de Coeur* (Five-star review)

"STOLEN WISHES is sheer pleasure with its interesting premise, engrossing twists and turns, lovable characters, and simmering passion."

—*Rendezvous*

"Deb Stover's ingenuity and cleverness soar in this heart-warming story. . . ."

—*Romantic Times* (A *Romantic Times* Top Pick)

Applause for ANOTHER DAWN:

"Clever, intelligent, intriguing and romantic."

—*Romantic Times* (A *Romantic Times* Top Pick)

"Deb Stover writes as if she has divine guidance. . . ."

—*Affaire de Coeur* (Five-star review)

"ANOTHER DAWN is gripping and wonderful!"

—JoAnn Ross, author of HOMEPLACE

Raves for SOME LIKE IT HOTTER:

"Tremendous! Five stars!"

—*Affair de Coeur* (Five-star review)

"Fun, fast-paced, sexy . . . sizzling passion . . . a terrific read."

—Kristin Hannah, author of ON MYSTIC LAKE

"Extraordinary! A haunting, heart-wrenching, utterly beautiful example of time travel at its very best!"

—Maggie Shayne, author of ETERNITY and INFINITY

"SOME LIKE IT HOTTER is everything the title promises and more."

—*Rendezvous*

Books by Deb Stover

SHADES OF ROSE
A WILLING SPIRIT
SOME LIKE IT HOTTER
ALMOST AN ANGEL
ANOTHER DAWN
STOLEN WISHES
A MATTER OF TRUST
A MOMENT IN TIME

Published by Pinnacle and Zebra Books

This book is for all the wonderful booksellers and readers who write to tell me you want more time travels. Special thanks to the subscribers of the READ list. You're the best!

As always, my eternal gratitude to the talented WYRD Sisters, who tell me when it works and when it doesn't—especially Paula Gill and Pam McCutcheon—and to my family for your patience and unwavering support.

And thanks to Tomasita Ortiz—an editor with excellent taste and an abundance of much appreciated moxie.

Chapter One

Sunlight slammed into Jackie with all the finesse of a sledgehammer. She flopped onto her back and covered her eyes. Not much help there.

Groaning, she struggled to a sitting position and stretched, gradually opening her eyes. With the sheet wrapped around her, she staggered to the window and pushed aside the tattered curtain. The dirt road and endless sea of pine trees jarred her memory.

Oh, yeah. She knew where she was. Sort of. A cultural oasis. A log cabin in the Rocky Mountains of Colorado.

"Why'd I let you talk me into this?" she muttered, glancing back at the rumpled bed.

The *empty* rumpled bed.

Her heart dropped into her stomach, then vaulted to her throat. Suspicion slithered through her as she walked to the closet and threw open the door. His clothes were gone.

"Perfect."

Then another far more disturbing realization struck and she rushed back to the window. The empty driveway confirmed her fears. "My car. He stole my *car!*"

Tears stung her eyes, and her head pounded a rhythm that would've put Phil Collins to shame. Her stomach clenched and burned, forcing bile to her throat.

As if she didn't have enough problems.

"Well, this is a high point in your life, Jackie," she said in her best imitation of Great-Aunt Pearl's voice. "After all, what did you expect from a man who calls himself Blade? How could you be so stupid?"

Looking for love in all the wrong places again?

Add one more man to the not-so-long list of those Jackie Clarke had foolishly trusted in her lifetime, starting with her father. "Nothing like family tradition."

With a sigh, she jerked on her T-shirt and jeans, then went through the only other room in the cabin and out the back door. This lovers' hideaway—sans electricity, phone, and indoor plumbing—had only the most modern conveniences.

For about a hundred years ago.

But the outhouse was the least of her problems. Being abandoned in a cabin somewhere in the Rocky Mountains was a hell of a lot more pressing than spending quality time with an outhouse.

Oh, joy.

Picking her way barefoot through the damp grass, she gave the outhouse what she hoped was her most scathing glance. Then she held her breath, ducked inside, and answered the call of nature.

This was all Blade's fault.

The cabin allegedly belonged to Blade's uncle. Somehow, she had trouble believing the con artist could possibly have any family. The place probably belonged to his last conquest.

Gullible woman number one hundred and thirty-seven.

She stepped from the outhouse and gulped fresh air.

Why'd you fall for it, Clarke?

Simple. Blade Smith had swept her off her feet. She glanced at her bare toes and wiggled them. His dark good looks, sexy voice, and artsy-fartsy way had wooed her big-time.

Let me take you away from all this, sweetcakes, he'd said. His lack of originality should've been her first warning. *I must paint you. You will be my masterpiece.* More bull.

And he'd said he loved her. And *that,* as they said, had clinched it.

She swallowed the lump in her throat and drew a steadying breath. She wouldn't cry. This wasn't the first mistake she'd ever made, and it probably wouldn't be the last. She just had to develop a tougher shell.

Blade had charmed her just when she'd needed charming most. So Jackie had left her partner in charge of their beauty shop and used her savings to fund Blade's excursion through never-never land.

"Smooth move, Tinkerbell."

With a sigh, she walked back inside and scrounged around the kitchen. At least he'd left her some groceries and the gas grill. Now if only she could figure out a way to put wheels on the thing and drive it down the mountain. She sighed. Right now she'd settle for a cup of strong coffee. A whole pot *might* help her think straight.

After her third cup, she ate a cold English muffin and went back to the bedroom to inventory her belongings. Just how much had Blade left her?

One thing was a safe bet—he'd taken all her money.

She turned her fanny pack upside down over the bed. "Yep." He even had her wallet and credit cards.

Not that they'd do him any good. A smug smile tugged at the corners of her mouth. Every single one of them was maxed out. "Thank God for small favors."

Her gaze shifted to the mirror on the wall and she groaned, lifting her trembling hand to her hair. Why had she let him talk her into dyeing her hair, too?

Red. Neon red.

For inspiration, he'd said. About the only thing it inspired in her was nausea. Until she returned to civilization and beauty supplies, she was stuck with it, and her dark roots were already showing.

Dismissing her appearance, she looked out the window again. The cloudless blue sky mocked her with the promise of a beautiful day. "Nice day for a hike." She'd have to drive back later for her clothes. Right now she needed to travel light. It was a long walk down the mountain. Still, she was healthy. No reason to think she couldn't handle a little exercise.

Damn Blade all to hell. Murderous thoughts fueled her as she stuffed a few items into her fanny pack, and realized one positive thing might come from this experience.

Her foolishness would provide Great-Aunt Pearl with enough material to razz Jackie for the rest of her life. Both their lives. And then some. After the old woman died, she'd undoubtedly return to haunt her. "Oh, now, that's just what I need."

Jackie sat on the edge of the bed, tears building in

her eyes, threatening to overflow any moment. At thirty-three, she should've known better than to let a creep like Blade take advantage of her this way. This wasn't at all like her. The old Jackie had been a dreamer.

But those dreams were dead.

"Fool." When she'd walked down the aisle so long ago, dreams had filled her young, idealistic mind. For eight years since the divorce, she'd worked. Period. No love life—nothing.

Just the kind of woman a con man would choose as a target. That made her a . . . victim. A shudder of revulsion rippled through her, barely saving her from drowning in self-pity.

"Wrong scenario, kid." She dried her eyes with the backs of her hands and stood. "Time to hit the road."

After tying her cheap hiking boots, she opened the door and stepped outside. *The great outdoors. Oh, goody.* Shading her eyes, she looked west. Dark clouds now marred the horizon beyond the next ridge.

She shrugged. *What the hell?* A little rain couldn't make her day any worse. Armed with her comb, compact, and Midol, she started along the trail.

The cabin quickly vanished behind her, swallowed by the thick forest of pine and aspen. "Stop looking behind you, stupid." She needed to concentrate on finding her way to the highway, where she knew the nearest town was to her left. At least she'd paid some attention during the drive up here.

When she hadn't been gazing into Blade's dark, deceitful eyes.

A fork in the road brought her to a standstill. She didn't remember this. Which way had they come? Both roads were equally rutted by the passage of four-wheel-drive vehicles. After a few minutes, she shook her head and chose the left fork . . . and prayed. It *looked* right.

She rubbed her upper arms, wishing for something heavier than her thin jacket, but her warmer coat and gloves were in her car. With Blade. The temperature was definitely dropping, and clouds now shrouded the area with heavy gray.

One small flake drifted languidly to the ground.

Jackie shook her head in disbelief. "No, it can't be." Resolutely, she continued along the mountain road, the plunging temperature numbing her fingers and toes. She buckled her fanny pack around her waist and tucked one hand under each armpit to warm them.

Another flake.

"No, no, *no!*"

She walked faster. The flakes were fruitful and multiplied. Now there was no denying the facts. *Snow.*

"Criminy, it's June." It was the very beginning of June, though, and snow still capped the highest peaks in the distance. She stopped to look around. The heavy clouds hung lower now, veiling the treetops.

But something else even more worrisome nagged at her. The farther she walked, the less familiar her surroundings looked. She paused.

She'd chosen the wrong fork. *Damn.*

"Decision time, Clarke." If she went much farther, she'd never be able to find her way back with the road covered in snow. Shoot, she had enough trouble finding her way to the mall.

But what if she managed to find her way back to the cabin and the snow piled up so high she couldn't leave?

Snowed in.

Without her electric blanket.

But it was June. No matter how much it snowed, it couldn't last long. And the farther down the mountain she went, the warmer it would be. Right?

As she stood in the middle of the unfamiliar road and contemplated her dilemma, the wet spring snow soaked her jacket and hair.

"Damn."

Even if this road wasn't the same one they'd driven up, it still had to lead to civilization. Eventually. Deciding not to waste precious time backtracking, she closed her eyes for a brief prayer, then reopened them and put one foot in front of the other.

Frustration permeated Jackie like lotion toner on a seek-and-destroy mission for dark roots, as she continued along the rutted mountain road. Snow quickly covered the ground, making her pray again that she'd made the right decision.

She squinted through the white stuff, straining to identify the dark silhouettes ahead. They weren't trees. Dare she hope . . . ?

She quickened her pace, falling flat on her face twice before she was able to identify the definite shapes of several structures. Calling out in the awesome silence, she hoped someone would hear and lead her to shelter.

Nothing. No sound at all came from the cluster of buildings. Whatever it was—a ranch, maybe?—no one was home. It didn't matter. She'd break in, if necessary.

Nearly numb, Jackie staggered to the nearest building and stumbled to her knees. An upward glance confirmed that she would find no shelter in this building. It had no roof.

Abandoned. Like her.

Fear sliced through her. Surely one of the buildings

was whole and safe. After struggling to her feet, she turned and stomped toward the next one. Only two walls still stood against the harsh Rocky Mountain weather.

"I don't believe this."

She was so tired, but she remembered reading something about people getting sleepy before they died from hypothermia. Well, she wasn't ready to die. Not until she made Blade pay for what he'd done.

A new surge of anger fueled her. After a few minutes, she summoned what remained of her strength and lurched toward the next building. If she died up here, she wouldn't be able to get revenge.

And her aunt would really get some mileage out of this one with her women's circle at church.

Jackie had no intention of being that generous.

Her heart raced as she studied the next structure. Hope filled her. This building had a porch, and all the walls appeared intact. She reached for the handle and jiggled it, holding her breath as the door squeaked in protest. After a good shove, it swung open and she scrambled inside. The interior was dry and warm—comparatively speaking.

After closing the door against the wind, she unbuckled her fanny pack and dropped it, then slumped to the floor to catch her breath. Her feet and hands were completely numb. The way her luck was running, she'd probably lose all her fingers and toes.

Blade would pay for each and every one.

As her breathing slowed to a more reasonable rate, she examined her surroundings. *Dusty* was a supreme understatement, but the place was totally dry. Who cared about a little dust?

She sneezed.

A bar ran the length of the room, with a tarnished

brass rail around its rim. Glasses and barrels lined the wall behind it.

A saloon. She laughed in disbelief. Just her luck to find an abandoned . . . ghost town?

She slowly rolled to one hip and rose, flexing her fingers and wiggling her toes. Maybe she didn't have frostbite after all. Everything seemed to be thawing nicely. *Like a Thanksgiving turkey.*

And she was definitely thankful, ghost town or not.

Stiff-legged, she walked toward the bar, inspecting the place. *Incredible.* Overturned tables and chairs filled the room; broken chandeliers hung from the rafters. A potbellied stove occupied one corner.

Her gaze followed the stovepipe through the wall high above. What were the chances of it being clean? She didn't want to burn down her only shelter, and the way her luck had been running . . .

A sinking sensation swept through her. It didn't matter anyway, because she had no matches. Just her luck they didn't teach fire building in beauty college.

With a sigh, she turned to look at the magnificent bar. Where were Little Joe, Hoss, and Adam? Better still, a bartender like Sam Malone from *Cheers* waiting to serve her a shot of whiskey to warm her bones?

It struck her as odd that this one building should be in such good shape—so to speak—while the others were completely collapsing. Curious, she walked behind the bar and looked at the shelves beneath it.

A book grabbed her attention. She pulled it out and set it on the bar, pluming dust into her face. Coughing and waving her hand to clear the air, she flipped open the black leather cover.

It was a script called *The Legend of Devil's Gulch.* That explained a few things. Obviously a movie crew had used the saloon. They must've done a little restoration on the place.

She looked upward at the roof. *Thank God.*

Wondering what other useful items might have been left behind, Jackie searched through the shelves and produced a bottle of whiskey. A sealed bottle of whiskey.

"This is progress." She placed the bottle on the bar and continued her search. Now if only she could find a can of soup, or anything else nonperishable and edible.

After completing her unsuccessful search of the bar, she turned around. A portrait on the wall seized her attention. Tentatively, she reached up and wiped a layer of dirt away with her bare hand.

"Nude, of course. I should've known." She shook her head and sighed. "Men are pigs. Sheesh."

As she studied the painting, heat bloomed in her face. Blade had painted Jackie in the nude. What was he doing with that painting now? Who was he showing it to?

"Damn." It didn't matter. Right now only survival mattered. But what if he tried to blackmail Aunt Pearl with it? Jackie covered her face for a second and groaned.

She couldn't help wondering if the woman in the portrait had been foolish about men, too. She studied the woman's face. Her eyes appeared intelligent, and a smug smile tilted the corners of her red lips.

No, *foolish* definitely wasn't the word to describe this woman. In fact, she exuded self-assurance. "I'll bet you had men falling at your feet. Bet you kicked them in the balls when they got out of line, too."

The woman's hair was as red as Jackie's, certainly

not natural. Henna, probably. Though beautiful, she was fat by today's standards. Rubenesque.

And except for a feather boa draped across her breasts and pelvic area, the woman was as naked as Jackie had been while modeling for Blade. "Who talked you out of your clothes, lady? One of Blade's ancestors, no doubt."

Buxom didn't begin to describe the woman's bustline. Jackie looked at her own medium-size assets beneath her damp, clinging T-shirt. Blade hadn't seemed to mind.

He'd said he loved her. Asked her to marry him. Wanted her to have his babies. Her eyes burned and she blinked rapidly. *No tears, Clarke. No tears.*

"To *hell* with Blade."

She looked up at the woman in the portrait again. A strange but powerful sense of déjà vu suddenly swept through her. She couldn't shake it.

A gold plate on the frame drew her gaze. She rubbed her thumb across it until the words became legible through the grime: *Lolita Belle, 1891.*

"Yeah, right." She snickered and shook her head. Lolita Belle had obviously been a stage name. Jackie looked up at the woman's face again, wondering exactly what type of performances had been her specialty.

"Lolita, were you a . . . lady of the evening?" Jackie waggled her eyebrows suggestively. "Aunt Pearl would've been in her element trying to convince you to mend your wicked ways." She laughed at her own foolishness.

"Instead, she just had pitiful me to work on." She sighed and turned away from the portrait. Standing around talking to an antique painting wasn't doing her a bit of good.

A particularly fierce blast of wind rattled the shutters, prompting Jackie to go to the window and peer through the louvered slats. The wind whipped the snow around in a furious pattern. She couldn't even see beyond the porch.

"Oh, boy. What am I going to do up here with no food?"

Shivering, she moved away from the window. "And no heat?" She could go longer without food than she could without heat. Water would be no problem with all the snow outside, but how would she melt it?

"I can't win for losing."

Her stomach rumbled, reminding her she hadn't eaten anything since her cold breakfast. At least it was dry inside, though definitely not warm. In fact, the temperature was dropping steadily. When night came she'd freeze.

Tears pricked her eyes, but she blinked them into submission. She couldn't—*wouldn't*—allow Blade to get away with this.

When she turned toward the back of the room, hope spiraled through her. Hidden in the shadows, an archway opened to another room at the back. To the right, a winding staircase led to the second floor.

"You dummy," she muttered.

With any luck, the back room might be a kitchen. What treasures besides the whiskey had the movie crew left behind? Food? Heat?

She quickened her pace to match her pulse, walking through a cobweb stretched across the doorway. "Yuck." Peeling the sticky threads away from her hair, she stepped into the room.

A kitchen. On a table in the center of the room sat a cardboard box. She rushed over and looked inside. A half dozen cans with pop-tops greeted her. Retrieving one, she read the label.

"Vienna sausages." She hadn't eaten anything that heavily laced with cholesterol in over a decade, but right now she didn't care. A slightly shortened life-span was better than a severely shortened one. Besides, she had to stay alive long enough to exact vengeance.

She examined the cans closely. One of them was badly dented, so she set it aside, not wanting to tempt fate *that* much. There were no expiration dates on the labels, so she'd have to trust her eyes and sense of smell to steer her clear of food poisoning.

"Oh, gee, that gives me a not-so-warm fuzzy." Grimacing, she popped up the metal ring on one can and peeled back the lid. When she looked inside, all she saw were Vienna sausages, nothing furry. She took a tentative sniff and sighed in relief. Carefully, she pulled a sausage from the can and turned it over several times. She could either die of food poisoning or starvation.

Her stomach growled angrily.

"All right." She pulled one out and took a bite. The little fat-laden thing tasted fabulous. She finished one and dug for another. Then another.

"Don't be a pig, Clarke." She set down the can, knowing the contents wouldn't spoil, since the room temperature rivaled that of any refrigerator she'd ever owned. She placed a full can on top of the open one to protect its contents.

There, she felt stronger now. Having food in her stomach made her feel warmer, too. At least she wouldn't starve to death for a while.

She explored the rest of the ground floor, but the

steps were too rickety for her taste, so she skipped a tour of the second floor.

Angry and bored, she opened the whiskey and took a tentative sip. She swallowed and waved her hand in front of her mouth.

Unaccustomed to whiskey, she was surprised by the sudden warmth that surged through her cold body. Saint Bernards supposedly carried brandy to freezing people. Right? She furrowed her brow, trying to remember whether medical science still endorsed that practice.

Looking at the bottle's amber contents and black label, she shrugged. "What the hell?" It made her *feel* warmer. She took another drink. It went down much smoother this time. In fact, it wasn't half bad.

Bottle clutched in her hand, she turned to look at Lolita again. "Who *were* you?" She looked at the woman's bright red hair. "Only your hairdresser knows for sure." Jackie winked and raised the bottle toward Lolita. "Here's to helping Mother Nature. I'm all for it"—she touched her own hair and grimaced—"as you can see."

She lifted the bottle to her lips again and took a mouthful, swaying to one side with the effort.

"Steady as she goes, Clarke." She raised the bottle and admired its sparkling contents through the dim light coming through the louvered shutters. Tipping the bottle again, she gulped a huge swallow, then gave a very unladylike belch. "Oops. Hic. 'Scuse me." She saluted Lolita.

"I bet you knew how to pick men." Jackie rolled her eyes, noticing the mirror off to one side for the first time. She staggered over a few steps and stared at herself.

"Yuck, Clarke." She raised her eyebrows and tilted

her head back, but the image looking back at her didn't improve. "You're a—*hic!*—mess." There were bags under her eyes, and the dark green T-shirt just wasn't her color.

Her hair looked even worse now, if that was possible. Plastered to one side of her head wasn't exactly the style she would've chosen for herself. She closed her eyes tightly, then reopened them to study her appropriately warped reflection. Her wild, shoulder-length hair was still red. Really red.

Lolita red.

Looking back at Lolita, she sighed. "I need something to do. I'll bet the newest Anne Stuart romance is out by now."

Of course, she'd thought Blade would keep her much too busy for reading. And he had . . . for a while.

"Bastard."

She placed her fanny pack and the whiskey bottle on the bar while she searched for her compact and a less warped mirror. "Aha. There you are."

Blade had practically begged her to go red, but she'd resisted for a while. Narrowing her eyes, she peered at herself in the small mirror. She should've resisted a lot harder. Furiously, she powdered her shiny nose and looked again. Nothing helped.

Red hair and Jackie Clarke just didn't complement each other. She looked back at Lolita. Adrenaline rushed through her veins as she studied the portrait. "Hey, my hair is pretty close to your shade.

"What do you think? Of course, this is only temporary. I make a foxy brunette. Could even give you a run for your money." She lifted one corner of her mouth and snarled. "Even if you did get in line twice when they were handing out boobs." She shot Lolita's feather-draped breasts a caustic look. "Make that three times."

With her bottle of whiskey in tow, she marched out to the kitchen in search of . . . something. She positioned her open compact on the table and shivered. "I'm freezing my ass off in the middle of nowhere, drinking alone, and talking to a dead woman. Aunt Pearl'd have a cow. What do you think?"

The mirror didn't answer.

"So tell me, Jackie," she said solemnly. "What is it with you and men?" Rolling her eyes, she shook her head. "Gee, I wish I knew."

Oh, maybe she did know, just a little. She wanted to love and be loved. She wanted a family like the one she would have if she hadn't miscarried. Of course, that marriage was doomed from the start, as Aunt Pearl had claimed.

Knock it off, Clarke.

Enough reminiscing—she was freezing. There had to be a way to start a fire. Surely there'd been a few smokers on the movie crew. What better place to keep matches than in the kitchen for cooking?

Several discarded boxes littered the room. She kicked them over with the toe of her boot, fearing she might disturb a hibernating rat or something. One of the boxes clattered as it fell over, making her leap back and stop breathing.

After a moment, she inched forward and nudged the box around with her toe until she could see inside. "Oh, my God," she whispered.

In the middle of several layers of crumpled newspaper was a kerosene lamp, a box of matches, and a bottle of kerosene. *Let there be light.* Her luck was definitely improving.

She retrieved the contents of the box and placed

the objects on the table. Carefully, she removed the top of the lamp and filled the reservoir with oil. After replacing the top, she turned up the wick and fished a match out of the box.

Then she remembered how much warmer it was in the other room. She went back, placed her newfound treasures on the bar in front of Lolita, and lit the lamp.

After a moment, a nice golden glow surrounded her. Now all she needed was some heat and a miracle. There was enough broken furniture in here to make a nice fire.

She gulped. What if she burned the place down? "Oh, hell, Clarke." Chewing her lower lip, she gathered a few of the smaller pieces of wood and stuffed them into the stove. Then she tore the last few pages out of the script and crumpled them, placing the paper beneath the wood.

Muttering a prayer, she struck a match and tossed it in, watching eagerly as the greedy flames devoured the paper, then went after the dry wood. She studied the stovepipe. *So far, so good.*

She shot Lolita a questioning glance. "Well, what do you think? I could've been an Eagle Scout. So now what am I supposed to do with myself?"

It was getting dark outside. Hoping the darkness simply meant dusk instead of more snow, Jackie went to the shutters and peered outside. The snow had stopped and patches of sky showed through the clouds, but she wouldn't be going anywhere in the dark. The sun slowly disappeared behind the highest mountain peak, bathing the small valley in shadow.

A dark shape ran by, contrasting against the snow. Was it a deer? She wiped the glass and looked, but whatever it was had disappeared around the side of the building.

It grew darker by the second, and Jackie shivered from more than merely cold. She was alone in the mountains, stranded.

"Thank goodness I found the lamp." She turned around and noticed the script she'd left on the bar. With a shrug, she dragged a battered chair to the stove and wiped some of the dust from the seat. "Please don't let it be a horror story." Her imagination was fertile enough without feeding it any Stephen King-like fodder.

It promised to be a long, cold night. After placing a few more splintered pieces of furniture on the fire, she settled into the chair with the script in her lap, scooting the lamp closer.

Cast of characters, she read. "Lolita Belle? Hmm. So somebody wrote the bimbo's life story." Relishing the fire's radiant heat, she allowed herself to be sucked into the story. It was an old-fashioned romantic adventure, but when she reached the end she groaned.

She'd used the last few pages to light the fire. Now she would never learn what happened to Lolita Belle. "Shoot."

An odd, crackling sound came from overhead. Frowning, Jackie looked up at the ceiling, bewildered at first by the bright orange fingers spreading across the cracked surface.

Reality finally registered and she dropped the script, jumping to her feet so fast the chair crashed to the floor. The building was on fire. She had to get out fast. The crackling became a roar as the greedy flames lapped at the old structure. She was surrounded.

Jackie dropped to her knees—the heat became

unbearable. Coughing, she crawled toward the bar, remembering a window along that wall. Her skin stung from the intense heat, and her throat burned. Tears streamed down her face as the same prayer played through her head again and again.

God, help me. Please help me. All she'd wanted was some heat and a miracle.

Behind the bar, the air was somewhat cooler and the smoke less suffocating. She drew several deep breaths before she rose.

Blazing timbers collapsed into the center of the room and she screamed. Regaining some control, she felt along the wall for the window she'd seen earlier. Somewhere . . .

Another crash—the building was falling down around her. She was going to burn. Freezing out in the wilderness would have been better than this.

"Where's that frigging window?" Tears and smoke blinded her as she felt along the wall, ducking lower to escape the intense heat. She felt something and straightened. A frame, but not the window.

Something large plummeted to the bar, struck her shoulder, and slammed her against the wall. Both she and Lolita slid to the floor together.

Dizziness gripped her and she held her head as she turned to look at the painting one more time. "This is it," she whispered, knowing she would die tonight. There was no escape.

The flames bathed the portrait in a red-orange glow, and Lolita's face faded before Jackie's eyes. Barely conscious, Jackie reached toward the portrait as a face reappeared.

Not Lolita's.

The face staring back from the canvas now was a

mirrored image. Dazed, Jackie touched her likeness just as something seized her. *God, help me.*

Powerful and swift, the force delivered her from the flames.

Darkness bathed her in blessed coolness. No longer frightened, Jackie closed her eyes.

And prepared to face death.

Chapter Two

Voices—loud ones—ganged up on Jackie. Then she remembered the fire! Her heart bolted and her stomach lurched upward to press against it.

I'm alive. Under the circumstances, that was a miracle in itself. Maybe the voices belonged to paramedics coming to her rescue. She struggled to open her eyes, but they declined to cooperate. Considering that the entire Sahara Desert must've filtered in beneath her lids during the night, she could understand their reluctance.

"She shore don't look like I reckoned she would," a man said.

Jackie managed to open one gritty eye, but quickly closed it to regroup. She must be dreaming. For a second, she'd thought she was at a Wild West amusement park.

But this was far from amusing.

"Scrawny thing, but who else could she be?" This time a woman's voice intruded.

I'm asleep and this is a dream. Jackie would simply ignore the voices until she could wake herself. Though that seemed her wisest course of action, wisdom and patience had never been her strengths. She couldn't resist peeking once more. Partly opening both eyes, she peered through a sticky veil of smudged mascara, confirming that she was still in the saloon.

Gray beard stubble covered the man's face; a dark stain shaded one side of his chin. *Yuck.* Why couldn't she dream about attractive men?

Yeah, like Blade? On second thought, maybe ugly was safer. Even Aunt Pearl might approve of ugly.

"Well, I reckon it must be her." The unattractive owner of the gruff voice stood less than a foot away, peering down at Jackie as if she were a side of beef.

I'm not asleep. But she had to be. *God, please let me be asleep.* Allowing her eyes a few minutes to tear and refocus, she blinked several times and forced them open completely.

"Well, it's about time," the woman said, coming closer to stare down at Jackie. "Don't just stand there—help her up, Zeb."

Grumbling, the filthy man—apparently the Zeb in question—reached down and grabbed Jackie's hand. A moment later she found herself being hauled to her feet, which seemed less than capable of supporting her weight this morning.

She wavered and the man grabbed her arm to steady her. His stench was unbelievable, and up close, his gap-toothed appearance did even less to restore her faith in a benevolent god. "Who—"

"What are you wearin'?" The woman shooed Zeb away and gripped Jackie's other arm. "You're a mess.

We'd better get you cleaned up real quick-like, before Rupert gets a look at what he paid for."

"Rupert who?" Jackie blinked again, trying to determine what sort of bizarre rescue team had found her, but after examining the woman's clothing, she realized the magnitude of her error.

The middle-aged woman wore a bright red dress adorned with gold braid at its single shoulder and at the hem. Her impressive cleavage left almost nothing to speculation, but the feathers protruding from the back of her blond hairdo had exactly the opposite effect, sending Jackie's speculative nature into warp speed. "What . . . Who . . ."

"C'mon, let's get you upstairs before Rupert gets here and sees you. We weren't expectin' you for weeks yet."

"You were expecting me?" Had Blade contacted these people? *Fat chance.* Besides, how could Blade have known Jackie'd end up here? Wherever *here* was.

The woman shook her head and clicked her tongue as if scolding a small child. "Now tell me, where in tarnation did you get them clothes? Mercy sakes alive!"

Jackie glanced down at her Levi's. "What's wrong with my clothes?" They were perfectly ordinary, though filthy, clothes, especially in comparison to the woman's Miss Kitty getup.

"Well, if you don't know, I reckon there ain't no point in discussin' it right now."

Zeb laughed along with two other men leaning against the bar. Jackie hadn't noticed them earlier, but they stared at her now with lechery written plainly across their grungy faces.

My God, I'm in hell. That fire had burned her alive—

cremated her. What else could it be? She was worm's meat, as Aunt Pearl would've said while in one of her Shakespearean moods.

"Where's your trunk, honey?" The woman's voice was somewhat reassuring, though her condescending manner did nothing to inspire Jackie's confidence.

"Is this . . . hell?"

The woman furrowed her brow and shook her head. "You must've been on one helluva drunk."

"Please answer me. Is this hell?"

"Nope, but sometimes it sure feels like it, especially Saturday night after payday."

Jackie scanned her surroundings, confirming that she was still in the saloon, though it appeared far different now than it had last night. For one thing, it was relatively clean, and there were no broken bits of furniture strewn about the room. No trace of fire damage. *Impossible.* Who'd have thought hell could be an improvement? "Weird."

"Hmm." With a sigh, the woman guided Jackie toward the stairs.

The gleaming, sturdy, totally unburned stairs.

"Holy—" Stunned, Jackie jerked herself free of the woman's grasp and backed away. This was her wake-up call—time for some answers. Hell or not, she had a right to know before she took another step. "I want to know who you are and what's going on. *Now!*"

The woman folded her arms across her middle and pursed her lips together in a thin line. "My, ain't we high and mighty?"

"No, we . . . ain't." Jackie shook her head and took another backward step, holding one hand up in front of her as if to ward off an attacker. Her arms and legs trembled and her head pounded with relentless pain. *Dead people don't feel pain, do they?*

But if she was still alive, then all this was even more inconceivable. First Blade, the freak blizzard, the fire—now this.

Whatever *this* was.

"Who are you and where am I?" she repeated.

"As if you don't know."

"I don't."

A flicker of compassion suddenly appeared in the woman's eyes, but cynicism quickly displaced it. "Whatever you say, honey. I'm Miss Dottie Elam."

Dottie, of course. She looked like a Dottie. Or maybe Mae West.

Dottie kept her gaze pinned on Jackie. "I'd be willing to bet you know where you are, but I'll tell you anyway. This here's the Gold Mine Saloon."

"Gold Mine?" *A bad joke, for sure.* Jackie dragged her fingers through her tangled hair, wincing when she caught sight of a flaming red curl dangling before her eyes. It was like something from her worst nightmare.

For a few blissful moments, she'd forgotten about her most recent act as a licensed, and somewhat misguided, beautician. "Oh, no." It was even worse—brighter—than she remembered. With both hands, she pulled several strands forward and stared. "God, it's *really* bad."

"Well, I've seen better, that's for sure. You are the strangest thing." Dottie shook her head and sighed. "Suit yourself, but considerin' what Rupert paid to bring you out here, I'd think you might want to look a little better when you meet him."

"Paid?" Jackie barked a derisive laugh and looked anxiously toward the men at the bar again. *No help there.* "Not even Donald Trump could pay me enough to make me come here on purpose."

"Huh, well, I don't know about this Donald Trump, but I reckon Rupert'll have somethin' to say about that, Miss Lolita Belle."

Jackie's mouth fell open and the skin around her lips tingled. A cold lump formed in the pit of her stomach and grew, spreading to her limbs before she managed to draw a deep enough breath to dispel the strange sensation. She remembered the face in the portrait fading, then returning as her own. An hallucination. "Lolita . . . ?"

Slowly, as if her life depended on it, Jackie turned to face the bar again. She blinked several times. Nothing but a moose head hung where Lolita's risqué portrait had been.

"Where . . . is . . . she?" Jackie walked to the bar, ignoring the rude snickers from the grimy trio. "What kind of sick game is this?" She whirled to face Dottie again, holding her hands out to her sides in a silent plea. "If you're in cahoots with Blade, I'm afraid you're too late. He cleaned me out."

Dottie threw her head back and laughed. Loud. "Blade? What kind of name is that?"

"Who *are* you?" Jackie repeated, tears stinging her gritty eyes.

The doors to the saloon swung open, and a short, stocky man strode in, a cigar clamped between his teeth. "Well, who the devil are *you*?"

Jackie met the man's critical gaze with far more bravado than she felt. Mustering what remained of her dignity—now *there* was a word—she swallowed the lump in her throat and lifted her chin a notch. For some reason, the weasely little man raised her hackles. Maybe that was what she needed—a challenge. Something to piss her off royally.

His suit—or costume—looked expensive, though severely dated, with a flashy brocade vest. A string tie adorned a white collar that appeared stiff enough to stand on its own in a hurricane.

My God, he thinks he's Maverick.

"Well," he repeated, "are you going to tell me who you are, or make me guess?"

"Guess." Jackie refused to allow her gaze to waver.

He chuckled and shook his head, shifting the unlit cigar from one corner of his mouth to the other, then back again. "Well, I'll be." His expression grew serious, and something resembling alarm registered in his small, dark eyes. "Dottie, you don't suppose . . . ?"

Miss Dottie heaved a mournful sigh, obviously playing the martyr in this piece. "Who else could she be? I'll tell you one thing for sure—she's already a lot more trouble than she's worth."

The man strolled purposefully toward Jackie, his gaze dipping to her T-shirt—no, *through* her T-shirt. His ruddy face suddenly paled, and deep wrinkles appeared on his brow, where a dark lock of silver-streaked hair fell across it like an exclamation point.

"Well, I'll be damned," he muttered, rolling the cigar around in his mouth again. His face darkened by several more degrees, and his eyes snapped with obvious fury. "I've been had. Your handbills exaggerated your, uh, attributes. At the very least!"

"What the hell are you—"

"With all due respect, madam," the weasel continued, "the illustration you sent showed you even more, shall we say, endowed than Dottie here."

Fury and embarrassment spiked through Jackie. How dare he? "I'm *endowed* enough, and I never sent you any illustrations, you creep." Was he talking about Blade's preliminary sketches? It didn't matter. "Where the hell are your famous tits?"

Jackie clenched her fists, wondering what he meant by *famous.* "Right where they've always been, you creep." She'd had enough of this—more than enough. "Just who the hell do you think you are?"

He took a threatening step, both hands on his hips. "The man who paid your train and stage fare, Miss Belle. Rupert P. Goodfellow."

Miss Belle. Him, too? "Never heard of you, and I haven't ridden on a train since I was ten." Jackie took a sidestep, shooting an anxious glance at the door. Every instinct she possessed screamed, *Run!* Something was very wrong here—something a lot more serious than the predicament she'd found herself in yesterday.

And she felt like crap. Besides her headache, she was half-starved and would gladly welcome a visit to the outhouse she'd bitched about yesterday.

"By God, I should demand a full refund. Every cent." He threw a caustic look at Dottie. "Get me one of them handbills."

"I . . . " Dottie ducked her head and glanced aside at Zeb. "I gave 'em to the miners."

"All of them?" Rupert rolled his eyes toward the ceiling and yanked the cigar from his mouth. "You didn't save even one?"

Dottie straightened and met his gaze, though her chin quivered slightly. "I just done what you told me to, Rupert."

He sighed and nodded. "Yeah, I reckon you did." Shoving the cigar back in his mouth, he turned on Jackie again. "Miss Belle, either you produce your world-famous attributes"—he cupped his hands some distance from his chest—"or prepare to return my—"

"That's it—I'm outta here." Jackie summoned energy from God only knew where and stomped to the door.

"Get her, boys."

Jackie heard the Brothers Grime shuffle away from the bar. That was her cue. She bolted through the swinging doors, into the bright sunlight . . . and froze. Not a hint of yesterday's snow remained anywhere. In fact, the ground was bare and dry.

"C'mon back, Miss Lolita," Zeb called, his boots pounding the boardwalk with his steady approach.

"The hell I will." Jackie's voice was barely more than a strangled whisper. She had to get out of here before she lost what remained of her sanity. Even Blade had been better than this. Without taking time to think, she dashed down the steps and into the street.

The very busy street.

Jackie heard the wagon's approach, saw the gigantic horse bearing down on her, but she couldn't move. Her feet refused to budge.

"Look out!"

Strong arms wrapped around her from behind, hauling her back to the relative safety of the boardwalk. Renewed terror quickly displaced her moment of relief, and she twisted and kicked at the man who still held her. She had to escape.

"Hold on there." His voice was different—definitely not Zeb's. And he smelled a lot better, too.

Jackie ceased her struggle and turned very slowly to face her rescuer. Her heart beat at an alarming rate, a combination of fear and exertion.

Recognition left her momentarily stunned. It

couldn't be. A white hat shaded piercing blue eyes; his face was clean-shaven and his jaw square.

He was gorgeous.

And familiar.

"Mel Gibson?"

Cole didn't understand what made her stop fighting him, but his bruised ribs were relieved. For such a little mite, she packed one hell of a wallop. "Name's Cole Morrison—did you say Gibson?"

"Mel Gibson."

She looked up at him with wide gray eyes—pleading eyes—and he loosened his grip.

"Mel Gibson, the actor?" she repeated.

"Actor? Never had much use for their kind." Cole flashed her a crooked grin, catching sight of a group from the Gold Mine Saloon hovering nearby. "You with them?" He aimed his thumb at the peculiar gathering.

"Huh." She rolled her eyes. "Not hardly." A look of confusion came over her face. "Please help me."

"I, uh . . ." Cole studied her face, then glanced at Goodfellow and company again. The whole lot of them reminded him of vultures. Hungry ones. "Well, I might. That depends on what kind of help you need."

She knitted her brow in obvious bewilderment. "First, just tell me where I am."

"You don't know?"

She shook her head. "Please? Where am I?" Her expression revealed the seriousness of her question. *"Please?"*

He studied her for a few seconds, wondering who she was and how she'd ended up here without knowing where she was. "This is Devil's Gulch, Colorado, ma'am. Where'd you think you were?"

Obviously taken aback, she blinked several times and covered her face with both hands. "The script," she said quietly, dragging her fingers down her face until the red inner rims of her eyes glared back at him.

"Script?" What in blazes was she talking about?

"That painting, the saloon, Devil's Gulch . . ." She laughed, though it sounded more like a sob or a crazy person's laugh. "My God, I must be asleep and dreaming that stupid frigging script, and I don't even know how it *ends.*"

Cole rubbed his chin with thumb and forefinger, contemplating this curious creature. Wearing men's jeans and a stretchy shirt unlike anything he'd ever seen before, she looked like an unkempt boy who needed to visit the barber in a bad way. Elizabeth would've had Cole's balls on a hot tin plate if he'd ever allowed their son to appear in public looking like that.

Of course, he knew without a doubt that this was no boy. Granted, he was surprised as heck to find his hands filled with womanly softness when he'd hauled her out of the road. In passing, he never would've guessed, but touching her was another matter entirely. Not an unpleasant matter by any means.

Upon closer inspection, she wasn't as young as he'd originally thought either. And Lord knew he'd *never* seen hair that color. It couldn't be real—it was even brighter than his newest pair of red flannels.

She looked at him again with those wide eyes of hers. There was something disturbing about her and her eyes—something that almost made him feel things he wasn't able to feel anymore.

"Where's the nearest bus station or airport?" She grabbed his forearm and held on tight. "A police station? A phone? Yes, that's what I need first. Please get me to a phone and I'll call someone—anyone but Aunt Pearl."

Bus? Airport? Phone? Shaking his head, Cole decided she needed more help than he was able to offer. Rupert Goodfellow stepped forward and inclined his head toward the woman.

"We've had enough excitement now. I think we'd best get you upstairs where you can rest," the saloonkeeper said. The look he flashed Cole held a warning.

Cole stared long and hard at Goodfellow's eyes. The runt was up to something—something involving this strange woman. It went against his grain to accommodate the man. Besides, if there was one thing Cole hated, it was being threatened.

"I'm not going anywhere with you," the woman said, sidling closer to Cole. "God, if I didn't know better, I'd swear you're all in on this with Blade. I don't know what's going on here, but I'm not Lolita Belle."

Lolita Belle? Cole looked at her with renewed interest. Was it possible? He cast a questioning glance at the saloonkeeper.

Goodfellow's eyes narrowed, and he clamped down on his cigar so hard the tip probably broke off in his mouth. "As much as I wish you weren't Lolita Belle, I can't imagine who else you could be."

"Are you?" Cole asked, watching her expression closely for any sign that she might be lying.

"Definitely not. This jerk thinks I am, but that's ridiculous."

Cole's instincts insisted she told the truth, though

common sense called him a fool. He studied Goodfellow again. "Well?" He jabbed his thumb toward the woman. "Is she Lolita Belle? Really?"

Goodfellow shook his head and yanked the cigar from his mouth. "Damned if I know." With a sigh, he cocked his head toward the Gold Mine Saloon. "Dottie here says she found her asleep on the floor this morning, even though she isn't supposed to be here for weeks yet. Besides, who else *could* she be with hair that color?"

"Yeah, well, she doesn't . . . isn't . . . Hell." From the corner of his eye, Cole studied the woman's nicely shaped bosom. The famous singer reportedly had breasts the size of melons, though that was probably an exaggeration. Still, this woman could claim only nice-size tomatoes. *Very* nice. "I thought . . ."

Goodfellow wheezed a cynical chuckle. "Yeah, you and me both. Those handbills she sent sure had me fooled."

Cole wanted to laugh. Badly. It served Goodfellow right, but one look at the woman's frightened expression sobered him. Something was wrong here. How could anyone as famous as Lolita Belle end up here in Devil's Gulch without knowing where she was? Or who she was, for that matter?

But this woman's problem was none of his business. Well, that wasn't entirely true, though he'd have to wait for confirmation.

"She sure as hell better sing like a nightingale—that's all I can say." Bitterness laced Goodfellow's words. "You think the miners'll pay to hear her sing if they don't have the . . . other to look at?"

"I . . . dunno." Cole felt uncomfortable talking about the woman as if she weren't there. "I reckon there's only one way to find out."

"Yeah, let's just hope I can get my money's worth out of this deal somehow." Goodfellow shot the woman a dubious glare and shook his head. "Personally, I wouldn't pay a cent to hear her sing looking like that. All we can do is hope she cleans up good."

"You son of a bitch."

The woman's fierce whisper made Cole smile. Maybe she wasn't ladylike, but she definitely had spunk. And from the look of things, she was going to need her spunk . . . and a whole lot more.

Dottie stepped around Goodfellow and grabbed the supposed Miss Belle's upper arm. "C'mon, honey," she said in a patronizing tone. "Let's get you a hot bath and some food, then we'll talk about all this."

The woman jerked her arm from Dottie's grasp. "Get your hands off me."

"See what I mean, Rupert?" Dottie gave Goodfellow a smug look. "I told you she ain't worth all the trouble she's causin'."

"She sure as hell had better be—that's all I can say." Goodfellow reached out to grab her himself, but she dodged him.

"Don't you touch me."

Though her words sounded tough and clipped, she appeared dangerously close to tears. *Damn.* If there was one thing Cole Morrison couldn't stand, it was a bawling woman. Hell, he knew the reason, too—something his late wife had learned very early in their marriage—he'd never been able to say no to a crying woman. Yeah, it was way past time for him to distance himself from this.

He hated the guilt pressing down on him, but he needed to get home to Todd. Goodfellow might be a mercenary bastard, but Cole felt confident that at least no harm would come to the woman.

But what if it did? He hesitated, silently kicking his own ass for giving the woman a second thought. *Get the hell out while the gettin's good.*

With a nod of resignation to Goodfellow, Cole gnashed his teeth and walked away. He heard the woman's startled protest, but he kept walking. He had to—this was none of his concern.

Unless she turned out to be who she claimed she wasn't.

Zeb and Rupert each took an arm and literally hauled Jackie back into the Gold Mine Saloon. "Get your filthy hands off me," she shouted, but no one seemed to have heard her. What was going on here? How could the ghost town she'd stumbled across the day before have suddenly become a boomtown?

"Well, Miss Belle—Lolita," Rupert said, depositing her in a chair near a familiar cast-iron stove.

I'm not crazy, she reasserted. *Not.*

She glanced around the saloon again, digging into her memory for fragments of everything she'd noticed last night. The whiskey, Vienna sausages, her stupid red hair . . .

"Since you're here early, we might as well have the artist get to work on your portrait." Rupert stood back to stare at her, tapping his chin with his finger. "Where's your trunk? You certainly can't perform in . . . that. I did take the liberty of having some items delivered, but they certainly won't fit."

Jackie was too tired to argue any more, so she drew a deep breath and simply stared at the man. After a few moments of total silence, his face darkened and she saw fury etched across his features. Again.

Insistent tears burned and threatened to spill from her eyes, but she blinked them back. She was determined not to let this asshole see her cry. "I told you, I'm not Lolita Belle." Jackie rested her chin in her hands and sighed. "I came in here last night to get out of a blizzard. There was a terrible fire . . . and now you're here. What the *hell* is going on?"

"Blizzard?" Rupert frowned and shook his head. "It's been a dry spring—we haven't had snow since early April."

"Bull." Jackie straightened and flashed him what she hoped came close to what her aunt would call an uppity glare. "I walked down the mountain in a blizzard yesterday and came in here to keep from freezing to death." Her voice rose with each syllable and she shot to her feet. "How dare you call me a liar?"

Rupert placed a hand on each of her shoulders and pressed her back into the chair. "I *own* you, Miss Belle," he said from between clenched teeth and his cigar. "Until I recover every cent I've sunk into bringing you here, you're mine. Understand?"

His tone permitted no argument, yet how could Jackie agree to this lunacy? "I don't get it." She shook her head in numbed outrage and her tears escaped—*damn traitors*—but she wiped them away before anyone could see. *You're pissed, Jackie—do not let them see you cry. Aunt Pearl said big girls don't cry. I am a big girl. Dammit.*

"Just help me understand this—who are you and how did you get here?" She drew a shaky breath. "For that matter, how did this town get here?"

Rupert chuckled and shook his head. "You're

good—one helluva performer. Maybe your handbills weren't *all* lies." A nasty smile spread across his face, and he shoved his cigar back into the corner of his mouth. "I don't know your game, Miss Belle, but you'd better come through, if you know what's good for you."

"Is that a threat?" Anger finally succeeded in forcing her tears to beat a hasty retreat, and she folded her arms across her growling stomach. Her bladder was so full it was about to abandon ship, and her head felt like rap music with the bass set to kill. Putting it simply, she felt like total crap.

"A promise, Miss Belle." He leaned toward her. "Now where is your trunk? For that matter, how'd you get here? The stage isn't due until three o'clock."

"What stage? I walked here." Jackie swept the room with her gaze again. It was almost as if . . .

No.

Still, the people, the saloon, Lolita . . .

She thought about the fire that had consumed the building—*this* building. What bizarre aftermath had it left behind? Could it be? Had the fire somehow thrown her back in time?

No, not the fire. The painting. She swallowed and tried to steady her breathing. *Time.* It was the only thing that made sense, in a twisted sort of way. "I don't believe this."

"Trust me, that makes two of us." Rupert's sneer was even worse now than before. "I've commissioned an artist to paint your portrait. Since you can't perform until either your trunk arrives or we can provide other attire, you can pose for your portrait."

"Portrait?" In her mind, Jackie pictured Lolita's smug smile, her mutant breasts, all that bare flesh. . . . "Oh, no. You can't be serious."

"I'm dead serious, Miss Belle." Rupert's expression had changed from furious to cocky. "The beauty of it is, you won't need any clothes at all for that."

Jackie stared long and hard at Rupert, then shifted her gaze to Dottie and the ever-present trio of goons. The polished bar, the unbroken furniture, no sign of a fire . . .

Evidence?

She had to know the truth. "What . . . year is it?" A roaring sound began in her head as she watched the flash of amusement in Rupert's eyes. "Answer me. Then . . . "

"Then what?" The man had a used-car-salesman air about him—he obviously smelled a hot deal in the making. "Well?"

Jackie held her breath for a moment, then said, "Then I'll pose for your damn portrait."

He nodded. "The year, Miss Belle, is 1891."

Chapter Three

Stunned, Jackie allowed Dottie to lead her up the stairs that had been engulfed in flames last night.

No, not last night.

Her escort opened a door near the end of the hall, and Jackie followed her inside. "This can't be happening," she whispered, looking around the room. Dark green flocked paper covered the walls, its intricate pattern broken only by two long, narrow windows flanking an ornate dressing table.

"Rupert had this room fixed up special . . . just for you." Disgust tinged Dottie's voice. "Lord only knows why men can't appreciate what's right in front of them."

Numbness filled Jackie—identical to when she'd first realized Lolita's portrait was missing. "This just can't be. . . ."

"What's the matter? Rupert said green was your favorite color. Was that a lie, too?" After an accusing glance at Jackie's bustline, Dottie flounced across the room to a tall wardrobe and threw open the doors. "I suppose you'll have to wear somethin' after your bath."

Taking a bath sounded so . . . normal. Jackie pressed her hand against her breastbone, feeling the solid thud of her heart and her erratic breathing. She was alive—this was real.

No, I won't let it be real.

Shifting her gaze from Dottie to the open window, Jackie saw the curtains fluttering in the gentle breeze. She brought her hand to her hair and pulled a strand forward to stare. Still red.

A reality check, Clarke?

"I'm not dead."

Dottie snorted and dropped a red velvet robe on the bed beside Jackie. "No, you ain't dead, but you might be if you don't figure out a way to give Rupert his money's worth outta this deal."

What color-blind idiot had selected a red robe for a redhead? Biting her lower lip, Jackie curbed the urge to snap at her reluctant hostess. She closed her eyes and forced herself to recap last night's events. Again.

Snow. Lolita. The fire . . .

"Did anything . . . strange happen here last night?" Jackie looked up at Dottie, hoping against hope for a miracle—or at least some answers.

"Well, you must've come sometime last night or early this mornin'." Dottie shrugged. "That's strange enough, especially since I remember lockin' the door."

Jackie sighed, shoving her hair behind her ears where she couldn't see it. "A storm, or maybe a . . . a fire?"

Dottie frowned and shook her head. "Nah. No fires I've heard about, and we ain't had rain or snow for weeks. Now *that's* strange. No storms at all, but I'd say we're overdue for a good one."

Pressing her index fingers against both temples, Jackie closed her eyes again to think. "Okay, so it's 1891." There, she'd said it, but she still didn't believe it. "What's the exact date?"

Dottie heaved an impatient sigh. "May seventh."

"It can't be." As Jackie opened her eyes, a wave of dizziness assaulted her with all the savoir faire of the Denver Broncos' offensive line. "Yesterday was June eleventh."

"No, today is the seventh of May, just like I said." The woman looked up at the ceiling, then met Jackie's gaze with an unspoken and unmistakable challenge. "Just because I don't talk as fine and pretty as you don't mean I can't tell what day it is. You'd best not be forgettin' that either, Miss Loli—"

"I'm *not* Lolita." Jackie's voice rose with each syllable. Somehow, she had to make these people understand, even if *she* didn't. "My name is Jackie Clarke—not Lolita Belle. Got it?"

"Sounds like a man's name." A nasty smile twisted Dottie's face, and her whiskey-colored eyes glittered menacingly. "You better watch yourself. That handsome Cole Morrison ain't around to save you now."

"Save me from what? Certain insanity?" Jackie covered her face and drew a long, slow breath through the spaces between her fingers. "I'm tired and I need to use the bathroom."

"You're really somethin'." Disapproval came through loud and clear in Dottie's tone. "Maybe *this*'ll teach Rupert a lesson he won't soon forget."

Jackie held a hand to the top of her head as she

stood. The sudden change in elevation increased the pain in her skull to the atomic level. Minimum. "My kingdom for a couple of ibuprofen."

"Ibu-what?"

"Never mind." Why had she taken off her fanny pack? *Talk about stupid.* Jackie rubbed her temples again, but found little relief from the constant and increasing throb. "Did you say something about a bath? And where do you pee around here?" Maybe a hot bath would kill the pain.

"Water closet's down the hall." Dottie waved her hand in front of her face. "I don't reckon you can wait till Saturday for a bath. Do you?"

Jackie drew a deep breath and released it very slowly. "Saturday? I take a shower or bath every morning."

"*Every* day?"

Jackie couldn't prevent the smug smile that tugged at the corners of her mouth. Mean old Dottie deserved every single inconvenience Jackie could create. And then some. "Yes, every single day."

"Don't your skin just curl up and *die* from all that water?" Dottie shuddered with enough force to make her ample bosom put on quite a show. "You'll probably get scales like a trout."

Jackie shrugged and prayed for her head to stop its ceaseless pounding. Then a terrifying thought barged into her mind—one that might possibly explain the pain in her head.

She was in a coma. *I'm not crazy.* She had to wake up and maintain her sanity long enough to put Blade behind bars. What happened after that was anybody's guess.

"That's it."

"What's what? You really got scales?"

Jackie sighed and thought. Her headache eased a little. She frowned, trying to ignore Dottie's continued staring. But what if she wasn't in a coma? How could she be certain?

Simple. She couldn't. "Damn."

"Rupert don't cotton to his girls swearin'."

"I'm not one of Rupert's girls." Jackie waved her hand in dismissal, trying to convince herself this was all part of her coma.

"We'll have to wait and see what he has to say about that." Dottie turned and sashayed toward the door, her round backside swinging like Mae West's at her finest. "Zeb'll fetch your water."

"Wonder how clean it'll be by the time it gets here," Jackie muttered.

"What'd you say?"

"Nothing important."

Dottie opened the door, then paused. "If I was you, I'd start prayin' real fast." After a moment, she looked over her shoulder, a crooked grin twisting her painted lips. "Either that, or ask that snake-oil salesman on the edge of town if he's got somethin' that'll grow you a big bosom real fast."

Jackie summoned her fiercest gaze and directed it at Dottie. "Yeah, and maybe he has something to cure jealousy, too. Hmm?"

"Jealousy?" Dottie's smile vanished and her nostrils flared. "You might have Rupert fooled, honey, but I see right through you."

"Yeah, right." The urge to blurt out the truth invaded Jackie, making her stomach clench and her adrenaline-laced blood sing through her veins. Instead she chose silence, knowing she had to sort through all this herself before sharing it with the world.

"Suit yourself." Dottie slipped through the door, pulling it shut behind her, and Jackie seized the opportunity to visit the water closet.

After putting the facilities through their paces, she returned to her room—for now, at least. She walked slowly to the window and peered out at the bustling little town. It was still there—Devil's Gulch, Colorado. "What the hell happened to me?"

Wagons and horses, men in work clothes, a few women in long dresses, and an abundance of dust filled the street below. *Incredible.* "Yeah, a coma." She nodded, trying—and failing—to convince herself again.

It was possible, though. If this was all part of a coma, then she'd either come out of it . . . or die. Eventually.

Lovely thought.

And if this was real . . . ?

Jackie swallowed and turned to look around the room again. Could she really have traveled back in time?

It was a possibility she had to face.

"Think, Jackie." She shuffled over to the bed and flopped onto her back, gripping her head with both hands.

If she had truly traveled through time, then she had to make the best of her situation . . . such as it was. Rupert P. Goodfellow thought she was the famous Lolita Belle—sans *Guinness Book of World Records*-size breasts. At least Jackie's mistaken identity had secured her temporary shelter. Besides, if she forced herself to think logically about all this—a greater challenge than getting Aunt Pearl into a male strip joint, for sure—it made sense for Jackie to stay put and play along.

Maybe she was no rocket scientist, but she'd

watched enough television to know it took either a time machine or a portal—a tunnel?—to travel through time. She was bound and determined to stay close to her exit. Except that the painting didn't exist. Yet. One more reason for her to pose in the nude. Again.

"Get a grip, Clarke." She rested the back of her hand against her forehead and closed her eyes, summoning everything she could remember about *Quantum Leap* and *Back to the Future.* But instead of Scott Bakula and Michael J. Fox, she saw Mel Gibson—rather, the man who'd hauled her fanny out of the street earlier.

"Cole . . . something. Morrison, that's it." At least his name wasn't Blade. Now that would've put a decidedly horrific slant to this entire predicament. "That sorry son of a bitch. This is all his fault."

A shuffling sound from the hall and a knock at the door jerked her to the present. *Past-present?* "What a mess." Jackie sat up and swung her feet to the floor just as the door opened.

Dottie sashayed in, followed by the ever-filthy Zeb pushing a bathtub on squeaky wheels. Fingers of steam drifted up from the water's surface.

A bath would make Jackie feel better, and maybe it would finish off her headache. Of course, she could always drown herself, but it'd be just her luck that this was really just a coma, after all.

Dottie dropped some towels on the bed beside the robe, then pointed to a collection of bottles on the dresser. "Fancy stuff Rupert ordered for you. Zeb'll come back to fetch the water later."

Zeb waggled his woolly eyebrows. "I could just stay an'—"

Jackie leveled her gaze at him. "Out, you pervert."

She drew a deep breath. "But thank you for the water."

Zeb looked almost as surprised as Dottie by Jackie's gratitude. *Good.* If she was going to stay here for a while, she'd better start making nice with the natives. Even mean old Dottie.

"And thank you, Dottie . . . for everything."

A look of total confusion flitted across the woman's face, then she sighed. "You're welcome." After a moment, she narrowed her gaze and flashed Jackie a wicked grin. "Rupert'll be up after your bath to take you to the artist. He works in a cabin on the edge of town—says it gives him inspiration."

Like Blade. "Today?"

"Yep, and that robe's *all* you'll be needin'." Dottie turned toward the door. "But you won't even need that for very long."

"Damn." Jackie watched the pair leave, laughing all the way. The image of Lolita's portrait flashed into her brain and made her wince.

After a moment, she jerked herself from a state of near shock and rushed across the room to lock the door. Somehow, some way, she had to endure posing for that portrait. If it was her time portal, it was also her only hope.

And just what would happen when the real Lolita put in an appearance?

Groaning, Jackie stripped off her clothes and stepped into the tub. She had to think of something. Fast. As much as she hated it here, the last thing she wanted was to lose access to her time. When the real and appropriately endowed Lolita showed up, Goodfellow would toss Jackie and her B cups out on her butt. She had to buy some time before—

"Waitaminute." A shiver raced through her, despite

the water's warmth. If she didn't know better, she might think she was starting to believe this.

Cole gave the reins a gentle tug until the mare his wife had named Ruth came to a reluctant stop. "Don't worry, girl," he said, patting the side of her neck, "you'll get those oats soon."

The horse stretched her neck to reach the early blades of grass around the base of a small aspen tree. The weather had been downright peculiar, though Cole wasn't complaining. Normally the high country was still covered with snow this time of year. Now only the highest peaks had any at all, and it was melting fast.

The dry weather enabled him to work in the mine almost every day. Not that all his work had done him any good. Sighing, he pushed his hat back farther on his head and scanned the horizon. All these years of mining the same claim had netted him barely enough gold to keep his son fed and clothed.

Todd deserved better than this. Elizabeth's last words barged into Cole's thoughts, tying his gut into an unwieldy knot.

Promise me, Cole, she'd said, clinging to life barely long enough to make her plea. *Make sure Todd gets decent schooling and a better life than this. Promise.*

And he had promised.

Though she'd asked him earlier to take their son home to St. Louis, he hadn't promised her that. Guilt pressed down on him and he sighed. Clicking his tongue, he gathered the reins in one hand and urged the mare into a slow walk up the rocky trail.

And he should have kept his promise. Not a day

passed that he didn't kick himself in the ass for breaking that vow to his dying wife. "Ah, Elizabeth."

Selling the claim probably was the wisest thing to do, because it certainly hadn't yielded the gold he needed to start the ranch he and Elizabeth had always planned. His dilemma had tormented him since her death. He could either return to St. Louis to beg his father-in-law for a job in the mercantile, or he could keep digging in that damned hole he called a mine.

But what of their dream? He and Elizabeth had come to Colorado shortly after Todd's birth with one dream in mind. All they'd wanted was enough gold to go to Oregon and start a ranch—something to pass down to their son.

Something to make them all proud.

Pride. What good was pride, after all? It couldn't fill a boy's belly . . . and it sure as hell couldn't warm a man's bed at night.

He flexed his gloved hand, suddenly remembering how it had felt to touch that woman in town. His gut clenched, and an insistent tugging commenced in his groin. Problem was, he hadn't been with a woman at all since Elizabeth. . . .

Long, lonely years without a woman could make a man want anything in a skirt. Hell, that woman in town hadn't even been *wearing* a skirt.

Still, her compelling softness filling his hand had triggered his need in a big way. In search of comfort, he shifted in the saddle. It was past time for him to get on with his life.

But not with Lolita Belle. She was a legend. Miners and cowboys alike had whispered about her at card tables, on the trail, and underground for years.

Cole tried to rid himself of the nagging voice in his head. That woman couldn't be Lolita. Not a chance.

At least, he sure hoped not.

Shading his eyes, he looked beyond the familiar boulder jutting out from the side of the mountain. He was almost there. *Home.* At least for now. Smoke curled upward from the chimney, vanishing in the clear mountain air.

Todd would be setting the table for their noon meal, knowing his father should be home by now. He always helped out without being told. Elizabeth would've been proud of the boy.

Stopping the horse again on the ridge, Cole gazed longingly at the flowers his wife had planted around the front of the cabin. The puny things looked so out of place there, but she'd been determined to bring civilization to their temporary home.

Temporary. Then why had Cole let it become so damned permanent?

This was no place to raise a boy. Todd needed schooling and a real home. His grandparents could give him that in St. Louis. All Cole had to do was put his tail between his legs and slink on back there.

Gnashing his teeth, he shifted his gaze to the well-worn trail leading from the back of the cabin up the side of the mountain.

His claim. All their dreams rested in that hole. "Fool." Shaking his head, he nudged the mare with his heels, and she cantered eagerly to the log shelter that served as a stable, not far from the cabin.

He'd been offered an alternative. It was there for the taking. All Cole had to do was agree to the dirty job, and he'd receive enough pay—gold!—to live his and Elizabeth's dream. If he didn't take it, the only way to keep his promise to Elizabeth would be to return to St. Louis with his pride in shreds.

Or he could do this one job and take his son to Oregon for the life he and Elizabeth had planned.

Choice, Morrison? He swallowed hard and dismounted, releasing the cinch and sliding the saddle off the mare's back. With a grunt, he swung the saddle onto a rail, then led the horse to the trough. She wasn't overheated, so he let her drink her fill while he poured her ration of oats into the feed box.

Merriweather had offered him his and Elizabeth's dream in a not-so-neat little package. Cole never should've trusted that traveling preacher enough to unburden his troubles. Things ate at a man, and Cole had reached his limit about the time that preacher came along. Next thing Cole knew, he'd told the kind-faced man everything.

Including his own failures.

The old fart had spilled Cole's desperation at the next watering hole, and Merriweather had been listening. Cole had to hand it to old Merriweather—he sure as hell knew how to pull a man's strings.

Cole released a long sigh. The money from that job was more than he could refuse, and it wasn't as if actual harm would come to anyone because of it. Still, the mere thought of it made his gut burn. If only he hadn't—

"Pa."

Cole turned around just in time to catch a flying nine-year-old body. He gave his son a hug and allowed himself a moment to admire the boy's dark blond hair, so much like his mother's. Though Elizabeth was gone from this world, a part of her lived on in their son.

"I'm starved," Cole said, ruffling the boy's hair. "What'd you cook?" He flashed Todd a grin when the boy groaned.

"Cookin's woman's work." The boy looked down at his bare feet, then lifted his face to squint into the sun.

"That's a fact." Cole walked slowly toward the cabin, knowing without looking that his son was at his side. It was a fine feeling—a damned fine one. "But I reckon it's a good thing for a man to know how to take care of himself, too." He knew that all too well.

"Yes, sir." Todd gave a sigh much larger than his size. "I sure get sick of it, though."

"Nah, you just get sick of *my* cooking."

They both laughed as Cole opened the door and stepped into the cabin's dim interior. His laughter stilled as his gaze focused on the ladder that led to the loft. In his mind's eye, he mentally followed each rung to the top, remembering Elizabeth's last night on this earth with him . . . and his wretched promise. The lump in his throat seemed unbearable as he struggled against it, suddenly thankful for the dim interior.

Todd slipped past him, dragging Cole's attention from the ladder . . . and from the past. The boy grabbed something off the mantel and hurried back.

"I almost forgot," Todd said, holding a folded piece of paper in his outstretched hand. "A man brought this while you was in town."

Cole hated the thought of anyone coming to the cabin while Todd was here alone. In St. Louis, Elizabeth's mother could care for Todd while Cole worked—yet another reason to give up that stupid dream and get on with his promise.

After clearing his throat, Cole asked, "What man?"

"Never seen him before." With a shrug, Todd padded barefoot across the rough wood floor and took two tin soup plates down from the shelf beside the stove.

While his son served their meal, Cole unfolded the letter and took a backward step into the light from the open doorway. The bold pen strokes leaped off the page and straight to Cole's gut. "Damn," he whispered.

Anyone else would've considered the message cryptic, but Cole knew exactly what the four words meant. After he reread the page, his gaze migrated back up the ladder to the loft he'd shared with his wife.

He no longer had a choice. This note had stolen that luxury from him, just as surely as a thief with a six-shooter. Removing his hat and hanging it on a peg near the door, Cole stuffed the note into his pocket and washed his hands in the basin near the hearth.

Those four words were his commandment. It was time for Cole Morrison to live up to the promise he'd made his wife. The handwriting was burned into his brain. Even as he took a seat at the table with his son, he saw the words clearly in his mind.

I'll double the money. The only other marks were the familiar initials at the bottom of the page.

"Can we go fishin' today?" Todd spooned beans into his mouth, oblivious to his father's torment.

Thank God for that.

Cole shook his head. "Not today, son." He forced a spoonful of beans into his mouth and chewed furiously. "I have to go back to town." He had a job to do.

"Again?" Todd gave a sound of disgust, then continued eating with far less enthusiasm.

Cole hated himself. If he'd kept his promise years ago, this wouldn't be happening, and his son wouldn't be disappointed in him. "I'll make it up to you," he said, and meant it.

"All right." Todd brightened and attacked his food.

In St. Louis, Todd could eat his meals at a real table with proper utensils. The boy would never be hungry, and he'd have a grand variety of things to eat.

Cole's appetite beat a hasty retreat, and he pushed away from the table. He crossed the room and took his rifle down from the rack over the hearth. As he turned around, he saw the look of concern on his son's face.

"I saw a bear on my way up the trail earlier," he lied, hating himself. "Nothing meaner than a bear just waking up in the spring."

Todd's eyes grew round and he nodded. "That's for sure."

"I'll be back before dark." Cole hesitated and touched the boy's shoulder. He hated leaving Todd alone again so soon. "You stay inside, just in case that bear decides to come up here looking for something to fill his belly."

"Oh, Pa." Todd made a face of utter disgust that crawled into a special corner of his father's heart.

"You look just like your ma when you do that." With a grin, Cole grabbed his hat and walked out the door.

Praying.

Jackie shifted uncomfortably on the satin pillows, making absolutely certain the feather boa covered all her assets—such as they were. Most women lived their entire lives without posing for a lurid portrait, but Jackie Clarke had the dubious honor of doing it twice in the same week.

In two different centuries.

First Blade, now Henri. Her gaze locked onto the obese man behind the canvas.

"Sacre bleu," he muttered for at least the hundredth time. "Monsieur Goodfellow assured me you would be . . . more . . ." He stuck the brush between his teeth and held both hands cupped out in front of his chest.

Far away from his chest.

"Well, I'm not, so get over it." Jackie flashed him a nasty smile—the nastiest one she could summon. "So use your imagination, Frenchie—you're an artist, aren't you?"

He jerked the paintbrush from between his teeth. *"Mon Dieu."* Dabbing furiously at his palette, he muttered a string of what Jackie felt certain weren't nice things, even if they were in French. "And that hair." More French. "How did it get to be such an atrocious shade?"

Jackie winced. *Touché.* "It's standard equipment," she fibbed, biting the inside of her cheek to keep herself from saying what she really thought. "Keep your opinions to yourself and paint. I'd like to get out of these feathers ASAP."

"Asap?"

"As soon as possible." She lifted her eyebrows and sighed. "Like, yesterday would be nice."

Actually, yesterday was pure hell, but today is even worse.

More French. *Good.* As long as he was happy . . .

"I simply cannot paint without . . . inspiration." He threw the brush and palette crashing to the floor, splattering paint across the room. "Come back tomorrow at the same time. Wait here until Zeb comes to claim you. Oh, how my head aches. Why did I ever leave Paris?"

Muttering to himself, Henri waddled to the back of the cabin and slammed the door.

"Cool." Keeping the feathers wrapped strategically around her body, Jackie swung her feet to the floor and reached for her jeans. Old Dottie had no idea that Jackie had worn her own filthy clothes beneath the velvet robe.

With the white boa draped around her neck, Jackie wiggled into her jeans and buttoned the fly, then slipped on her socks and hiking boots. A noise from outside made her adjust the boa to cover herself just before the door burst open.

A man—a tall one—filled the doorway. A white hat was pulled low over his eyes, and a bandanna covered his mouth and nose. Only twin blue slits were visible on his face. He held a rifle in his hands, though it wasn't aimed at her. Exactly.

"Oh, no, you don't," she said, knowing the script was in force again. "I'm *not* Lolita. You've got the wrong woman, buster. Be patient—she'll be along in a few weeks."

"You're coming with me." His voice was muffled, but his words were clear. Unmistakable. "Now."

"I don't believe this." Jackie knew she should fear the kidnapper, but her anger took command. "You want Lolita—I'm Jackie. Trust me on this. I'm only a thirty-four B. You want the forty-four D ones. They're worth the wait. I've seen—"

"Hush." His words sounded more confused than angry. "Just hush your mouth and get yourself out the door."

"I'm not dressed."

Henri chose that moment to open the door. "I've changed my mind, mademoiselle," the artist said dramatically. "We will continue the—"

"That's far enough." The rifle shifted toward the artist. "Stay right there."

Henri's eyes rolled into the back of his head and he fell forward, landing with a loud splat when his face hit the wood floor.

Right on top of Jackie's T-shirt and the velvet robe.

"Come on," the kidnapper ordered. "Now."

Jackie looked down at the unconscious painter and, more important, at the edge of her ugly dark green T-shirt. "My clothes." She pointed ineffectively with her left hand, but the kidnapper seemed indifferent to her request.

Henri moaned, and Jackie found the kidnapper's gloved hand around her upper arm, feathers and all. He propelled her out the door and into the bright sunlight, in all her half-naked glory.

"My clothes," she repeated, but found herself slung unceremoniously onto a horse. *A horse?* She didn't know how to ride a horse. All thoughts of clothes and time travel fled in light of more urgent matters.

Like survival.

A second later, the kidnapper shoved his rifle into a slot on the side of his saddle and swung himself up behind her. He reached around Jackie and grabbed the reins, snapped them once, and did something with his feet to launch the horse.

"Noooooooo." Jackie clung to the saddle horn and gasped for breath, no longer holding the boa. It flapped in the breeze around her and her captor.

"Hold those damned feathers before you spook the horse," he said in her ear.

Suddenly aware of his proximity and her monstrous vulnerability, Jackie quieted and gathered the feathers closer, tucking the ends under her inner thighs to secure them across her breasts. Without slowing its pace, the horse galloped up a rocky incline that didn't even resemble a trail. Jackie could barely breathe, and her skin was starting to itch where the feathers touched it. The constant jarring motion of the horse was making her stomach queasy, and she was just plain sick and tired of her adventure.

"I want to go home," she whispered between breaths. "I've had all of this I'm going to put up with."

Nothing. The least he could do was acknowledge her.

"I said, I want to go home."

Still nothing.

As the horse plunged over a fallen tree and down into a ravine, Jackie reached and passed her limit. She sucked in a deep breath, closed her eyes, and let loose the loudest, shrillest scream of her life.

"Jesus, woman." The horse balked and reared as the kidnapper pulled on the reins, trying to calm the beast. "Hush, you're spooking my mare."

She knew it was risky—well, more than risky—but rather than listen to reason, Jackie sucked in yet another breath and screamed even louder.

The horse reared again, pawing the air high above them. Jackie stared at the flailing hooves, almost ready to admit she might have pushed her luck just a little too far.

"Easy, girl," the kidnapper said in a soothing tone.

Was he speaking to her?

"That's a good old girl."

Old girl? Jackie whipped her head around to stare at the man, whose face was still hidden from view. When she opened her mouth to talk, he clamped his gloved hand over it.

Dust mingled with the scent of sweat and leather,

nearly suffocating her. His glittering eyes narrowed and he leaned very close. "If you promise to be quiet, I'll let go. If you don't . . ."

A shudder rippled through Jackie and she nodded, certain he intended to do something horrible to her at any moment.

"That's better," he said softly, moving his hand away from her mouth. The kerchief twitched slightly.

The bastard is laughing.

Something inside her snapped. How dared he? Her life had been completely destroyed, and now the Sundance Kid, or whatever he called himself, was *laughing.*

Rage, irrational but commanding, gripped her, and she screamed even louder than before. Her throat protested the harsh treatment, even as the surge of adrenaline made her feel superhuman. Let him laugh, she thought.

The horse went berserk, and Jackie clawed the air for something more substantial than ostrich feathers. But this time even she knew the beast wouldn't stop.

No, this time the huge animal was going all the way over.

With two humans to cushion its fall.

Chapter Four

Cole tightened his grip around Lolita's waist and released the reins. The mare had gone berserk, and no amount of expert handling would make any difference.

Ruth's body twisted one way and Cole lunged the other, hauling the woman with him. Preventing a fall now was impossible. Hitting the ground hard would be one helluva lot better than being crushed to death.

He curled his body around Miss Lolita's, praying he'd land beneath her and a safe distance from flailing hooves. His shoulder slammed into a rock—pain pierced through his bones. Ignoring the pain as best he could, he pulled the woman's slight form closer to his chest as his body absorbed the shock of their fall.

Pain shot down his arm, but he didn't loosen his grip. The woman was just crazy enough to get them both killed, given half a chance. And he had no intention of giving her that chance.

The horse's shrill neigh reminded Cole of the continued threat. He looked up just in time to see Ruth's descent. She seemed to hang in the air, frozen for several seconds. Nothing could prevent the animal from going down.

Cole scrambled farther down the rocky incline, away from the shadow cast by the horse's broad back. Everything seemed to slow almost to a standstill as he watched.

Cole yanked Miss Lolita from the path of destruction. The mare landed on her side, grunting as she hit the rocks. Her hooves shot a spray of rocks and dirt down the incline, stinging Cole's face and the side of his neck. After a moment, Ruth fell silent.

Cole clenched his teeth, knowing he had to see if the mare was hurt as badly as he feared. He couldn't—wouldn't—let her suffer. "Damn," he muttered, feeling the woman tense against him. "You all right?"

She nodded against his sore shoulder and lifted her head to look at him. Dirt covered her face, and she blew a feather from the corner of her mouth. That wild red hair fell in disarray around her small face. At this moment, she more closely resembled a woman raised by wolves—or maybe ostriches—than a famous saloon singer.

"I have to see about my horse," he said.

The sound of sliding rocks jerked Cole's attention back to the animal. He held his breath as the graceful mare swung herself to a standing position with surprising ease.

"She's all right," the woman said, relief giving her voice a breathy quality that seeped right through Cole's bones.

Miss Lolita's gray eyes sparkled like silver in the sunlight. The sight purloined his breath, and his heart slammed against his ribs. Other than to lift her head, she hadn't moved since their fall. Still sprawled atop him, her hips were pressed intimately against his.

What the hell was he thinking? Cole needed to put some distance between them damned fast. "My mare," he repeated, reaching for Miss Lolita's shoulder to ease away her soft, appealing weight.

But the roundness that filled his palm was far too lush and pliable for a shoulder. Surprised, he looked down to where his hand pressed against her round breast, her dusky brown nipple peeking tantalizingly between two of his gloved fingers.

Cole's throat went dry and lightning whipped through his body, straight to his groin. Then his gaze met hers again, where he found shock and something more displayed in her silver eyes. The something more made him wonder how she would taste. How soft her flesh would feel beneath his lips . . .

The sun blazed down on them, and sweat trickled along the long, pale column of her throat. He followed the moisture's trail, feeling himself grow harder with each beat of his heart until the droplet vanished amid a riotous tangle of feathers.

He ached to remove his glove and close his hand around her breast, to roll her onto her back and cover her with his length, to press himself into her receptive body. . . .

Deep. Hard. Fast.

"Copping a feel, cowboy?" she whispered, her gaze drifting toward his impudent hand.

Self-disgust and humiliation shot through him, and he shifted his hand from her breast to her shoulder. "Pardon." *Hellfire and damnation.* He'd been *much* too long without a woman. Avoiding her gaze, he shifted her weight from him and rose, dragging her none too gently up beside him. Careful not to look upon her nakedness again, he released her arm and drew one end of her feather wrap over her shoulder.

Though he'd held her softness for only a few startling moments, the feel of her was burned into his palm right through his leather glove. The savageness of his sudden desire had shaken him senseless enough to make him forget far more important matters.

Like Ruth. Furious with himself, Cole turned away from Miss Lolita. The mare stood quietly. Guilt was an ugly mistress, and she seemed uglier than usual as he climbed the rocky slope. It sure as hell wasn't like him to think about bedding a woman when his horse could be suffering.

Murmuring in a gentle tone, he removed one glove and slowly approached Ruth. Once certain she wouldn't go crazy again, he checked the mare's head and neck, then examined every inch of her. Holding his breath, he reached down to feel each of her legs from top to bottom, praying he wouldn't find what he dreaded. Stooping made him realize that his butt had taken the brunt of their fall.

Other than some scrapes, she was sound. "Thank God," he muttered aloud. "You're all right, old girl."

"It's my fault." Miss Lolita's voice came from right beside him. "I—"

"Quiet." Cole glanced up at her and blinked. At least she wasn't leaking tears all over the place. A crying woman was just what he *didn't* need.

When he returned his attention to the mare where it belonged, his bandanna slipped down to reveal his identity to his hostage. *Hostage.* The word tasted vile, though he hadn't spoken it aloud.

He was a kidnapper.

He yanked the wayward piece of cloth back over his face as if to hide his shame even from himself. *Fat lot of good that'll do.*

"*You?* Don't bother hiding now, because I saw you."

Shame slithered through him as he stroked Ruth's neck. "Damn." Though he knew he shouldn't, he slipped the bandanna back down, then lifted his head to meet Miss Lolita's accusing gaze.

"I never figured you for a kidnapper." Miss Lolita moved closer, shifting her gaze to the horse. "Is she really all right?"

"Yes, thank God." Cole ran his hands along the mare's front legs again. Smiling, he returned to Ruth's head and looked into her soft brown eyes. "Well, old girl, feel like a little walk?"

Clicking his tongue, he gathered the reins and applied firm but gentle pressure until the mare took a few steps. He looked back over his shoulder for any signs of pain. "By God, she really is all right."

"I'm sorry, I didn't mean to hurt your horse," Miss Lolita said. "But you shouldn't have kidnapped me."

Kidnapped. Cole swallowed hard, wishing like hell his bandanna hadn't slipped. Doing this filthy deed anonymously had been one thing, but doing it as Cole Morrison, father of Todd, was quite another. All the more reason he should be ashamed.

Only a coward would hide behind a mask.

"Why'd you kidnap me?" She moved closer, her face flushing with obvious anger. "I'm *not* Lolita, dammit."

He looked at her again, remembering the feel of her firm flesh filling his hand—nice and full, but definitely not what men who'd seen Lolita claimed. Could she be telling the truth?

His gaze swept over her face, and her bizarre red hair startled him back to reality. She *had* to be Lolita Belle. Only a saloon singer would dye her hair. A decent woman wouldn't even consider it, and especially not that glaring shade.

"You're in demand, Miss Lolita," he murmured, trying to justify the sordid mess to himself. And failing. He lifted his uninjured shoulder and averted his gaze. "The price was right."

"You filthy pig." Her voice trembled. "I have to get back to that hellhole and see that portrait finished so I can go . . . go home."

"Now, don't you start bawling." He sighed and didn't allow himself to confirm whether her ruby lips quivered, or any sparkling tears streamed down her rosy cheeks. Surrendering, he faced her. "Just . . . don't."

"Why the hell should I listen to you?" Her eyes snapped and her nostrils flared.

She wasn't crying, but her rage was a palpable thing. Cole had a hunch she could commit murder about now. "Look, nobody's going to hurt you. Hell, they all love you, though God only knows why."

"Excuse me?" She put one hand on her hip and lifted her chin a notch. "They don't want *me*, they want Lolita Belle. I'm not—"

"Yeah, you already said that." He clenched his teeth until they ached, then released a long sigh. "Look, I didn't want to do this, but I . . . I really need the money. You're still going to perform and get paid, so what difference does it make to you if that's at the Gold Mine Saloon or the Silver Spur?"

"What, no Caesar's Palace?"

Her feathers shifted, offering him a brief glimpse of heaven. Cole held his breath as a shudder of longing rippled through him, and he tried to ignore the ornery throb between his legs.

"I'm *not* Lolita Belle. My name is Jackie Clarke and I'm a hairdresser, you fool."

His gaze returned to her hair, so bright it hurt his eyes out here in the sunshine. One corner of his mouth lifted and he arched his brow. "Jack's a man's name, and I don't believe a real hairdresser would do . . . *that* to her hair."

"Shit."

"And you sure talk like a saloon singer."

"What the hell is that supposed to mean?" She scratched her chest. "I'm getting a frigging rash from these feathers."

"My ma would've washed your mouth out with soap by now."

"Bite me." She actually smirked.

His gaze drifted down the length of her again, and a powerful urge to do a lot more than bite her waylaid him. He drew a shaky breath and said, "No, but thanks for offering, ma'am."

"Ha! I don't give a damn that you look like Mel Gibson." She looked up at him through eyes like lethal gray daggers. "Well, you're taller than Mel, but that doesn't mean every woman with a pulse wants to jump your bones. Get over it, cowboy."

"You had your chance," he said, ignoring her second reference to someone named Mel. "Why didn't you make a run for it while I was checking on Ruth here?"

"I . . . I had to stay and make sure she was all right."

"That speaks well of you, ma'am." He nodded and looked over the length of her again. Even though she was a bit on the scrawny side by most standards, she was curvy in all the right places. A fine-looking woman . . . except for the hair. "Ruth's fine."

"Good, then I'll be on my way."

"Nope." He folded his arms and shook his head. "I can't let you do that. I promised to deliver you to Lost Creek, and deliver you I will."

"You son of a . . ." She lifted her fist as if to strike him, then started scratching again instead. "If this is a dream or a coma, then how the hell can I have a rash?" Her tone shifted from fury to uncertainty in the space of a heartbeat.

Cole chuckled. "Trust me, this is no dream." *More like a nightmare.*

"My God." Her eyes widened and her lower lip trembled.

"Don't you start bawling." Cole shoved his hat back farther on his head. "The horse is all right, and we're due at the Silver Spur."

"My rash is real. You're real. *This* is all real," she whispered, her voice trembling, though no tears streamed down her face. "Impossible, but . . . *real.*"

"Yes, ma'am, I reckon you could say that." *Dear Lord, please don't let her start bawling. I swear I won't hurt her and I'll never kidnap another soul as long as I live if you just don't let her bawl. Amen.*

Of course, Cole never planned to kidnap anyone again anyway. This was far more adventure than he could stand.

"I . . . What . . . What am I going to do?"

The terror in her voice and eyes gave him pause. He rubbed the back of his neck. "For starters, let's haul ourselves back on Ruth here and be on our way."

As if in a trance, she met his gaze. "But I don't know how."

Her sudden shift in demeanor worried him. Was Miss Lolita addled in the mind? Well, once he delivered her to Merriweather at the Silver Spur, she would no longer be Cole's problem. The sooner, the better. He sucked in a deep breath and held it.

No matter how much he wanted to touch her again.

It's true, it's true, it's true, true, true. . . . Jackie's lament played over and over again through her mind as she sat stoically in front of her kidnapper on top of a smelly horse. Somehow, she really was stuck back in time and being taken by force to sing in a saloon.

And she had a rash. Absently she scratched again, knowing her chest, shoulders, and back would be raw by the time she shed these ridiculous feathers. She'd kill for a tube of hydrocortisone cream, but they probably didn't have such luxuries in 1891. They didn't even have malls, movie theaters, or high-tech beauty salons. If she didn't sing for her supper, what the hell would she do? But she wouldn't cry, dammit. Instead she sniffled.

"Will you quit that bawl—"

"I'm *not* bawling. Just shut up and drive this thing, cowboy." She didn't bother looking back. "Somebody paid you to kidnap me?"

"That's right, but do we have to call it that?"

"Kidnapping?" She snorted. What had Dottie called him? Oh, yes, Cole Morrison. "What would you prefer I call it, Mr. Morrison?"

"Shit," he snapped, open disgust making the word sound more vile than usual.

"Now who needs his mouth washed out with soap?"

"How'd you learn my name?"

"Dottie told me." Jackie clutched the saddle horn

fiercely as the horse scaled another rocky slope. It certainly wasn't hard to see why they called these the *Rocky* Mountains.

"You know, Miss Lolita, the miners will pay dearly to hear you sing, but if you talk to them the way you've been talking to me, you'll find yourself without a job."

Jackie snorted again, then chewed her lower lip as reality reared its ugly head for an encore performance. She had to be practical about this. If she didn't play along and pretend to be Lolita Belle, she'd be the Wild West equivalent to a bag lady. "Damn."

"Seems we both could stand a little taste of lye soap." His chuckle was warm and not the least bit condescending.

Jackie kept chewing her lip, trying not to remember how she'd felt lying atop this handsome beefcake a short while ago. And he'd even copped a feel, though she figured that had been accidental. With all these feathers, it was hard enough for *her* to determine what was shoulder and what wasn't. That surge of heat she'd noticed had been simple fear, of course. No reason to let another deceitful man turn her not-so-pretty head.

Cole Morrison was no better than Blade—after all, he was male—and she'd better not forget that. *Survival, Jackie.* "So . . . you think the miners will actually pay to hear me sing, huh?"

"That's what I've been told." Cole urged the horse over a fallen tree, then took a fork that led into a dense forest of pine and aspen. "You're a legend in these parts."

"Legend?" *The Legend of Devil's Gulch?* She shivered as the cool mountain air encircled her bare and feather-covered skin. The rash stung and itched like mad, but she struggled against the urge to scratch any more. She was raw enough. "I doubt they'll feel the same way once they hear me sing." Not to mention their likely reaction to seeing her less-than-huge attributes.

"Well, that isn't my problem."

She glanced back over her shoulder, drawing a sharp breath when she met his piercing blue gaze. *God, he's gorgeous.* Swallowing the lump in her throat, she summoned Blade's image to the forefront of her gray matter and renewed her sense of indignance.

"No, of course it isn't your problem, Mr. Morrison." She flashed a false smile and batted her lashes at warp speed. "You're just delivering the merchandise. Right?" Somewhat vindicated by his flinch and grimace, she faced forward again.

"Touché, Miss Lolita. Touché."

"Why, you don't sound very pleased with your success, Mr. Morrison."

"Would you stop calling me that?"

"But isn't that your name, Mr. Morrison?" His sigh tickled the back of her neck and the curve of her bare shoulder.

"Yep, that's my name." He shifted his weight and momentarily tightened his arms around her as he adjusted his grip on the reins. "Like I told you earlier, I didn't want to do this, but they kept raising the ante until I couldn't say no. I have . . . obligations."

"Money talks, eh?" Jackie cleared her throat. She needed to keep a clear head and determine a way to get back to the Gold Mine Saloon and make sure Lolita's portrait—and *her* time portal—became reality, with or without Lolita's impressive cleavage. Running away would be stupid, considering what had happened to her last time she wandered into the mountains alone. With a sigh, she asked, "How much did the owner of the Silver Spur pay you to kidnap me?"

"I'd rather not say."

"Don't I have a right to know how much I'm worth?" *Sounds like white slavery.*

"No, ma'am, I don't reckon you do."

She heard him grinding his teeth, and satisfaction oozed through her. Good, she wanted him to feel guilty. Her only hope was to convince him to take her back to Devil's Gulch, and she'd use any means necessary.

Remembering the shocked expression on his face when he'd realized where his hand was, she squirmed. *Any means, Jackie?* Her belly roiled and a chill chased itself down her spine even as an insistent and irritating warmth settled deep and low and fast. *Talk about internal contradiction.*

Damn.

Cole Morrison was a handsome devil, but so was Blade. Jackie closed her eyes for a moment. *No way.* She'd fallen easily into Blade's deceptive arms, but not because she was loose, as Aunt Pearl would have proclaimed. No, she'd fallen victim to Blade's charms simply because she wanted to be loved. Always had.

Fool.

She couldn't use sex to convince Cole to do her bidding. Couldn't and wouldn't. Her eyes popped open and she commanded her hormones to surrender unconditionally, knowing they wouldn't listen. Her only choice was to ignore them as best she could.

But what if using her body was the only way to convince Cole to help her? No, she had to think, use her brain instead of her body, and forget her irksome libido once and for all.

Kidnapper or not, she suspected he was a man with a conscience, and that this activity violated his sense of right and wrong. Why she believed that, she wasn't sure. It wasn't as if she had a good track record when it came to judging men. Even so, she had nothing to lose by appealing to his sense of fairness, if he actually had one.

And play on his guilt for all it was worth.

Cole urged Ruth into a slow trot when they emerged on the far side of the forest. A wide meadow sprinkled with wildflowers was the only thing between them and the tiny town of Lost Creek, where the largest building was the Silver Spur Saloon.

The sooner he deposited the mouthy Miss Lolita with her new employer, the happier he'd be. Then he'd take the promised gold home and plan their trip to Oregon. The mere thought of a ranch made him downright giddy.

The dream. His and Elizabeth's. With a bittersweet sigh, he nudged Ruth into a canter, eager to finish this sordid business.

"Do you mind?" Miss Lolita said, clutching the saddle horn with both hands. "It's all I can do to stay in the saddle without you galloping like a madman."

"This isn't a gallop, but Ruth can set a fair pace." He chuckled low. "Want to see?"

"Don't. You're killing me." Pain etched her words.

Cole slowed the mare, puzzled. "With all due respect, ma'am, Ruth's doing all the work."

"Yes, but you're bouncing my . . . Oh, never mind."

Once Ruth returned to a slow walk, Miss Lolita released the saddle horn and folded her arms across her chest. Heat suffused Cole's face as he realized exactly what had been bouncing. He cleared his throat and muttered, "Beg pardon, ma'am." She didn't say anything, but he felt her relax a little. "We'll be at the Silver Spur in no time."

"Go ahead; make my day." Bitter laughter erupted from the woman, but she didn't look back at him. "This is one helluva lot worse than a bad-hair day."

Even more confused, he shook his head. With hair the color of Miss Lolita's, every day must be a bad-hair day.

"Ah, I suppose that little oasis ahead is our destination."

Cole urged Ruth across the dry creek bed and onto a rutted dirt road. "Yep, straight ahead lies Lost Creek, Colorado."

"Oh, joy. Oh, rapture."

"Whatever you say, Miss Lolita."

"I'm *not* . . ." She left the declaration unfinished and shook her head. "Never mind."

They were less than a hundred yards from the edge of town when she held up one hand and said, "Wait." She looked over her shoulder, her eyes wide and pleading. "I don't suppose you have a spare shirt I could borrow?"

"No, I'm afraid not, ma'am." He understood her dilemma. Even a famous saloon singer must have had second thoughts about riding into town wearing only feathers and men's jeans.

She sighed and faced forward again. "Thanks anyway."

You son of a bitch, Morrison. No matter what kind of woman Lolita Belle was, he couldn't take her into town exposed this way. It was wrong. He nudged Ruth toward a clump of pines and dismounted, looping the reins over a low branch. Without speaking, he held his hands up to Miss Lolita, trying to ignore the lingering ache in his shoulder.

"What?" She tilted her head to one side and stared at him through those expressive eyes of hers. "You aren't going to try anything, are you?"

Cole blinked and narrowed his gaze until realization sliced through him. "Ma'am, I could've done that a long time ago if I'd been so inclined." He cleared his throat, trying not to remember just how inclined he'd felt with her softness filling his hand. Instead he reached for the buttons of his shirt and released them one at a time, tugging the tail out until it flapped in the breeze.

She arched a brow. "Then why are you taking off your clothes, cowboy?"

He shoved his hat farther back on his head. "First, I'm not a cowboy, at least not yet." He held up two fingers. "Second, I'm trying to do the gentlemanly thing here and give you the shirt off my back."

"Oh." A smile curved her lips as he slipped his hands around her tiny waist and lowered her to the ground, her feather-covered bosom coming dangerously close to his bare chest.

A knot formed in his throat at the transformation in her appearance when she smiled. Miss Lolita was . . . well . . . beautiful. He held his breath and released her to remove his shirt, wincing at the stabbing pain in his shoulder, then offered her the garment.

"Thanks." She smiled again.

"You're welcome." He stood there like a roped steer, sliding his suspenders back over his bare shoulders.

"You have a bruise." She bit her lower lip and

caressed his wounded shoulder with her now-tender gaze.

"It's nothing." He held his breath, reining in his rampant urges.

"I'm sorry I went crazy, but I didn't know what to do." She sighed and met his gaze again. "I didn't mean for you or Ruth to get hurt."

He couldn't believe this was the same woman who'd screamed loud enough to send his mare into hysteria earlier. He stared long and hard at Miss Lolita, then gave a curt nod, reminding himself he couldn't really be sure she wouldn't go crazy again. "It's all right now."

"Thanks." She made a twirling motion with her finger. "Uh, do you mind?"

"Oh, of course, ma'am." He half turned, then shot a look back over his shoulder. "You aren't going to try anything, are you?"

"Huh. Where would I go?" She rolled her eyes heavenward. "Getting lost in the frigging mountains is what got me in this mess in the first place."

She made less sense than that snake-oil salesman who came through town every spring and fall. "Good enough." He turned his back and folded his arms over his bare abdomen. A man could get mighty cold at night in these mountains without a shirt. He'd have to ask Merriweather for one. Now *that* was a name Cole wished he'd never heard. . . .

"All right, you can turn around now."

He pivoted and almost laughed at the ridiculous sight. His shirt engulfed her, hanging nearly to her knees and gaping open at the neckline, where he'd lost a button last summer and never bothered to replace it. She rolled the sleeves up just above her slender wrists, then put her hands on her hips.

"There, how do I look?"

Cole laughed. "Like a little boy wearing his pa's clothes."

"You know damn well I'm not a little boy," she said in a sultry tone, then bent down to retrieve the ostrich feathers at her feet. "Would you like to try wearing these itchy things for a while, Mr. Morrison?"

The reminder of his earlier indiscretion regarding her anatomy sent a flash of quicksilver between his legs. To make matters worse, her gaze raked his nakedness, and if he wasn't mistaken, she liked what she saw. *Damnation.*

"No," he whispered, his voice gruff and thick, "you definitely are not a boy." He took the feathers and draped them around a tree branch. "We'd better go on into town so I can get home before dark."

"Mmm, you do have a fine set of pecs, Mr. Morrison." She winked, then turned and put the wrong foot in the stirrup. After a few seconds of staring at her misplaced foot, she seemed to realize her error and switched. "I'm a quick study."

"Yeah, I can see that." Chuckling, he swung himself up behind the saddle and gathered the reins, then turned Ruth toward Lost Creek and the Silver Spur. "Uh, mind if I ask a question?"

"Go for it, big guy."

"What are pecs?"

Chapter Five

Jackie grew far too aware of Cole's shirtless state as they rode into the minuscule town of Lost Creek. The heat of his body seeped toward her, closing the short distance between her back and his impressive chest. His bare arms at her sides didn't help any either.

She'd never imagined a man wearing suspenders without a shirt would look so good. *Oh, my.* And they were red suspenders, too.

You're in big trouble, Clarke, and you can't keep your mind off this man. Self-disgust oozed through her, and she resisted the urge to scratch her rash. When she'd removed the boa to put on the shirt, she noticed angry red welts covering her chest and shoulders. Her back felt even worse. Of course, those welts would have to grow a lot before she'd live up to the real Lolita's legendary bustline.

Despite her situation, a grin tugged at the corners of

her mouth. Under other circumstances, she would've found this entire adventure utterly hilarious. *If* it were happening to someone else . . .

A few moments later, Cole brought the horse to a stop in front of a garish building painted fiery red with canary yellow trim. A sign arched over the swinging doors, telling her they'd reached their destination.

The Silver Spur seemed far too extravagant for such a small town, but it was just one more in a long series of the oxymorons she'd encountered. It wouldn't be the last, either.

"Why such a big saloon for such a small town?" she asked as Cole dismounted and looped the horse's reins over a hitching post.

"Competition's fierce." He chuckled quietly. "The miners live in shacks and cabins all over these hills, and all the towns are part of the Devil's Gulch Mining District."

His cockeyed grin gave him a rakish charm that nearly made her fall off the horse. "So the miners visit the various saloons in the area for, uh, relaxation and refreshment?" She hoped her voice didn't reveal her attraction to her own abductor.

"And entertainment." His expression grew solemn as he held his hands up to assist her. "In this case, you. The saloonkeepers all believe you're the key to success—that every miner in the area will spend his paycheck in the establishment where you're singing."

"Oh, yeah." She swallowed the lump in her throat as Cole gripped her waist to ease her descent. She had way too many problems now to think about how good it felt to have him so close. *Focus, Clarke.*

"Ouch." She rubbed her backside as her feet met

the ground. "My God, is that saddle made of concrete?"

"Just leather, ma'am."

At least the pain might keep her mind off his pecs. She directed a sideways glance. *Doubtful.*

Besides her aching butt and stiff legs, the main problem now was that she'd be expected to perform. How was she going to manage that? When Aunt Pearl had insisted she try out for the church choir during high school, she'd been asked—politely, of course—not to come back. The preacher's nasty daughter had muttered something about a dying cat.

Jackie hadn't been offended, because it was true. She couldn't sing. Period. In a word, she sucked. Except in the privacy of her own shower, she never sang, though she knew the words and tunes to almost every Broadway musical ever produced.

And now she had to hop up on the stage and entertain a bunch of drunken miners. At least, she hoped they would be drunk, because that was the only way they might be able to endure her singing.

"Well, here we are," he said, stopping suddenly to face her. "I just want to thank you for being so . . . understanding about this. Eventually." He grinned again.

A lump lodged in her throat, and Jackie managed a quick nod before he led her toward a pair of swinging doors. She should hate Cole Morrison, but she couldn't. It didn't take a rocket scientist to realize he'd never done anything dishonest before in his life. No way. Obviously he needed the money pretty badly and had his own reasons for taking the job. It didn't really matter, as long as she found her way back to Lolita's portrait—and her own time—sooner or later. Preferably sooner.

Holding her breath, Jackie followed Cole into the saloon. Tobacco smoke flavored with the stench of beer and whiskey struck her immediately. The Silver Spur wasn't nearly as large as the Gold Mine Saloon, but it was more extravagantly decorated. The now-familiar spittoons occupied every available corner, and several crystal chandeliers illuminated the gaudy interior; ornate carving adorned the bar and the stage.

The stage.

Jackie's blood turned to ice as she stared at the stage. Highly polished and elevated, it gleamed beneath the largest chandelier. Silver ropes held red velvet drapes to each side, and heavy fringe cascaded in a waterfall from the curtain's edges.

"Hey, is that her?" someone yelled.

Jackie looked around the saloon and found several intense gazes boring into her. A tremor skittered through her, and she felt Cole's hand press more firmly against the small of her back.

Was he trying to comfort her or steer her toward destiny? Jackie sighed and tried not to think about the fact that he'd soon be leaving her here among strangers. At least at the Gold Mine Saloon she'd had Dottie to keep her company, and that wasn't saying much. Looking around the Silver Spur, she didn't see any other women.

She was it.

"Oh, my God," she whispered.

"Here comes the owner now," Cole said, his hand still pressed against her back.

"You mean your employer?" She avoided Cole's gaze, but felt him wince. Her comment had found its mark, but for some reason that knowledge gave her no satisfaction. It should have, though, and that worried her.

Shifting her attention from her own inconsistent thoughts about her abductor, she spotted a rotund man dressed in a suit with a red-and-silver brocade vest and string tie emerge from the far side of the stage. The guy looked like a pale sumo wrestler. Only bigger. And dressed.

"Well, well, it took you long enough to get here, Morrison," the man said, his gaze riveted to Jackie as he spoke.

"We're here now."

"So you are, though I'm sure wondering why you gave away your shirt." The huge man inclined his head toward Jackie, his meaty jowls jiggling with the effort. "I'm Elwood Merriweather. You must be the famous Miss Lolita Belle." He took her hand, then bent over and planted a sloppy kiss on it.

Yuck.

As he straightened, he brought his gaze level with her chest, and his brows arched in surprise. After a moment his face flushed crimson, and by the time he was upright, he appeared outright skeptical.

"You *are* Miss Belle, aren't you?" He shot Cole an accusing glare even as he spoke to Jackie.

"She's the woman Goodfellow said was Lolita," Cole said. "He was even having her portrait painted."

"Not exactly what I expected." Merriweather sighed and gave her a sheepish grin. "I realize you don't have your trunk, considering the, uh, circumstances, but I've arranged for a wardrobe. I hope you'll be pleased." His florid coloring intensified again. "Though I daresay the garments will require some alteration."

"Yeah, I'll bet." Jackie pressed her lips into a thin line and vowed to say as little as possible. She had to do this until she returned to Devil's Gulch and Lolita's portrait.

The man faced Cole again, his brow furrowed. "Morrison, if you've brought me a ringer, I swear . . . "

"He hasn't." Jackie bit the inside of her cheek. Why the devil had she said that?

Merriweather lifted his chin a notch and folded his arms across his rotund abdomen. "Then perhaps you won't mind giving us a little demonstration, Miss Belle."

Several of the miners seated close enough to overhear echoed Merriweather's request.

"Now?" Jackie gave a nervous laugh and patted her hair. "I'm hardly dressed to entertain, sir. Surely you could allow me to freshen up." She batted her lashes at light speed and held her breath.

Merriweather stared at her for several moments. "No, I think not," he finally said. "Forgive me, ma'am, but I need to know that you're the real Lolita." He shot Cole a sidelong glance. "Before I fork over the gold."

"Just hop up there and sing something," her abductor urged, nudging her. "If you sing *real* pretty, maybe old Merriweather will loan me a shirt."

Jackie scowled at the humorous glint in Cole's eyes. He was laughing at her again. *Damn him.*

"We're waiting, Miss Belle," Merriweather said, his beady little eyes darkening.

Jackie's knees quaked as she climbed the steps at the side of the stage. How the hell was she going to manage this? Once they realized she was a fraud, she'd be out the door on her butt with nowhere to go. *God, please let them all be tone-deaf.*

The only songs she knew were from Broadway musicals that wouldn't be written for decades, and some old Peter, Paul, and Mary tunes her mother used to sing as lullabies.

With a sigh, Jackie perused the crowd of grubby, eager miners. They'd never grasp "Puff the Magic Dragon." The show tunes were a better bet.

Okay, Clarke. Maybe singing loud and smiling while she batted her lashes would help. After all, these men didn't have any other females to drool over. *Sheesh.*

She drew a deep breath and belted out the first verse and chorus of "I Could've Danced All Night" from *My Fair Lady.*

Dead silence filled the saloon, and Jackie's heart thundered in her head. Her moment of truth had arrived.

"Let's have another one," a scruffy man in the front row called, then blew her a kiss.

"Yeah, that was great," another miner said, moving closer to the stage. "More, Miss Lolita." He started clapping and the others joined in.

She sought out Cole Morrison, who had a look of utter bewilderment on his handsome face, as did Mr. Merriweather. Obviously they weren't as tone-deaf as the others. Thank heavens the miners were the ones she needed to impress.

She smiled and blew the men kisses, then bellowed her way through songs from *The Music Man, Carousel,* and *The Sound of Music.*

Breathless, she stood bewildered by the small crowd's adoration. They cheered, applauded, whistled, and a few men even shouted marriage proposals.

Amazed and feeling more than a little smug, Jackie

made her way through her audience and winked at Merriweather. "It looks like I've got what it takes, after all."

Cole chuckled and shook his head. "Definitely a crowd pleaser."

She warmed beneath his praise, though she knew he didn't really like her singing. What reasonably intelligent, hearing person would? Unless they were starved for the sight and sound of any woman. That was all that had saved her. She wasn't foolish enough to believe anything else.

"All right, you're Lolita Belle," Merriweather said, scratching his bald head. "You'll start tonight."

"Nope." Jackie folded her arms and tilted her head to one side, praying her bravado would hit its mark. "It's not quite that simple, Mr. Merriweather."

"Oh, hell," Cole muttered under his breath, and rolled his eyes upward.

When he looked at Jackie again, she gave him a conspiratorial wink. Kidnapper or not, she liked the guy, and he was drop-dead gorgeous. Besides, she needed someone to take her back to Devil's Gulch when the time came. In short, she needed a friend.

"When can you start then, Miss Belle?" Merriweather pulled a handkerchief from his pocket and mopped perspiration from his bald head. "Tomorrow? The next day? When?"

Jackie drew a deep breath, praying she could pull this off and buy herself enough time to return to the correct century before she ever had to appear as Lolita in an official capacity. "I'll need three weeks to rest from my ordeal." She directed an accusing glare in Cole's direction. "Being kidnapped takes its toll on a girl, Mr. Merriweather." She gave a dramatic sigh and batted her lashes again. The man was a sucker for that, thank goodness.

"Three . . . weeks?" Merriweather mopped his brow and the back of his neck. "Three?"

"At least," Jackie said, sighing again. "Furthermore, I want you to guarantee a full house, and we'll need to agree on my cut of the take."

"Cut?" Merriweather looked upward and shook his head. "Twenty percent."

"Fifty," Jackie said without hesitating. She met Cole's gaze and he returned her earlier wink, turning her insides to something warm and mushy. "Fifty percent, Mr. Merriweather. That's only fair, considering how you hired someone to *kidnap* me and haul me across the wilderness without my clothes."

"I suppose that will give us time to have your clothes altered," Merriweather finally said, resignation sounding almost like defeat in his tone. He looked over his shoulder. "Tom, run fetch the tailor."

"Tailor?" Jackie echoed.

"We don't have a seamstress in Lost Creek, Miss Belle. I ordered your wardrobe from Denver." He loosened his tie and faced Cole. "We got us another problem, though."

"What's that?" Cole's eyes narrowed as he stared at Merriweather.

"Goodfellow will try to get her back."

"Yeah, I reckon he will at that." Cole stroked his chin with his thumb and forefinger. "That's your problem, Merriweather. I'll just collect my wages and be on my way."

Jackie closed her eyes, wishing there were some way to keep him here, though heaven knew what she'd do with him if she kept him. She opened her eyes and admired the dark hair curling on his broad expanse of chest. Well, she did know what she could do with him, but that was just the sort of behavior that had landed her in this trouble. Besides, she was looking for love and sex—not just sex.

Don't go there, Clarke.

"No, wait, Morrison," Merriweather said.

"Start counting my gold," Cole said, obviously avoiding Jackie's gaze.

He feels guilty. Good.

Merriweather surveyed the crowd, openly pleased with his customers' reaction to Jackie's performance. "How would you like to earn triple what I offered you to bring Miss Belle here?"

Surprise flickered across Cole's face. "You mean triple the double offer?"

"Yes, exactly." Merriweather lifted his chin and stared at Cole. "Triple. What do you say?"

Cole sighed and shifted his weight to his other foot, then raked his fingers through his dark hair. He gripped his hat in his free hand. "This sticks in my craw, Merriweather," he said. "I don't like being on the wrong side of the law."

"Triple, Morrison, and who says you broke any laws?" Merriweather looked like a used-car salesman moving in for the kill. "Think of that ranch you and your wife always wanted."

Wife? Is that why he needs the money?

"Let's leave my wife out of this. Let her rest in peace. I swear, if I ever lay eyes on that preacher again . . ." Cole rubbed the back of his neck, his muscles flexing and rippling in his arm and shoulder. "Exactly what do you expect me to do for that much money, Merriweather?"

Oh, nuts. He was available. Now she'd have even more trouble keeping her feelings under control where this man was concerned. Jackie chewed the inside of her lower lip as she waited for this latest development in her adventure through another dimension.

"Nothing dishonest," Merriweather said. "All you gotta do is keep Miss Belle hidden until her opening night."

Jackie's brows shot upward and she tried to meet Cole's gaze, but he quickly looked away. Did Merriweather's plan mean she'd remain in close proximity to this walking, living, breathing, unmarried Mel Gibson for three full weeks?

If so, she was in *big* trouble.

"How the devil am I supposed to keep her hidden for three weeks?"

"Shh, keep your voice down," Merriweather said, looking around the room nervously. Seeming convinced that no one was eavesdropping, he leaned closer. "Just take her to your place and keep her there until opening night. Nobody'll ever guess."

"My . . . place?" The words sounded like a curse from Cole's lips.

"Of course. You see anybody in here you know?"

Cole looked around and shook his head. "Nope."

"Then no one will ever suspect straight-arrow Cole Morrison," Merriweather continued, his eyes glowing with blatant avarice. "And, by damn, that preacher gets a lifetime of free drinks."

"I dunno." Cole slapped his hat against his thigh, and his cheeks colored.

My God, he's blushing. There was something incredibly sexy about a man who blushed. *Damn.* She was pitiful. They were talking about her life, and all she could do was stare at Cole's chest and shoulders. Had her staring made him blush?

But what choice did she have but to play along? Besides, three weeks might be enough time to convince Cole to return her to Devil's Gulch. This really was her only hope.

"*Triple* the money, Morrison." Merriweather held up three beefy fingers. "Triple. In gold."

Cole met Jackie's gaze for the first time in several minutes and she shrugged, trying to appear nonchalant about the whole thing. "All right." He sighed. "I don't like it, but I'll do it on one condition."

"Fine, fine, as soon as the tailor is finished taking a few measurements for the alterations, you two can be on your way." Merriweather faced Jackie again. "Three weeks from tonight, a full house, and fifty percent of the take. Deal, Miss Belle?"

Jackie drew a deep breath and nodded. "Deal."

"I *said* there's one condition," Cole said, his voice tinged with impatience.

"Yes, of course. One condition. What?" Merriweather waited, but Cole's glare was for Jackie.

"What?" she echoed, wondering why he thought she had any control over anything in this mess.

He moved so close she could smell him. Feel him. Almost taste him. Jackie's breath froze even as her body warmed. It took every ounce of self-restraint she could muster to keep from leaning into all that bare chest. His eyes darkened and his nostrils flared slightly.

What a man.

He shook his finger in her face. "You can stay at my place only if you make a solemn vow."

"What?" she repeated. "Do you think I'm going to compromise your virtue or something?"

Merriweather guffawed.

Cole leaned even closer, his eyes glittering dangerously. "No singing."

Jackie couldn't prevent her laughter, but Cole was the only one wearing a deadly serious expression. "Okay, no singing." She held her hands up in surrender. She'd agree to almost anything to gain more time to charm Cole into taking her back to Devil's Gulch.

Merriweather mopped his eyes dry and stopped laughing. "Then it's settled. I'll see you both back here in three weeks." He pointed a finger at Cole. "And if you deliver her safe and sound then, the gold is yours."

"Not so fast, Merriweather. What about what you already owe me?" Cole towered over the saloon owner, his expression stern.

"Wouldn't you rather have a lot more later than a little now?" Merriweather asked in a patronizing tone.

Cole leaned closer. "I'd rather have *both.*"

Merriweather gave a snort and nodded. "Very well, I'll get the first installment."

"*And* a shirt."

"And a shirt." Merriweather rolled his eyes. "Oh, there's the tailor now, Miss Belle, to take your measurements. Wilson, you can use my office."

A small man carrying a case followed Merriweather, and Jackie gathered she was expected to join them. With a shrug, she obeyed, figuring it best to cooperate now and savor her freedom later. Silently, she was grateful that Cole followed close behind. For some reason she trusted him. Strange emotion for a woman to feel toward her kidnapper.

Dark and gaudily carved mahogany furnishings occupied Merriweather's office. The seat cushions and drapes were the same red velvet with silver trim as the stage curtain. At least the rotund man was consistent with his horrible taste.

Cole pulled on a stiffly starched shirt more than a few sizes too large and tucked it into the waistband of his jeans, then slipped his suspenders back in place. Jackie stifled her sigh of regret that his muscular chest was no longer on display.

But she had the next three weeks alone with Cole. A tiny shiver of excitement raced through her, and she silenced Aunt Pearl's voice in the back of her mind.

I don't have to listen to you while I'm here. She'd deal with Aunt Pearl later, after she returned to her own time. Now she was a free agent with only her own conscience to guide her.

Scary thought.

In truth, her own conscience was more than enough to keep her in line. Besides, hadn't she learned her lesson with Blade? No more men for Jackie Clarke. *Too much trouble.*

Then why couldn't she convince her hormones of that?

The fitting wasn't nearly as humiliating as she'd expected, though the tailor did grumble about how much he'd have to alter to make the gowns fit her more modest bust and hips. Jackie amazed herself by keeping her comments to herself, though she grew increasingly aware of Cole's approving gaze aimed in her direction.

The man made her hot. *Get a grip, Clarke.* Forcibly quelling her rampant libido, she endured the fitting in stony silence. Finally she and Cole were making their way back through the front room of the Silver Spur. Long shadows stretched across the room as they maneuvered their way through the crowd of gawking miners. These guys were worse than the Brothers Grime back at the Gold Mine Saloon. Almost.

Only a few yards from the swinging front doors, a chill washed over her, and the fine hairs on the back of her neck stood on end. Someone was staring at her. She almost laughed. Of course, an entire roomful of men was staring at her. However, her uneasiness persisted, and she looked toward a card game in the corner.

A pair of hauntingly familiar dark eyes met her questioning gaze. Her heart slammed into her chest, and a cold sweat coated her skin. A desert overtook her mouth and throat, and no amount of swallowing provided relief.

"Come on, it's late," Cole said, steering her toward the doors.

Jackie watched those dark eyes following her until she emerged into the late-afternoon light. The cool mountain air revived her and she shook her head, denying what she'd seen as Cole helped her into the saddle and swung himself up behind her.

"You sure got quiet all of a sudden," he said, nudging the horse away from the Silver Spur and the town of Lost Creek. "I don't reckon it'll last, though."

Jackie looked back, leaning to the side enough to see past Cole. She half expected to find the dark-eyed man in hot pursuit, but the lone street stretched empty behind them. It had to have been her imagination. She faced forward again, willing her hands to cease their trembling and her pulse to slow to a moderate pace.

Anxiety made way for another emotion, one she hadn't felt since before her trip through the looking glass—rather, Lolita's portrait—anger. And a raging thirst for revenge.

She clenched her teeth, gripping the saddle horn until her knuckles whitened and her fingers ached. Was it possible? Could he really be here, too? The man's dark eyes, his unshaven face, his inky hair merged in her mind's eye to taunt her.

Blade.

Chapter Six

Cole rushed the mare as much as he dared through the darkening mountain pass. Todd would be worried. Besides, Cole never left his son alone this late. The little guy might be self-reliant, but he was still just a child.

"Did you see that man?" Miss Lolita asked after an uncharacteristically long silence.

"Which man? The place was crawling with men."

"The one in the corner who was staring at me."

He chuckled. "They were all staring."

"Yes, but . . ." She sighed, her shoulders slumping. "Never mind. It must've been my imagination."

Something was obviously worrying the woman, but Cole sensed she didn't want to talk about it. Thinking back, he couldn't remember anyone, other than Merriweather himself, being rude or unseemly toward her. Maybe she did recognize the man she was worried about. A woman like her must know more than her share.

Heat crept up Cole's neck to his face. The woman's personal life was none of his business, but for some blamed reason it bothered the hell out of him to think of her *being* with a lot of men.

She's a saloon singer. She made her living by entertaining men.

Did she entertain them in other ways, too?

Dang it all. He didn't want to know, and it didn't—shouldn't—matter to him anyway.

And how the devil was Cole supposed to explain Miss Lolita to a nine-year-old boy? He slowed the horse as they rounded the final curve before the ground leveled out again. The last thing in the world Cole wanted was for his son to know his father had stooped to kidnapping for a few gold nuggets.

More than just a few. The money Merriweather had promised him would be enough to allow him and Todd to leave Devil's Gulch and head for Oregon. He'd probably have enough left to buy some land and a few hundred head of cattle before winter.

His spirits lifted. The woman wasn't being harmed, after all, and she'd negotiated a respectable deal with old Merriweather herself. Cole chuckled quietly, remembering how the miners had responded to that racket she called singing. After that, Miss Lolita had been able to name her price. And so she had.

Damned peculiar. A man would have to be either deaf or starving for the sight *and* sound of a woman to enjoy Miss Lolita's voice. She had a way about her, though. His mother would've called it charm. In fact, if not for the crazy red hair and her chosen profession, he suspected his mother would've liked her.

Actually, the more time he spent with her, the more *he* liked her.

"How much farther?" she asked, glancing back over her shoulder.

"Just up yonder." He pointed up the sloping trail that led to his cabin, suddenly wary that someone might see them climbing the mountain. The sun had nearly set, and darkness bathed the lower valleys, but the higher they went, the lighter the sky.

Her hair was like a signal fire to anybody searching for her, and he'd be willing to bet money these mountains were crawling with men on the lookout for the famous Lolita Belle. Without another thought, he yanked off his hat and put it on her head.

"Hey, why'd you do that?"

"Don't want anybody to recognize you."

She nodded and adjusted the hat's angle, tucking her hair up under it. "There, better?"

She looked back and flashed him that big, open smile of hers. He caught his breath. Without that dyed hair hanging around her face, she looked like a different woman. Her eyes were large and expressive, fringed with thick, inky lashes. Her lips were full and the color of rubies. Beckoning.

Kissable.

Rein yourself in, Morrison. He'd definitely been too long without a woman. She faced forward again, and one red curl slipped from the back of the hat, helping him put things in perspective. She was a saloon singer who dyed her hair—not the kind of woman he could take up with even if he wanted to.

And the more he thought about her, the more he wanted to.

He recalled the way her womanly softness had filled his hand, with her dusky nipple peeking between his gloved fingers. Tauntingly. A powerful ache commenced between his legs. Considering he was *behind* the saddle, one wrong move could cause him more physical distress than he'd known in a decade. Of course, having this particular woman around day and night for three weeks was bound to cause him a passel more physical distress before this was finished.

"Are we there yet?" she asked again, turning enough to show her profile in the twilight. "I need to, uh . . . "

He nodded, comprehending what she hadn't said. "Just beyond that outcropping."

"Hot damn."

"Miss Lolita . . . ?"

She sighed but didn't look at him. "What?"

"I'd appreciate it if you'd watch your language and such while you're at my cabin."

She laughed quietly. "You don't talk like a Sunday-school teacher yourself, Morrison."

"Well, that's a fact," he said, grinning. "But I do try to watch my language at home."

She half turned again, arching a brow. "Why? I thought you lived alone."

He shook his head. "My wife died a few years ago, but I have a son."

She twisted more, her eyes widening and her lips curving into another smile. "Really? That's great. I always . . . wanted a child."

Cole fell silent as the cabin came into view. Miss Lolita wanted a child? She was full of surprises. "I need your word, ma'am." He brought Ruth to a stop on the rise just above the house.

"My word?" She blinked; then her mouth formed a circle. "Oh, right. About my, uh, behavior. Sure, I'll be good. *Very* good."

Fire ignited between Cole's legs, and he drew a deep breath, then released it very slowly. "I'll bet," he said gruffly, "but you know what I mean."

"Sorry. I will watch my language and behavior while I'm at your cabin." Her smile widened and she fluttered her lashes the way she had at Merriweather and the miners.

"Thank you. I appreciate it." Cole cleared his throat.

"Anything for you, big guy."

Liquid fire crept up his neck from his stiff collar and settled in both ears. "Calling me that isn't exactly what I'd call behaving."

She winked. "I'll be good. Cross my heart." She drew an imaginary X over her chest. Between those tempting breasts . . .

He had to keep his mind, his hands, and his gaze off her bosom. They were more enticing than any part of a woman's anatomy had a right to be. Full. Firm. Perfect.

Enough, Morrison. He wrenched his gaze from her chest to her face and realized she knew where he'd been looking. From that devilish gleam in her eyes, he'd be willing to bet she'd read his thoughts, too.

Determined to bring those guilty thoughts under control, he cleared his throat again. She'd promised to behave and, though he had no idea why, he trusted her. *Probably dangerous.* "Thanks."

She swung around and gasped just as the cabin came into clear focus. "Oh, Cole, it's beautiful."

The breathy, feminine quality of her voice and easy use of his given name struck a chord deep within his soul. His heart stuttered and skipped a beat. "Elizabeth—my wife—worked real hard to make those flowers grow up here," he said quietly. "Me and Todd have been carrying water to them ever since."

"That's a sweet tribute to her memory." She gave a dreamy sigh—another contrast to her saloon-singer persona. "How old is Todd?"

"Nine. Ten in August."

"He must miss his mother very much."

"Yeah." Cole swallowed hard. "We both do."

"I'm sorry."

"Me, too." He brought Ruth to a stop again as he scanned the cabin for any sign of Todd. "There's one more thing, Miss Lolita. I'd appreciate it if you wouldn't say anything to the boy about . . . about . . ."

"About why and *how* I came to, uh, visit?" She flashed him a crooked grin over her shoulder. "No sweat, big guy. I understand."

And, somehow, he knew she did. Bemused by this vexing and perplexing creature, he swung his leg over the horse's rump and reached up to assist Miss Lolita dismount. "Thank you, ma'am."

She winced as he lowered her to the ground in front of him. "Ouch."

"Beg pardon. Did I hurt you?"

"No, but 'ma'am' makes me sound as old as this saddle makes my fanny feel, cowboy."

He chuckled quietly as she stood there rubbing her backside. He tried not to think about how much he wanted to rub her backside for her. *Dangerous territory, Morrison.* "All right, Miss Lolita."

"Uh, how about calling me Ja—"

"Pa!"

Todd came rushing out the door, but skidded to a halt when he saw Miss Lolita. "I . . . I was worried about you," he said to Cole, though his questioning gaze never left the strange woman.

"Sorry, Todd," Cole said. "I was delayed in town."

Lantern light spilled out the open cabin door, framing the boy's lanky body. Finally Todd pointed at the woman. "Who's she?"

"Hello, Todd," Miss Lolita said in a gentle voice. "My name is Miss Clarke." She stepped closer and extended her hand to the child. "Your father brought me here to . . . to be your teacher for a while. You may call me Miss Jackie."

Miss Jackie? Teacher? Cole coughed and mopped perspiration from the back of his neck. What the hell was this woman up to now? He couldn't imagine what she could possibly teach anybody—well, at least not a nine-year-old boy.

"I don't need no teacher." Todd's tone held more than a trace of skepticism. "And Jackie's a man's name."

Like father, like son. A grin tugged at the corners of Cole's mouth. "Mind your manners."

"Jackie is short for Jacqueline," she said, still waiting for Todd to take her hand.

The boy shook her hand at last, tilting his head to one side as he continued to stare. "You don't look like no teacher. You're wearing men's clothes, too."

Maybe she didn't look like a teacher, but Cole had to admit she sure sounded like one. Encouraged, he listened in silence to his son and his new "teacher."

"I believe you meant to say I don't look like *a* teacher," she corrected. "Double negatives are not allowed." Todd grimaced and she ruffled his hair. "And I think you could stand a trim, too."

"Pa," Todd whined, and Cole's level of confidence that this charade might work blossomed just like Elizabeth's columbine.

"Your ma said folks judge a man's worth by how

well he puts words together." Cole started toward the stable with Ruth in tow. "Learning to speak properly is more important than clothes or anything else. Except for knowing how to treat a lady and a horse, that is."

Miss Lolita coughed. "So I've been elevated to the same rank as a horse. Imagine that."

Todd laughed. Actually laughed. Cole stopped and whirled around to watch. His son seemed like a happy child most of the time, but he rarely laughed out loud this way. Something in Cole's chest swelled near bursting.

"Supper ready?" Cole called, needing to break the spell this strange woman had cast on them.

"Sure thing, Pa." Taking the woman's hand, the boy led his new "teacher" toward the small cabin's front door.

With a sigh, Cole clicked his tongue at Ruth and decided he'd better hurry before their guest said something she shouldn't. Just before the pair vanished through the opening, Miss Lolita—no, he'd best start thinking of her as "Miss Jackie"—waggled her fingers at Cole in an exaggerated way.

His breath caught on a gasp as blood rushed from his head to his loins like a mountain stream during spring thaw. For three weeks he would live in this tiny cabin with a woman as mystifying and stimulating—Lord help him—as any he'd ever known.

With only a nine-year-old boy as chaperon.

Jackie was determined to charm both the Morrison males until they were ready to do anything she asked—like return her to Devil's Gulch for her portrait sitting. Pretty unfair of fate to send her back to a time before her portal existed. However, if that were true, then how had she landed here in the first place? *Don't think about it, Clarke. It probably violates the prime directive.*

Squinting, she shook her head and banished the confusing thoughts. She had enough to worry about just surviving in this time without trying to understand how and why she was here.

The cabin was one open room downstairs with a loft that ran its entire width upstairs. A pair of shuttered windows flanked the front door, and two narrow bunks were pushed against the back wall under the loft, separated by a bookshelf built floor to ceiling. The shelves were filled with books and magazines, seeming out of place in a miner's cabin. But then, she'd already surmised that Cole Morrison was anything but typical.

A rectangular table, a pair of benches, a rocking chair, a barrel, and a pie safe were the only other furnishings. Clothing hung from pegs along the back wall between the bunks; pots and pans occupied the walls nearest the fireplace.

"Home away from home," she muttered. The cabin was pure Americana. The one where Blade had abandoned her was decorated in early Garage Sale.

Blade. The memory of his look-alike slammed into her, and her blood turned frigid all over again. It couldn't have been Blade. Could it?

"Miss Jackie, I hope you like beans and corn bread," Todd said, ladling beans and broth onto tin plates from an iron kettle suspended over the fire.

"Beans are fine, Todd," she said, forcing thoughts of Blade and time travel from her mind. "First tell me where the, uh, outhouse is, then I'll wash up and give you a hand. Deal?"

The boy's narrow shoulders lifted in a shrug and he flashed her a gap-toothed grin. "Straight out back. Take a light. It's getting dark, and we get bears around this time of year."

Bears? She gulped as Todd lit a second lantern and handed it to her. The boy's expression more closely resembled that of an adult than a child. "You're pretty grown up for nine," she said.

Another shrug, but no grin this time. "I gotta help Pa any way I can."

Jackie's throat clogged. This little boy had lost his mother and lived in isolation with his father. Her heart opened to him, but she closed her eyes and sent out an emotional torpedo. Mission: search and destroy her caring genes. She'd opened her heart to Blade and look where that had landed her.

Abandoned. Unloved. Alone. Status quo.

She went out the back door, found the outhouse—she'd thought her days with outhouses were gone forever—took care of business, then hurried back inside. She considered herself lucky not to have seen a single bear during her adventure.

Cole still wasn't there, but Todd greeted her with another boyish grin. *What a cute kid.*

"You gonna wear Pa's hat all night, Miss Jackie?"

I just might. For some reason, she didn't want to show Todd her hair. This was the Victorian era—*ladies* didn't dye their hair, and especially not such a brazen shade. *Brazen, Clarke?*

"What can I do to help?" she asked, ignoring his comment about the hat. For now.

"There's cups and fresh water over there." He inclined his head toward the barrel near the back door. "Pa hauled fresh water from the spring this morning."

"Three cups of water, then?" Jackie hoped they wouldn't all contract hepatitis. She'd never tasted water from a spring before—a well, yes, but never a spring. Did those bears Todd had mentioned relieve themselves in the spring? With a surrendering shudder, she took the cups Todd had indicated and dipped them into the barrel, then placed them on the table. "What else can I do?"

Todd deftly filled another cup with dark, steaming liquid and placed it on the table. "Pa always wants coffee."

"That he does."

The sound of Cole's voice startled Jackie, and she whirled around to find him watching her. His gaze was wary but gentle. He actually feared she might betray him to his son, even though she'd given her word. Why did the knowledge that he didn't completely trust her hurt? It shouldn't matter.

Another thought—a devious one—formed in her mind. Could she use the threat of telling Todd to coerce Cole into taking her back? She hated the idea immediately, but had to admit it made sense. Todd's opinion of his father was obviously Cole's weak spot. Jackie should wield that power. She should.

But she didn't want to.

She gave Cole a weak smile, remembering to play her role—but just what was her role? Temptress? No, "desperate woman" was a better fit. She sighed, convincing herself that she could pull off "temptress" with the best of them.

His gaze lifted to his hat still perched on her head and he cocked a questioning brow. *Damn.* She had to remove the hat now. No more excuses.

With a sigh, she slipped the hat from her head and handed it to its rightful owner. Cole stood there filling the doorway and the cabin with his incredibly macho presence. Despite his impressive size and strength, there was something endearing about a man who raised his son alone, who carried water to his dead wife's flowers, and who watched his language at home.

You need to torpedo those f-ing caring genes again, Clarke.

With a nod, Cole took the hat and hung it on a peg near the door. "I washed up outside and I'm starved," he said. "Let's eat."

Jackie followed him to the table and slid onto the bench beside Todd. She felt his gaze on her and she knew why. *Dammit.* Sighing, she half turned and gave him a wan smile. His eyes were wide and his mouth agape.

"It isn't nice to stare, Todd," Cole said quietly, reaching for his coffee and taking a sip.

"I . . . ain't never seen hair that color before." Todd's incredulous tone matched his expression.

"Don't say 'ain't,' " Jackie whispered, and took a sip of her water. At least it didn't taste like bear pee. Not that she knew what bear pee tasted like, of course.

"How'd your hair get that color?" Todd pressed.

"An accident." Jackie glowered at Cole, noticing the way his lips twitched and his eyes twinkled. He was laughing at her. *Damn him.* "I didn't mean for it to turn exactly this color."

"You mean you *dyed* your hair?" Todd's obvious shock stung. "I didn't know teachers did—"

"Miss Jackie told you it was an accident, Todd. That's enough." Cole took another sip of coffee, then set his cup down and folded his hands in front of him. "Did I miss the blessing?"

"No, sir."

"Well?"

Jackie smiled to herself while Todd muttered a brief

prayer. Cole had rescued her, even though he'd been silently laughing at her, too. She owed him one. She peered through her lashes at his dark head across the table from her.

"Amen," Todd said, grabbing the corn bread.

"Amen," Cole echoed, looking up to capture Jackie's gaze with his drop-dead-gorgeous eyes. Bedroom eyes.

Her breath caught, and heat settled low and heavy in her belly. Maybe she owed him more than one? The man oozed sex appeal, and she had a hunch he didn't even know it. That made him all the more desirable.

All the more dangerous.

Blade had recognized and used his looks as a highly effective weapon. Against *her.* Deep down—really deep—she'd probably known all along that their fling would never be anything permanent. The truth was, she'd been starving for male affection and had easily fallen victim to his charms.

And now a man every bit as good-looking—all right, even better—was charming her without even trying. And he was a *nice* man, not a con artist. Anyone could see that by the way he treated his son.

But he's also a kidnapper.

Then why didn't she feel like a hostage?

She narrowed her gaze, watching Cole crumble a piece of corn bread over his beans. He scooped up a spoonful and raised it toward his lips, stopping halfway there to meet her gaze.

His lips curved in a boyish grin that stole her breath, then he resumed eating. On the other hand, maybe he *did* know what he was doing to her. He certainly knew when and how to apply his killer smile. Her only defense was to turn his flirtations right back at him. Maybe a bit risky, but what fun . . .

Summoning what she hoped was a sultry expression, she slipped the tip of her tongue across her lower lip, then pursed her lips into a kissable pout and reached for her spoon. He didn't move while she ate her beans and half a piece of corn bread. She reached for her water and took a sip, peering at him over the cup's metal rim. His Adam's apple traveled the length of his throat and back again, his blue eyes darkening to cobalt. No doubt about it—Cole Morrison wanted her.

Heat suffused her as her flirtation backfired with a vengeance. She wanted him, too. Badly.

She was in big trouble.

Her sip of water trickled down the wrong way, and she coughed, setting her cup aside and reaching for the square of blue fabric she assumed was her napkin. Tears gathered in her eyes, and Todd reached over to pound her back right between her shoulder blades.

"You all right, Miss Jackie?" the boy asked.

Jackie nodded and ventured a peek at Cole, who sat there grinning again, his expression far less intense now. He folded his arms across his trim abs and leaned back, a smug, knowing glint in his eyes. Then the man had the audacity to wink at her.

Oh, yeah, Clarke, you're in really *big trouble.*

Chapter Seven

Cole retreated to the cabin's small front porch and gazed up at the stars. The evening air was cool and still; an owl hooted in the distance. From inside, he heard his son laughing again at the mystery woman's strange bedtime story about space travel and someone named Yoda. Cole couldn't recall a character by that name in Jules Verne's most recent novel, and he'd read it three times.

Who was Jackie Clarke, and how had she ended up as a very bad saloon singer named Lolita Belle? Lolita was obviously a stage name, and a successful one at that. Recalling the miners' response to her singing, he chuckled quietly and shook his head. There was just no accounting for taste.

"May the Force be with you, Grasshopper," Lolita-Jackie said from inside the cabin. "Live long and prosper, and nanu-nanu."

Todd's giggles approached the hysterical point,

and guilt pressed down on Cole. His son was being cheated out of his childhood. Lolita-Jackie or whoever was a welcome change in the boy's life.

Imagine that. A saloon singer had brought more joy to his son's life in one evening than Cole had in the years since Elizabeth's death. He shoved his hands into his pockets and leaned against a post.

Cole hadn't planned for Todd to grow up so fast, but the boy had always insisted on helping. Come to think of it, Todd might have learned to cook just to avoid his pa's lousy attempts. A wistful smile tugged at Cole's lips, and he sighed, determined to help his son learn to be a child again.

"He's ready for his dad to tuck him in," Lolita-Jackie said from the doorway.

Cole spun around on his heel and stared at her. Lamplight spilled out around her from inside, igniting her red hair until it glowed. He could barely see her expression, but he could've sworn he saw concern in her eyes. She stepped onto the porch, and Cole slipped inside, trying not to dwell on the cause of her concern . . . if it existed at all.

Todd was tucked into his bunk, his hands folded across his chest and his eyes wide open. Lying in bed with his hair tousled, the boy looked like the child he was, rather than the miniature adult he'd become since his mother's death.

"Thanks, Pa," Todd whispered as Cole bent down to kiss his son's forehead.

"For what?" Cole tucked the quilt more securely around the boy's bony shoulders.

"For bringing me a teacher who tells funny stories."

As long as those funny stories weren't about saloons . . . Cole straightened, gazing down at his son.

"You're welcome." His voice sounded gruff, and he cleared his throat again. "Now get some shut-eye."

"Pa?"

"What?"

"Why don't you let Miss Jackie read some of your sto—"

"No." Cole bit the inside of his cheek. "Nobody wants to look at those."

"But—"

"No. Now get some sleep."

"All right." Disappointment dimmed the light in the boy's eyes. "Night, Pa."

Cole squeezed his son's shoulder, his heart racing and his gut clenching. He'd never shared that secret side of himself with any outsider. "I'll think about it. All right?"

Todd smiled his mother's smile, and Cole's heart broke all over again.

"Night, Pa."

"Night, son."

Cole blew out the lamp nearest the bed, but left the one on the hearth burning. He had to make sure Lolita-Jackie understood where she was to sleep, and what would be expected of her starting tomorrow.

She was the one who'd told Todd she was his teacher. Now, by damn, she'd have to live up to the boy's expectations. Cole paused near the door, clenching and unclenching his fists.

And so help him, if the woman hurt Todd in any way . . .

"Cole, come look quick," she called from outside, her voice washing over him like a cool breeze. "It's a shooting star."

Perplexing didn't begin to describe this woman, and he silently chastised himself for thinking she might harm Todd. He knew without knowing why that she would treat his son well.

Cole joined her at the porch rail, but he didn't even try to see the shooting star. Instead he gazed at her profile bathed in moonlight and starlight.

She was looking up toward the sky, her small nose and full lips clearly defined by the silver moonlight. Her hair appeared dark and colorless, thank goodness, and he breathed a sigh of relief. He could almost forget her chosen profession and the circumstances that had brought her here when that red hair wasn't staring him in the face.

"Ah, you missed it." She turned and smiled, her teeth gleaming in the darkness. "I made a wish."

"Did you now?" What would a woman like her wish for? She probably had plenty of money tucked away somewhere, and he knew firsthand that the miners adored her. What more could she want that she didn't already have? He remembered her comment about wanting a child. Was that her wish?

"I can't tell you what my wish is, or it won't come true." Her voice fell to a faint whisper, and she looked away again. "Pretty stupid of me to be wishing for anything anyway."

He heard something in her voice he hadn't noticed since that first morning he'd dragged her out of the street in front of the Gold Mine Saloon—fear and futility. He thought back to that morning, her insistence that she wasn't Lolita, and her plea for his help. He'd turned his back on her then, and later he'd kidnapped her for pay.

You're lower than low, Morrison. He couldn't undo what he'd already done, but he could try to make amends, especially since she'd inadvertently become his son's teacher and a houseguest, rather than—he winced—a hostage.

"I want to apologize, Miss Lolita," he said quietly, not wanting his son to overhear.

"Call me Jackie, please," she said. "Apologize for what? Kidnapping me?"

"Partly." He nodded and looked up at the stars. "And for not believing you when you asked me for help." He felt her gaze on him, but he didn't look at her. "I'm still not clear why you needed help, or why you insist you aren't Lolita, but a gentleman doesn't turn away from a lady in distress." Repentant, he faced her. "I did."

"Why, Cole Morrison, are you calling me a lady?"

Her tone was light, but he heard the intense undercurrent she kept barely in check. "Yes, ma'am," he said, remembering the way Todd had taken to her. "I reckon I am."

"I'm flattered." She turned away and looked toward the mountains, towering dark masses against the star-strewn sky. "I probably don't deserve that distinction, though. My great-aunt certainly never thought so."

"Well, maybe she doesn't know everything." He touched her arm and she turned to face him again. "And I thank you for being so good to Todd."

"He's an adorable little boy." She smiled again, rubbing her hands along her upper arms. "He has his daddy's killer smile."

Cole chuckled. "Killer, huh?"

"At the very least."

He sighed. "Anyway, I just wanted to tell you I'm sorry about . . . everything."

She nodded, tilting her head to one side to gaze

up at him. "Gee, maybe you can even start believing I'm not Lolita now."

One corner of his mouth tugged upward. "Oh, I wouldn't say that."

She punched him on the arm. "Cad."

"Ow." He rubbed the offended spot, though it didn't hurt at all. "I believe your real name is Jacqueline Clarke, as you say, but that Lolita Belle is your stage name."

She stared at him in silence for several moments. "And if I tell you I never have been Lolita . . . ?"

He remained silent, remembering the miners' reaction to her performance, her wanton pose wearing nothing but feathers for that French painter, and the saloon owners' battle for her appearance at their establishments. Slowly he shook his head. "I want to believe you, but I can't."

To his amazement, she didn't argue with him, but her lips narrowed and her jaw twitched slightly. After a moment of silence, she tilted her head back and looked up at the sky again. "It sure is pretty up here."

"It is when you're above ground."

"You don't have to mine anymore," she said matter-of-factly. "You have all that g—"

"Shhh." He gnashed his teeth in frustration. "Beg pardon. I really don't have any right to ask you to keep my secret after what . . . after . . . but I don't want—"

"I know, I know." She sighed again. "Sorry."

He couldn't suppress a chuckle. "Thanks, but it sure isn't your fault. I'm the one who said I'm sorry . . . and I meant it."

"Apology almost accepted." She laughed quietly, facing him again. "Brother, you don't know the half of it, though. Men started doing me dirty long before you ever came into the picture."

Guilt pressed down on him again. He *had* done her dirty. "Maybe someday you'd like to tell me about it."

She shrugged. "I might, but if you refuse to believe I'm not Lolita, then you sure wouldn't buy the rest of my crazy story." She shook her head. "Half the time I can't believe it myself."

"Truth is stranger than fiction?"

She laughed again. "That's for sure. In fact, I was reading a story sort of like what's happening to me just before . . . "

"Before what?"

"Ah, never mind."

He felt her withdrawal as surely as if she'd slammed a door in his face. There was a lot more behind the story of Lolita Belle than anyone knew—of that he was certain.

"I might tell you about my adventure, Cole," she said quietly, turning to stare at him, "but only if you tell me what made a nice guy like you willing to do Merriweather's dirty work."

"Easy enough." His gut clenched and burned. "I made someone a promise, and I need money to keep it."

She looked out at something only she could see. "And I made *myself* a promise to get revenge against somebody . . . and I aim to keep that promise."

He studied her profile, wondering if she also wanted revenge against him. No, that didn't make sense after the way she'd bartered with Elwood Merriweather and left Lost Creek with him willingly. There was something more she wasn't saying.

"Enough about that." She pivoted toward him

again. "What sort of things should I teach Todd while I'm here?" she asked, obviously wanting to change the subject.

"Everything, I reckon." Cole rammed his hands into his pockets again, trying not to think about his transgressions. "He can read and cipher some, but he needs to learn to talk properly, and I want him to read well enough to really enjoy books."

"Yeah, I noticed that collection of yours in there," she said. "You read all those books, Cole?"

He smiled sadly. "Many, many times."

" 'Still waters run deep,' " she murmured.

He faced her, catching the glimmer of a smile in her moonlit eyes. "I guess you could say that."

"So you aren't really planning to dig in that hole of yours anymore, are you?"

"You mean the mine?" He shrugged. "I have to."

"But what about the . . . you know?"

"I can't count on that until I have it," he said, pulling his hands out of his pockets to grip the porch rail. "Something could go wrong, and my son's future is too important."

"As long as he has a father like you, he'll do fine." She reached over and covered his hand with hers. "Something could go wrong, Cole. You're right about that. If it does, I want you to know I'm sorry, though I still don't know exactly why you need the money so badly."

Why would she be sorry? He was the kidnapper, the desperate man in search of a futile dream. He sighed, but warmth crept up his arm from her touch, and his gaze dropped to where her silvery white hand covered his darker one. "I want to trust you. I really want to."

"I won't run away, Cole," she whispered. "I promise."

"I appreciate that, though I don't understand it."

"There's a lot about me you can't possibly understand, cowboy." She eased her hand away and hugged herself as if chilled.

"You cold?"

"Not on the outside."

Something swelled in his chest, and he ached to reach out to her, to pull her small frame against his chest, to hold her and protect her against the whole world. But he knew that if he touched her now it wouldn't stop there. He burned to taste her lips, to feel the softness of her body pressed against his, to lose himself in her womanly flesh.

The pressure in his chest turned south within the span of two heartbeats. His blood rushed to his groin, tugging until he was hard enough to dig ore. Raking his fingers through his hair, he drew a deep breath and released it very slowly.

"Well, if you're determined to work in your mine, then Todd and I will be fine here." Her voice sounded strained, filled with something undefinable. "We'll start reading some of those books for starters."

"Good." He drew another deep breath, regaining some semblance of self-control. "And thanks."

"Don't thank me, because I'm going to ask you for a favor later. Consider yourself warned."

He stared at her, wondering what favor she could possibly ask of him. Her freedom? She could've taken that many times since reaching the cabin, if she'd wanted. "What is it?"

"Later, cowboy. For now, you've given me a lot to think about," she whispered. "Thanks."

She'd given him one hell of a lot to think about,

too. And want. His eyes dipped to his oversize shirt that still covered her slender body. Hungrily, his gaze settled on the open collar just above her full bosom. This woman would definitely leave a permanent mark on the Morrison males.

He only hoped he lived to tell about it.

By the time Jackie climbed the ladder to the loft, exhaustion made her legs feel as though they weighed a thousand pounds apiece. Garbed in a soft cotton gown that had belonged to Cole's wife, she flopped onto the narrow bunk shoved against the wall beneath the eves.

And stared at the ceiling.

When Cole had offered her his dead wife's clothing, she'd been unable to refuse. She couldn't very well traipse around in his shirt and her filthy jeans indefinitely.

Not indefinitely—temporarily, Clarke. This is only temporary.

Somehow she would determine a way to return to her own time, to indoor plumbing, and to freezers full of ice cream and ice makers. This primitive Americana scene was for people made of tougher stuff.

And why was she being so damned cooperative with Cole Morrison? This was nuts. Okay, she knew why—she was attracted to her kidnapper. Talk about shallow. Obviously she still hadn't learned her lesson about men.

But Cole Morrison wasn't Blade Smith. Thank God. Her eyes drifted closed on a sigh, but sleep continued to elude her. Vivid memories of Blade, of her stupidity, and of her great-aunt's constant criticism made her tense and very much awake.

Before being thrown back in time, she'd vowed to exact revenge against Blade. Sitting up in bed, she clenched her fists in her lap. Dammit, she still wanted that revenge. Blade had it coming, too.

A chill chased itself down her spine as she remembered that man in the Silver Spur. He couldn't have been Blade. Maybe an ancestor? But if he wasn't Blade, why had he stared at her so intently?

As if he knew her.

"Cut the crap, Clarke," she muttered, falling back on the bunk. The man might very well be one of Blade's ancestors. After all, he had claimed that the cabin where he abandoned her belonged to his family. However, there was no way his ancestors could know about her.

Unless he was here, too.

Impossible. But until she experienced time travel up close and personal, she'd believed *that* impossible, too. If she was here, then couldn't Blade be, too?

"No," she whispered, dragging her hands over her face, hoping to stop the crazy thoughts.

She had to concentrate on facts and on her present present. Fact number one: Cole planned to return her to Lost Creek for her opening night.

Fact number two: she had to get back to Devil's Gulch and her portrait sitting.

But how? She'd think about that later.

Fact number three: Cole Morrison expected her to stay here and play teacher to his adorable little boy. And she was actually looking forward to it.

Sucker.

Fact number four: if the real Lolita showed up before her opening night or her portrait was completed, she was up Shit Creek without a paddle. Plus, Cole wouldn't get paid, and for some crazy reason she wanted him to have the promised gold. Furthermore, once he learned she really wasn't Lolita, he'd have no more reason to keep her under his roof. She'd be homeless in a strange place and an even stranger time.

Damn.

She heard Cole close the door, and a scraping sound she couldn't identify followed. He was probably doing something to the fireplace. After a few moments, the scent of wood smoke drifted up to the loft. She heard the rustle of fabric as he undressed; then he blew out the lamp.

Did he sleep in the buff? A lump formed in her throat, and her pulse did the tango through her veins. She rolled onto her side, trying not to picture the way his bare chest had looked with those red suspenders. . . .

And failing.

It didn't help matters at all that she'd actually *seen* his bare chest when he'd given her his shirt earlier. The sexy image in her mind was more than her imagination. It was a pure, unabridged—and damned nice—memory.

After a moment, she heard him climb into his own bunk, and his sigh drifted up to the loft. She wrapped her arms around herself and bit her lower lip, forcing herself not to wish for the warmth of Cole's arms or the strength of his shoulder to rest her head upon.

But as sleep claimed her at last, her dreams found her running from Blade's double, straight into the protective circle of her captor's embrace.

Morning sun rays stretched across the loft, startling Jackie awake. She rubbed her eyes and crept to the edge of the loft to peer down. Cole and Todd sat at the table eating breakfast. She shouldn't have slept so late.

Then again, maybe it would be best if Cole left before she went downstairs. If she concentrated more on Todd and less on his handsome father, she'd be a lot less distracted. Maybe then she could develop a reasonable plan to find her way home again.

"I remember visiting Grandma and Grandpa in St. Louis," Todd said.

"Do you now?" Cole's smile was wistful, and he reached across the table to squeeze his son's hand. "You were still wet behind the ears then, but your ma would be proud that you remember her folks."

Jackie's eyes blurred, but she rubbed them clear again. Cole and Todd both obviously missed Elizabeth. Jackie fingered the lace at the neckline of her nightgown.

Elizabeth's nightgown . . .

"But I still remember." Todd reached for his cup and took a long drink. "I remember lots."

"I'm glad." Cole cleared his throat and refilled his coffee cup. "I want you always to remember your ma. She loved you more than anything."

Todd bowed his head for a moment, then looked up at his father again. "I remember when she died, too. And what you promised her."

"Oh?"

Cole looked nervous, as if he didn't want his son to remember this. Jackie listened more intently, sensing this was important.

A loud knock on the door made Jackie gasp. Cole glanced up at her before he went to the door. Their gazes met, and Jackie understood his silent plea. *Stay hidden.*

"Todd, go out back and get fresh water, please," his father said.

"But—"

"Do as I say, son."

Jackie held her breath as Todd obeyed his father and headed out the back door. Poor Cole still didn't want his son to know what he'd done, and he obviously didn't want her to know *why* he'd done it.

She inched back, peering through the floorboards as Cole opened the door. Recognizing the Brothers Grime from the Gold Mine Saloon, she held her breath. The last thing in the world she wanted was to go back with *them.*

Even if it would put her back where she started, and closer to her time portal? *Damn.* All she had to do was reveal herself to them, and they'd take her back to Goodfellow and that unfinished portrait. *Think, Jackie. Think!*

Good old Zeb said, "We're lookin' for Miss Lolita. You seen her, Morrison?"

"Miss Lolita?" Cole rubbed his chin, obviously planning to play dumb.

"Yeah, that crazy woman you kept from gettin' run down over to Devil's Gulch. Remember?"

Cole nodded slowly. "Sure, but why would you think she might be here?"

And why wasn't Jackie seizing this opportunity? *You're weak, Clarke.* All right, she knew why. She didn't want to expose Cole as a kidnapper. After all, he was a single father. What would happen to Todd if his father went to jail? No matter how much she needed to see that portrait completed, she couldn't bring herself to jeopardize the Morrisons. She'd find a way to do it herself, without incriminating Cole.

Even if he had kidnapped her.

She rested her forehead against the cool wood. *I'm a stupid, trusting fool.* Even so, she remained silent.

"Goodfellow reckoned maybe you changed yer mind 'bout helpin' her, since she asked you," Zeb's equally filthy cohort said. "Did ya?"

"Nope." Cole straightened to his full and impressive height. "I have work to do. Tell Goodfellow he sent you two on a wild-goose chase."

"I told him so," Zeb said, slapping his thigh. "But he's hell-bent on findin' her by the time that Frenchman's hand heals."

"Frenchman?" Cole asked.

"Yep, that fancy painter feller." Zeb chuckled and shook his head. " 'Pears he broke his little finger when he fell, and he swears he can't hold his paintbrush just yet."

"When was he hurt?"

"The day Miss Lolita disappeared," Zeb continued. "He said some man with a rifle took her, then he fell and broke his finger."

"That's too bad about his finger." Genuine regret sounded in Cole's voice, and Jackie suspected he blamed himself for Henri's injury.

Zeb's comrade snorted with obvious disgust. "Goldurned pantywaist, if'n you ask me."

"The Frenchman'll mend," Zeb said. "And we gotta fetch Miss Lolita back there before he does."

"I can't help you with that," Cole said quietly.

"You give a yell if you hear from her," Zeb said. "Hear?"

"Maybe."

Zeb chuckled as the pair left.

Jackie had to admit that Cole Morrison was one smooth operator. Was he conning her with his single-daddy charm as well? No—that would make him no better than Blade, and she refused to believe that.

Cole closed the door behind the Brothers Grime, but stepped to the side to peek through the window as Jackie climbed down the ladder.

"So old Rupert is looking for me, huh?" She paused behind Cole and peered over his shoulder. "Those guys give me the willies."

"Willies?" Cole glanced back at her, his eyes widening as they drifted languidly down to her bare toes, then back to her face.

Probably the first time he's seen a woman in his dead wife's nightgown. Guilt made her breath catch, and her heart pressed upward. His gaze dipped to her breasts, and she wondered how transparent the worn fabric was in the bright light of morning. Was he wondering what she had on underneath the soft white cotton? Shaking herself, she closed her eyes, then remembered his question even if he didn't.

"Uh, 'willies' means they give me the creeps." Jackie watched the grungy pair until they were out of sight, then turned her attention to the breakfast table. "Is there any coffee?"

"On the fire."

Jackie poured herself a cup and took an appreciative sniff, then tasted it. "Yuck, Morrison, never apply for a job at Starbucks."

"Starbucks?"

"Never mind." She took another drink. "I'll get used to it, and caffeine is caffeine. Also my drug of choice."

"Drug? Caffeine?"

"Sorry, never mind."

Cole went to the back door and peered out at his son. "I'm going to the mine as soon as Todd gets back with the water." He rubbed his chin, a thoughtful expression on his handsome face. "I don't like strangers coming here when I'm not around."

"And I don't suppose you want anyone to see me either." She arched a brow when he looked at her sharply. "Let's face facts, Cole. You don't want Todd or anybody else to know it. If anybody sees me, they'll know who I am." Rather, who they thought she was. "And you don't want Todd to know the real reason I'm here."

A muscle twitched in his jaw. "All right, you found my weak spot." He pinned her with his gaze. "Now what do you plan to do about it?"

Jackie stared at him for several seconds, then sighed. "Nothing. Yet." She shook her head and set her coffee cup on the table. "I told you last night I plan to ask you for a favor, and I still do, but not just yet." *Dummy.* "I'll keep quiet, for now, if you'll tell me why you need that gold badly enough to resort to kidnapping."

"What makes you so sure I need a reason besides wanting the gold?"

"It doesn't take a rocket scientist to see that, Morrison," Jackie said quietly. "What did Merriweather call you? Oh, yeah—a straight arrow." She gave an emphatic nod. "So why'd you do it?"

"I . . ." Cole raked his fingers through his collar-length hair and gave her a sad smile. "It's a long story. I'll tell you tonight after Todd's asleep."

She studied his eyes, so blue she could drown in their depths, and as sincere as any she'd ever seen. No, this man wasn't a con artist, and he couldn't become one no matter how hard he tried. Sure, he'd kidnapped her, but every passing moment made her more certain he had a powerful motivation for doing so.

"Fair enough." She held out her right hand. He stared at it for a few moments, then shook it. The warmth of his hand sent shivers up her arm and skittering down her spine. "Tonight," she whispered, unable to prevent other possible and impossible meanings to that word from flooding her certainly addled mind.

But she had to stay focused—convince him to take her back to Devil's Gulch and that damned portrait, before it was too late.

He continued to hold her gaze as he held her hand, his expression intense and unwavering. "Tonight."

Chapter Eight

Jackie spent the entire morning with Todd, going through his father's impressive collection of books. Cole owned first editions by Mark Twain, Jules Verne, Herman Melville, James Fenimore Cooper, and others that would be rare collectibles in her time. The leather bindings were careworn, the pages obviously read and reread.

Cole Morrison was as intriguing as he was handsome. Any man who loved books as much as he obviously did wasn't meant to be a miner. There were books of poetry inscribed to Elizabeth, too. How and why had a couple like the Morrisons ended up here?

Todd stumbled over a word in the primer Jackie'd found among Cole's collection. He and Elizabeth must have been planning for their son's education when they'd hauled all these books to the top of a mountain.

"I think you've earned a break, kiddo," she said,

closing the book and setting it aside. "Hmm, where does your dad keep his scissors?"

"Ma's sewing basket's over there." Todd pointed to the top of the pie safe. "Whatcha need scissors for?"

"You'll see." Jackie retrieved the basket, containing various threads, yarns, and patches, and removed a pair of shears. She tested them on a scrap of fabric and nodded. "These'll do."

"For what?" Todd's expression could only be described as dubious.

"Todd, my man, grab your comb and haul that chair outside." She swung open the front door. "You're about to have a complimentary cut and style, sans blow-dry."

His eyes grew round and he shook his head.

"It's all right; I know what I'm doing." She put one hand on her hip and smiled at him. "I went to school to learn how to cut hair, Todd. Really."

"They got schools for stuff like that?"

Well, in my time they do. She couldn't be so sure about now. "You bet they do."

"Is that how your hair got that . . . that color?" Todd gave a loud gulp.

Jackie feigned indignance, patting the twin braids she'd coiled tightly around her head. She looked downright proper in the gray muslin dress with white cuffs and collar, and her hair restrained until its color was almost tame. Almost.

"I'll have you know that women pay lots of money to have their hair dyed this shade, young man." *Yeah, and they're out of their gourds, too.*

"They do?" He narrowed his eyes, clearly skeptical.

"Indeed, they do." She made a snipping motion with the shears and waggled her eyebrows. "I promise your hair won't change color, and your father will like it."

"Well . . ."

"And we'll cut his hair later."

Todd brightened and he flashed her a grin that could charm Mary Poppins out of her umbrella. "All right, but I want to watch you cut Pa's hair."

And keep me from jumping his gorgeous bones. "It's okay with me if it's okay with him."

"Okay?"

"All right."

Jackie positioned the chair in the shade while Todd poured pitchers of water over his head as she'd requested. What did they do for shampoo around here? Rubbing his wet hair with a square of fabric that passed for a towel, he came around the corner of the cabin with a look of pure terror in his eyes.

"You'd think you've never had a simple haircut before," Jackie said. "Sheesh. You're almost ten. Now plop your backside into this chair and be a man." She bit the inside of her lip to prevent herself from laughing when he nodded in silent horror and obeyed.

She draped a dry cloth around his shoulders and combed out his hair. "I'll bet your hair will turn as dark as your dad's when you get older."

"That's what Ma always said." Todd sounded calmer now.

A squeezing sensation clutched her heart. She hurt for this little boy, and wanted to make it all better. Her caring torpedoes were misfiring all over the place. "You miss your mom a lot."

"Yeah, and so does Pa."

"Yes, of course he does." An uncomfortable tightening commenced in her chest, but she refused to accept it as jealousy. Even Jackie Clarke wasn't insecure enough to be jealous of a dead woman.

Shaking the feeling, she started at Todd's nape, cutting the hair blunt and square, then tapering it toward the front with some strategic layering around his face. "Your hair has just enough curl in it to manage this style. It looks great."

She couldn't have planned a more beautiful day. The sky was crystal blue, birds sang, and the breeze was gentle and warm. A few puffy white clouds floated by, so close it seemed she could reach out and pluck one of them out of the sky.

When she was finished, she stood back to survey her work. "Todd, my man, you look good enough for prime-time television."

"What's tele—"

"Ah, nothing important." She winked and swept the comb through his drying locks once more.

A dark hand snaked before her and grabbed her wrist in a steel grip. Jackie's heart stopped, and she turned slowly to identify the owner of the hand.

Her gaze settled on a leather-clad man whose silver hair hung in braids nearly to his waist. His creased face was the color of bronze, and his eyes were as black as the cast-iron frying pans hanging in Cole's cabin.

"It's all right, Chief Byron," Todd said. "This is Miss Jackie. She's my teacher."

Byron? Jackie managed a shaky smile and met the old man's gaze. "Hi, I'm Jackie Clarke." She wiggled the fingers of the hand he still held prisoner. "Uh, could I have my hand back now, please?" At least he wasn't one of the Brothers Grime back for an encore.

"It's all right," Todd repeated, and the aging Native American released her hand.

Jackie rubbed her appendage until the circulation was restored. "Pleased to meet you, Chief." What was one supposed to say to Indian chiefs in 1891? Aunt Pearl's etiquette training had fallen a little short in this area. Jackie tried another tight smile and added, "Sir," for good measure.

He looked fierce. Old, sure, but still fierce. He had to be at least seventy, and his eyes were downright mean when he stared at her. But when he shifted his gaze from Jackie to Todd, a transformation took place.

Chief Byron's lips curved in a toothless grin and his obsidian eyes twinkled. "Did you let this white squaw scalp you, Son of Pale Eyes?"

"She didn't scalp me." Todd touched his head with both hands. "I gotta look." He raced inside, then returned a few seconds later. "Hey, I think it looks pretty good, Miss Jackie."

"Miss Jackie?" The chief pinned her with his intelligent gaze again, but he didn't seem nearly as fierce now. "That sounds like a white man's name."

Todd giggled and said, "That's what I said."

Jackie stuck her tongue out at him. "It's also what your father said."

Todd laughed even louder. After he regained his composure, he explained, "Chief Byron is a Ute Indian. When the government sent his tribe away to the reservation, he stayed here."

History in the making. She might not have finished college, but even this lowly hairdresser had read enough historical romance to value real history. "Why did you stay here?" *Alone?* Jackie Clarke understood *alone* too damned well.

"This is my home." Chief Byron gazed at a bird flying overhead, and when he looked at her again the light in his eyes appeared to have dimmed. "No matter what the white man may say."

Todd kicked the dirt at his feet. "You know how Pa feels about that."

"Pale Eyes is a wise man." Chief Byron smiled at Todd again. "So are you."

Todd blushed with obvious pleasure and ducked his head. "Miss Jackie's teaching me to read and write and do arithmetic."

The chief looked at her again and gave a curt nod before turning his gaze back to Todd. "Your mother taught me to read, write, and to speak in your tongue."

"Really?" Todd asked, his eyes widening.

The boy was obviously hungry for stories about his mother. Jackie's heart ached for him, because she knew all too well what it felt like to lose a parent at such a young age.

"Yes," the chief continued. "Wife of Pale Eyes—Elizabeth—named me Chief Byron the day of our first meeting."

"Why?" Though curious about his name, Jackie was more interested in keeping the old man talking about Elizabeth for Todd's benefit. The boy hung on every blessed word. "Why Byron?"

"My real name is very long and begins with the letter B. Elizabeth taught me that, too." He gave a wistful sigh. "Elizabeth read to me from a book that brought tears to these old eyes." Chief Byron's wrinkled bronze skin represented a web of life experience. "The words reminded me of the mother of my sons."

Lord Byron? "Why, Chief, I do believe you're a romantic at heart," Jackie said, winking at Todd.

Chief Byron turned his dark gaze on Jackie again, surprise evident in his expression. "That was what

Elizabeth said. She taught me many things, but passed on with much yet to teach. We miss her."

"Maybe . . ." Todd hesitated, then cast a questioning glance at Jackie. "Maybe the chief can learn with me, Miss Jackie."

"I . . . don't see why not." Jackie gave a nervous laugh, wondering how she'd managed to make the leap from beauty-college grad to teacher.

"I would like that." Chief Byron's eyes twinkled with renewed interest and he smiled again. "Very much."

He was obviously a proud man who'd refused to leave his homeland with his tribe. Jackie had a lot of respect for anyone willing to stand his ground for something he believed in. Besides, the old guy looked lonely. Of course, she knew a man like him wouldn't take kindly to pity, and she made a silent vow to offer him only kindness and respect.

"Sure, why not?" She laughed, and Chief Byron gifted her with another of his toothless grins. "How about a haircut first?" She snipped the air with the scissors.

The chief slapped both hands over his braids, and his eyes flashed with horror. "Never."

Todd shifted closer to Jackie. "I don't think the chief takes kindly to teasing about his hair."

"No kidding, Sherlock?" Jackie smiled and lowered the scissors. "Just a little joke there, Chief Byron. No harm done."

The old Indian straightened to his full height and pinned her with his gaze. "Foolish squaw."

Squaw? That was twice. "With all due respect, Chief, I'm *nobody's* squaw."

"That was also what Elizabeth said." The chief's piercing gaze drifted down the length of her, and he arched a silver brow. "Maiden?" His tone was skeptical.

Jackie stiffened and flames flared in her cheeks. "Sure, why not?" *In my dreams.*

"Fire in your hair." The chief walked a half circle around her, then gave a nod and grunted. Twice.

God only knew what that meant.

"I believe this one will do, Son of Pale Eyes."

"Do?" Jackie swallowed, wondering what the old man was up to now. "Do for what?"

The chief chuckled and rubbed his leather-covered abdomen. "The sun is high. We eat now."

"Do for what?" Jackie repeated, following the chief and Todd into the cabin. "Hey, do for what?" Did he plan to scalp her in her sleep? No, of course not. *Get a grip, Clarke.*

Chief Byron peeked in the pot bubbling over the hot coals, then looked back over his shoulder. "Beans again. Next time I bring a rabbit."

"Thanks, Chief," Todd said, getting plates and cups for the table.

Jackie hurried over to help him. Leaning close, she whispered, "Do for what?"

Todd looked a little sheepish. "I think he thinks you're here to be . . . my new ma."

Jackie dropped the tin plate she'd been holding. "Oh, shit."

Cole stepped out of the dark mine and into the late-afternoon sunshine. He hadn't even taken a break for dinner today, but he didn't feel any closer to finding gold than on any other day.

His mine was nothing but a worthless hole in the ground. Elizabeth had known it all along, and she'd asked him to give it up and go back to St. Louis more times than he could count. Maybe she'd still be alive if he'd listened to her. His gut clenched and his chest tightened.

And Todd would be in a real school, instead of learning to read and write from a saloon singer. Gazing upward at the blue sky, Cole shook his head. With a sigh, he set his tools inside the cave entrance and headed down the trail toward the cabin.

He was a failure as a miner, and now he'd stooped to kidnapping. What next?

"Don't ask," he muttered to himself, stopping to wash beside the cabin. His father would've rolled over in his grave to see his only son digging in the ground instead of following in his scholarly footsteps. For that matter, Cole much preferred the company of books to that of dirt and rocks.

With a sigh, he stepped through the open front door of the cabin he called home. For now. Jackie sat at the table with Todd and Chief Byron. She had both males writing with chalk on slates.

Jackie looked up and smiled at Cole. His heart faltered at the transformation. Wearing a decent dress and her hair up, she looked like a different woman. And that smile of hers never failed to ambush him.

When she smiled and had her wild red hair tucked away, Jackie Clarke was one of the prettiest women he'd ever seen. That realization shocked him, but he didn't argue with himself. That would've been pointless.

Because he was right.

He felt her gaze still on him and returned her smile with a tentative one of his own. Much to his surprise, her cheeks pinkened and she averted her gaze. By God, Jackie Clarke seemed downright . . . demure.

Impossible.

She was up to something. Then Cole remembered their conversation from this morning. *Tonight,* she'd promised.

Tonight.

He swallowed the lump in his throat, then deliberately made enough noise to draw his son's attention.

"Pa." Todd jumped up and rushed over to hug him. "Miss Jackie's teachin' me and Chief Byron to read, write, and cipher."

"Is that a fact? Nice to see you, Chief."

"Greetings," the chief said, rising. "Woman with Fire in Her Hair will make good squaw, Pale Eyes. She will warm your bed when the snow covers the mountains, and give you many fine sons."

Jackie coughed, and Todd pounded her on the back until she waved him away. "I think the chief is operating under a misconception," she said at last.

"Hmm." Cole smiled at the chief and tried to remain calm. This wasn't easy, especially with Jackie and Todd in the room. "Chief, Miss Jackie is here only to teach—not to be my, uh, squaw." He glanced at Jackie and saw her nostrils flare and sparks dance in her eyes.

"Or wife." Cole gave a sheepish grin. "Honest."

Chief Byron appeared confused as he looked from Cole to Jackie, then back again. Finally he shrugged and said, "We will see, Pale Eyes. We will all see in time."

Time was something they didn't have. In three weeks, Jackie would be out of their lives, and Cole would have the gold necessary to take his son to Oregon. But the thought of never seeing Jackie again stung, and Cole turned his attention back to the old Indian.

Chief Byron's presence wasn't a surprise. He invited himself to dinner regularly, often bringing the main course along.

"You staying for supper, Chief?" The sooner Cole could change the subject, the better. He hung his hat on a peg near the door, avoiding his son's probing gaze for now. Later he'd have to speak with him about the chief's assumption.

"No, I must go now, before the sun is lower." The chief gave a weary sigh and looked back at Jackie. "Thank you for teaching me more words today, Miss Jackie."

"Will you come again, Chief?" Jackie smiled at the old man, and Cole realized the chief was as enamored of that smile as he.

"It will be my pleasure." The chief raised a hand to bid them farewell, but hesitated. "I have one question before I go," he said, looking at Cole.

"Sure."

"What meaning does the word 'shit' have?"

Todd dissolved into squeals of laughter, and Cole struggled to keep a straight face himself as Jackie turned every shade of crimson known to man and nature. She'd obviously had some difficulty remembering to watch her language, but he couldn't summon any anger, no matter how justified.

"Uh, well," Cole said, clearing his throat. "It's slang, Chief, and it's a word Miss Jackie promised not to use while she's here."

Todd fell silent and Jackie turned even redder.

"And a word your lovely Elizabeth chose not to teach me." The chief rubbed his chin, then looked at Cole again. "What meaning does it have?"

Cole escorted the chief outside and whispered the definition in the old man's ear. The chief grinned and nodded. "You will see that I am right. Woman with Fire in Her Hair—and mouth—will make a good squaw. She will warm your bed when the snow covers the mountains, and give you many fine sons."

Cole's breath caught in his throat, and he tried not to dwell on the notion of Jackie in his bed, or on his body's immediate and nearly explosive response to that thought.

"You sound like an Indian," he said gently, his voice hoarse. He knew his words would be taken as they were intended—as a jest.

"I am Ute." Chief Byron gave an emphatic nod. "Heed my words, Pale Eyes."

"Uh, thanks, Chief." Cole rubbed the back of his neck and reminded himself to breathe. "I'll definitely think about it." *Whether I like it or not.*

Unfortunately, he liked it. A lot.

He drew a deep breath and watched the chief walk slowly down the trail. Raking his fingers through his hair, Cole tried to banish thoughts of Jackie in his bed, then turned and stepped into the darkening cabin.

"I'm starved," he said, not looking at Jackie, fearing his lustful thoughts might reveal themselves in his eyes. "What's for supper?"

"Beans." Todd sighed.

"No, not just beans. Refried beans," Jackie said.

"What?" Cole watched her go to work. She put a spoonful of lard in the skillet, waiting until it melted, then scooped beans into the fat.

"I need a fork."

Todd passed her a fork and she started mashing the beans as they sizzled in the frying pan.

"Todd, mix up the corn bread," she said. "These won't take long. They'd be better with peppers and cheese. Oh, and what I wouldn't give for some hot and nasty nachos. And a Diet Coke. And pizza. And . . ."

Her voice drifted away. Cole stared at her and couldn't help but notice the huge tear trickling down her cheek. She wiped it away with the back of her hand and squared her shoulders, returning her attention to the beans she was mashing into oblivion.

Something heavy weighed on her heart, but her courage was obvious. Cole rubbed his whiskered jaw, wondering again about what she had wanted help with the first morning he'd laid eyes on her. What or who did she fear? And why? The man she'd believed was staring at her in the Silver Spur? Her past? The future? What?

Or maybe what Jackie feared most was herself. The fine hairs on the back of his neck prickled, and he glanced quickly at his son. Todd stood staring at Cole with an expression far too mature for a child. It almost seemed as if Todd understood Cole's feelings better than he did.

That would be a fine trick, since Cole didn't understand them himself. *Enough of this, Morrison.* "Looks like somebody cut your hair," he said to Todd, desperately needing to change the subject.

"Miss Jackie." The boy poured the corn-bread batter into an iron skillet and shoved it onto the glowing coals in the bottom of the fireplace. "She said she went to school to learn how to cut hair."

"Like a barber?" Cole glanced at her, but she continued to kneel before the fire, tending the beans. "It looks good. Thank you."

"You're next," she said without turning around.

Cole's cheeks warmed and his son giggled. At least some of his bothersome tension had passed. "All right, I'm willing," he said, giving an emphatic nod when Jackie glanced back over her shoulder. "I *am* willing. You can cut my hair, too."

She turned her back on him again. "Only if you bathe and wash your hair first."

Todd laughed again, and Cole pinned him with a fierce gaze that only made the boy laugh even harder. "Seems you've been doing a lot of laughing lately, boy." He couldn't suppress his own grin. He let his voice fall to a hoarse whisper. "Keep doing it."

He felt Jackie's gaze on him again and looked her way. Her gray eyes were wide and moist, her smile gentle and knowing, almost sad.

The heat in his face sank to his groin like lightning after a lone pine. "I reckon I have time to make it to the falls and back before we eat."

"Falls?" Jackie rose and moved the skillet to the table. "I'll heat these again just before we eat. What falls?"

"There's a small waterfall." Mountain snow runoff might dampen his body's spirits a mite. At least, he sure as hell hoped so.

"Sounds lovely." Her eyes brightened. "I'd like to see that sometime."

"Well, not now, if you really want me to wash up, ma'am." He held her gaze with his, struggling to breathe as her eyes darkened and her tongue swept out to moisten her lips. Her gaze dropped below his waist, and her lips curved ever so slightly.

Damn. Demure definitely wasn't the right word to describe this woman, no matter how she was dressed.

"That's awful cold water this time of year, Pa," Todd said, marking on his slate again. "Last spring you said we had to wait till Jul—"

"Never mind what I said," Cole interrupted. "Cold

water will clean just as good as warm." Not that water was ever really warm at this altitude.

"Don't catch a chill, cowboy," Jackie said, pursing her lips in a way that made his blood turn molten.

Without another word, Cole pivoted and marched out the door toward the falls. A chill was exactly what he needed, but the way his luck was running, he'd probably turn the water to steam instead.

The moment the falls came into view, he unbuttoned his shirt and tossed it into the low branches of a young aspen. His hat followed, then he kicked off his boots a few feet farther down the trail. By the time he reached the water, he had his clothes stripped away and walked into the steady stream without hesitation. The frigid water peppered his skin like buckshot, but he stood there and took it until his lust finally waned.

After washing himself and his hair as best he could without soap, it took several minutes to gather his clothes from the various trees. That only reminded him why he'd been in such an all-fired hurry in the first place—a reminder he sure as hell didn't need.

Gritting his teeth, he slipped his clothes on his shivering, damp body. He'd better hurry back before dark so Todd wouldn't worry.

But as he picked his way along the trail in the encroaching twilight, Chief Byron's words flashed through his mind again.

Woman with Fire in Her Hair—and mouth—will make a good squaw. She will warm your bed when the snow covers the mountains, and give you many fine sons.

Damn. The cold water's effect was only temporary.

* * *

Jackie's hands trembled as she turned the pages of *Huckleberry Finn.* She was far too nervous for a mature woman who had her head screwed on straight. *Right, Clarke.*

She glanced down at Todd, tucked in his bed for the night. The boy's lids drooped and he yawned.

"Looks to me like you'd better get some sleep now, kiddo," she said, rising. "I'll send your father in to say good night."

"Miss Jackie?"

"Yes?" She hesitated, warmed by the affection in Todd's eyes. Her caring torpedoes were obviously factory defects. Seconds. Or maybe even thirds.

"I'm glad you're here. Thank you."

What could she say? Was she glad to be here, stranded in 1891 without her blow-dryer or indoor plumbing? *Don't answer that.* "Thanks, Todd," she whispered instead, then hurried out to the porch, where Cole sat on the front step. "Todd's ready."

"I think you tuckered him out today." Cole rose, an impressive tower of a man against the darkening horizon.

"The feeling is mutual." Jackie still had the book clutched in her hand, and she extended it to Cole. "I need to put this away."

He took the book, his fingertips brushing against hers. Jackie closed her eyes as warmth seeped through her veins. These Morrison men were wreaking havoc on her self-control. The little guy was shattering her resistance to caring, and the big one had her libido in overdrive.

Nix on the libido, Clarke.

Cole paused, staring at her in the moonlight, then retreated inside. He returned a few minutes later without the book. "He's already asleep."

"I didn't think he'd last long, but he reminded me we didn't get to your haircut," Jackie said, rubbing her hands along her upper arms.

"Ah, that's right. Sorry."

"Tomorrow."

"Sure."

Enough small talk. Jackie drew a deep breath and girded her resolve. "Well, you promised to tell me why you need the gold badly enough to kid—"

"Wait." Cole closed the front door of the cabin, then took her hand and led her off the porch. They paused in a patch of moonlight at the edge of the forest. "It's pretty tonight."

"Yes, but a little cool." Jackie felt as nervous as a teenager on her first date. At least now she didn't have to worry about zits, but she had plenty of other things on her mind.

This is not a date. She gnashed her teeth and drew another deep breath. Cole might be a hunk and a half, but she had to keep things in perspective.

"Okay, cut the stalling," she said, summoning the stubborn streak she'd inherited from her mother. Unfortunately, Great-Aunt Pearl had it, too, which was probably why she and Jackie had always fought over every little thing. "Tell me why you agreed to be Merriweather's henchman."

"Ouch." Cole raked his fingers through his hair and gazed beyond her at something only he could see. "I suppose that's what I am."

"Color me clueless here, but you don't seem the type." She felt his gaze redirected now—toward her. "I don't think 'kidnapper' is listed on your résumé. Is it?" she pressed.

His chuckle sounded bitter in the peaceful night

air. "This is the first . . . and last time," he said after a long pause. "The very last."

"So why this time?" *And what can I do to convince you to give up the gold and take me back to Devil's Gulch instead?*

"A promise."

Jackie stared at him for several silent moments. Though she tried to resist it, she couldn't help but sense his pain. It was a palpable thing, as real as the gentle breeze that suddenly swept up the mountain pass and rustled the aspen leaves overhead.

"Why, Cole?" For some crazy reason, she needed to know. Though her instincts screamed for her to wrap her arms around him and share his pain, logic demanded she persist until she had all the ammunition necessary to convince him to do her bidding.

And she felt like a royal bitch about it.

"You promised me, too," she prompted, hating herself.

"You sure don't seem much like a famous saloon singer now." His voice was warm and husky, floating through the night air and hitting its mark.

Her heart.

"You promised." Her voice was barely more than a rasping whisper now.

He combed his fingers through his hair again, then shoved both hands into the front pockets of his jeans. "I . . . I need the money to give my son a decent life." He laughed again, with no trace of humor even now. "Elizabeth wanted . . . "

His dead wife. Jackie should've known. She squeezed her eyes shut for a few moments, then blinked away the moisture that had gathered in her lashes. "Elizabeth wanted what, Cole?" She kept her voice gentle, and she knew the reason for her gentleness was far more significant than merely the means to an end. She truly cared about this man and his son.

No, you can't care. Holding her breath, she suppressed the tremor that commenced from her very soul. "What did she want? What did you promise her?"

Cole turned away and braced his arms against a boulder. His shoulders were slumped, his head bowed. Jackie's heart broke right then and there.

She ached to wrap her arms around his slim waist, to offer any comfort she could possibly provide. Heat settled low in her belly and coiled through her loins. Altruistic thoughts vanished beneath a powerful onslaught of plain, old-fashioned need, physical *and* emotional. God help her.

The cool breeze wafted through the trees again, stirring her senses to a hunger so intense she could barely stand it. Her nipples strained against the stiff fabric of Cole's dead wife's dress, but that reminder didn't help to diminish the desire erupting within her. Instead, thoughts of Elizabeth Morrison waned, and carnal urges reigned supreme.

Cole remained quiet, like a statue attached to the boulder. Without thinking, she crept up behind him and slid her arms around his waist. She felt him tense even more as she rested her cheek against his muscular back, her breath catching. He felt so good, so solid, so warm. A sigh escaped her parted lips, carried upward by the breeze until quaffed by silvery moonlight.

She rubbed her cheek against the rough fabric of his shirt, felt the rumble in his chest before she heard it as a low, primal growl. He slipped from her arms and whirled around to face her, but she barely had time to mourn the loss of physical contact before she found herself wrapped in the warmth of his embrace and pressed intimately against his full length.

Chest to chest. Belly to belly. Pelvis to pelvis.

She'd known he was a man among men in more ways than one, but this intimate contact told her more than she could possibly have imagined. And she'd imagined plenty.

The moonlight bathed his dark head in silver, but she couldn't read the expression in his eyes. With one hand, he brushed the backs of his fingers against her cheek, the rough pad of his thumb along her temple to her jaw. Then he cupped her chin and lifted her face upward, lowering his lips toward hers one breathtaking inch at a time.

Jackie's innards turned to Great-Aunt Pearl's oatmeal, hot but the consistency of glue. Her knees trembled, and she doubted her ability to support her own weight as his warm, moist breath fanned her face and incited her hunger.

His lips were firm but gentle, shaping hers to his will. After a moment, the kiss grew to something with a power all its own, mouths open, tongues no longer timid. Feverish, desperate, wanton, they devoured each other, taking and giving, tasting and tantalizing.

Moaning, she wrapped her arms around his waist and clung to him, savoring the molten surge of her blood as he hardened and pulsed against her. They would be so good together. If only the barrier of their clothing were gone, she could wrap her legs around his waist and take him deep inside her and hold him tight, lose herself in the bliss of mind-shattering sex.

Her breasts swelled against his rock-hard chest, and she ached to free them from the confines of this prudish dress. She wanted to be naked in his arms.

She wanted *him* naked in hers.

He brought his hand along the side of her rib cage and caressed her breast. Gently kneading her flesh, he eased his thumb between their bodies and brushed it against her taut nipple. Trembling with raw need, she moved her arms to his shoulders, twining them behind his neck, allowing more space for him to fondle her.

And he did. He stroked and plucked and manipulated her tender flesh until she moaned into his mouth and trembled against him. Just when she thought she'd go mad with wanting, he abandoned her breast and cradled her butt in his big, strong hands.

Straining on tiptoe, she met his lips more fully, burying her fingers in the fine, silky hairs at his nape. Growling again, he lifted her upward, holding her against his uncompromising arousal.

Jackie whimpered, wanting him to do so much more.

A shriek pierced the night, followed by a beastly growl, and this time it wasn't human. Cole jerked away and set her quickly on her feet. She wavered and almost fell, but he steadied her with both hands on her upper arms.

"Cougar," he whispered. "Be still."

Jackie stood frozen, still throbbing with unquenched passion, and stricken with terror at the thought of a cougar way too close for comfort. After several heart-stopping moments, Cole took her hand and they ran to the cabin. He opened the front door and they bolted inside.

Jackie's breathing came in rapid bursts, and she hoped she wouldn't wake Todd. Now Cole would climb the ladder with her and finish what they'd started. Safe from the cougar, all she could think of was the wild beast Cole had awakened within her.

Looking for love again, Clarke?

No, she couldn't be. She couldn't allow that. She'd never had sex just for the sake of sex. At least she'd always convinced herself there were other, deeper motives involved. Making love.

Dangerous thinking . . .

She started to speak, but he held a finger to his lips and shook his head. Then he leaned close and whispered, "Good night."

Stunned, Jackie obediently scaled the ladder to the loft. Maybe Cole planned to follow after he banked the fire and did all the usual things, as he had last night. She undressed and slipped into her bunk without donning the cotton nightgown, preparing herself emotionally and physically for her lover.

She listened to the same sounds she'd heard last night as he went about preparing the cabin for the night. The now-familiar scent of wood smoke wafted upward to her nostrils. Cole's hair would smell like that when he finally came to her. She took an appreciative sniff.

She heard the rustle of fabric as he undressed, and her pulse leaped, her body warming in anticipation. What would he think at finding her naked beneath her blanket? The thought brought a wicked smile to her lips as she waited.

And waited.

After a few minutes, he extinguished the lamp and she held her breath, waiting for the sound of him climbing the ladder. Instead she heard him climb into his own bed downstairs.

Disappointment made her throat and chest burn

and tighten as her desire abated. She knew he wanted her as much as she wanted him. Why hadn't he . . . ?

"You bastard," she whispered.

He'd used that kiss to distract her enough to avoid telling her the truth about why he'd kidnapped her. Fury washed through her, and she sat up to pull on her nightgown, buttoning it with jerky movements.

And she hadn't had a chance to ask him about taking her back to town. She was batting a thousand in failures with this guy.

When she lay back down to sleep, she stared at the dark ceiling for what seemed like hours. Cole Morrison had put her off tonight, but no more. Why, he'd actually *teased* her into thinking he wanted her. He'd tricked her.

Tonight he'd called the shots.

Tomorrow night was hers.

Chapter Nine

The moment Cole met the morning with one eye barely open, he grew instantly aware of two things.

First, the sun's angle as it slanted across the room told him he'd overslept. He hated to oversleep. It ruined his morning and made him grumpy the rest of the day. His father had always said a man who slept late was wasting his life. Cole tended to downplay most things his father had claimed, but he agreed with this one, to a certain extent. Of course, his father would've considered Cole's present vocation a total waste of his life, too.

Second, pinpricks of awareness erupted all over his body, alerting him that he was being watched. And, damnation, he knew without looking who was doing the watching. Remembering last night, he decided to feign sleep just a while longer, and surveyed his observer through his lashes.

He lay sprawled on his back with one hand across

his forehead and the other atop the quilt. One of his feet poked out from the covers, drawing his attention to the end of his bed, where something blue filled the space beyond his naked appendage.

He opened his eyes a fraction farther. That something blue was the wide skirt of a dress Elizabeth hadn't been able to wear after carrying Todd. She'd kept all the dresses from the early days of their marriage, vowing to fit into them again one day without letting out the seams. Of course, Cole had believed her beautiful even swollen with child. Especially then, in fact. His chest knotted in remembrance.

Now a notorious saloon singer wore Elizabeth's too-tight dress with ease. Maybe he should be offended, but he wasn't. Elizabeth would've been the first one to insist on giving the dress to someone in need. Considering that Lolita-Jackie had come wearing only jeans and feathers, she definitely qualified.

Cole gazed up the row of buttons, lingering at the twin mounds outlined by the soft fabric. His mouth went dry as he recalled last night. He had held her, touched her, and had ached to taste as well. His gaze meandered farther up to the square neckline that exposed an expanse of creamy skin. Perspiration trickled down the sides of his neck, and he licked his lips, remembering. . . .

That kiss. Another few minutes and he would've taken her right there on the ground like an ani—

"You going to lie there staring at me all morning, Morrison?" She reached down and trailed her fingernail along the bottom of his foot.

Todd giggled and Cole jerked his foot to safety beneath the covers, rolling onto his side in one smooth motion. No need to let anybody see his typical randy morning state. Then again, she'd probably already noticed. With a sigh, he swung his legs to the floor, keeping the quilt bunched in his lap.

Squinting, he glanced up at her. "Mind giving a man a little privacy?"

She cocked one brow and pursed her lips. "You got something to hide, big guy?"

Todd giggled again from his seat at the table, obviously missing the dual meaning. *Thank God.* Cole cleared his throat. "Yeah, I reckon I do. Ma'am." A moment later, his jeans smacked him across the face. Forcing a grin and gritting his teeth, he muttered, "Much obliged."

"No problem." Sarcasm edged her tone.

He glanced at her again and couldn't miss the steel glitter in her gray eyes. They looked downright silver this morning. Quicksilver. Her cheeks had a nice rosy flush, too. Anger agreed with her, but he kept his opinion safely to himself. Somehow he suspected it wouldn't be much appreciated just now.

"Well?" He arched a brow, waiting.

"Well, what?" She kept her arms folded and tapped her foot.

He held the jeans up suggestively, hoping she wouldn't make him spell it out in front of Todd. The woman was plain old-fashioned ornery this morning, and Cole's patience was wearing damned thin. "You get up on the wrong side of the bed this morning?"

Her jaw gaped open and her nostrils flared.

Uh-oh. He glanced over at his son, whose eyes widened.

"I'm gonna go tend Ruth," the boy wisely announced, then disappeared through the open door.

Jackie's lips twitched. "Smart kid you've got there, Morrison."

Cole couldn't prevent his grin. "That he is. A chip off the old . . ." He shot another look at Jackie's narrowed gaze. "Ah, never mind."

The woman burst out laughing. Shaking her head, she turned her back, her laughter subsiding. "You'd better get dressed and go dig in your mine some more."

He yanked on his jeans, then stood and buttoned them quickly, figuring she might turn around any second. That would be just like her, too—one surprise after another. Jackie probably drove every single man she met out of his mind.

And far be it for Cole Morrison to defy the laws of man and nature.

"I'm not going to the mine today," he said, deciding as he buttoned his shirt, then turning to observe her slim back and narrow waist.

She spun around to confront him again, surprise etched across her pretty face. "Why not? Today could be the big day. Gee, you might miss it." Sarcasm dripped from every syllable.

Chuckling, he shook his head and tugged the quilt neatly across his bed. "The same worthless rocks'll be there tomorrow." Who was he trying to convince anyway? Truth was, his heart wasn't in that damned mine.

And it never had been.

He straightened and found himself unable to tear his gaze away from Jackie. Sunlight flooded through the open door behind her, outlining her with golden fire. Her hair was pulled away from her face and tied loosely at her nape, the red tresses glinting in the morning light. With the sun at her back, her complexion softened right before his eyes, not that it had been rough before. Not at all.

But there was something so compelling about her this morning, he could barely keep his hands—and other things—to himself. Remembering last night didn't help matters any. His enthusiastic body twinged and throbbed, reminding him he hadn't even visited the outhouse yet this morning.

Yep, the woman is driving me mad.

Maybe he should go to the mine after all. He wrenched his gaze from hers and raked his fingers through his hair. "I don't know what got into me, sleeping so late." He stepped into his boot and stomped his foot, then imitated the process with the other.

"Something keep you awake last night, Morrison?" she asked, drawing his gaze back to her mouth.

Her lips had tasted sweet and spicy at the same time. Warm. Soft. He swallowed. Hard. "Slept like a babe," he lied, wondering how he managed to stay on his feet with all the memories firing through him.

"Oh, yeah, I'll bet." She arched both brows this time. "We already had breakfast. Fix your own, then we'll get to your hair."

"My hair?" He crossed the room and retrieved his hat from the peg near the door, hoping his hands didn't tremble as he jammed it onto his head.

"Yes. You managed to wiggle out of your haircut last night . . . among other things."

Her voice took on a husky, throaty quality that made him hold his breath and stare as she faced him again, moistening her lips with her tongue. Twice.

"Guess we forgot." He had to breathe.

She took a step toward him. Two. Three. Less than a foot away, she paused and said, "Guess we were . . . distracted." She pursed her lips into a pout and took another step, the tips of her breasts almost touching his chest.

Oh, shit. "Distract . . . ed?" That squeaky croak didn't sound a thing like him, and if she came any closer, he was going to grab her and—

"Hmm." She walked her fingers up the buttons on his shirtfront and released the top one with a deft movement of her thumb and forefinger. "Yes, don't you remember?"

"Remember?"

"You sound like a parrot, Morrison." Her eyes glittering dangerously, she gripped the points of his collar with both hands and gave a sharp tug, hauling him full against her. She brushed her lips across his so delicately he wasn't sure they'd actually made contact, then she severed any further doubt about their proximity by pressing herself against him so tightly they practically shared one skin. She wound her arms around the back of his neck. "Need me to refresh your memory, cowboy?" she whispered.

He was lost. Before his next heartbeat he covered her mouth with his, igniting a liquid inferno between them. A shudder dawned in the depths of his soul and shattered his pitiful excuse for self-restraint.

This woman drove him to want and do things he had no business wanting or doing. She muddled his thinking until he had no common sense left.

And, damnation, she felt good against him and tasted even better. Banishing the voices at the back of his mind that told him he should resist, he held her to him and deepened their kiss, amazed at how her method of kissing resembled a far more intimate act between man and woman.

An act he wanted to do with her. Now.

Soft, warm, stroking . . . she tormented and tantalized his tongue until he moaned into her mouth. All he could think of was having her womanly warmth surround another, much harder, part of him. She'd be hot and slick there, too. He knew that as surely as he knew the sun would set behind the mountains come evening. And she'd be tight. Oh, so tight . . .

"Pa, you coming?"

Jackie wrenched herself away so violently she sent Cole slamming against the wall. A smug, triumphant smile spread itself across her pretty face. "Now do you remember, cowboy?"

Right this moment, he hated Jackie Clarke—hated her with all the passion she'd dredged out of him since she'd barged into his life. To hell with who'd kidnapped whom. He pointed at her with his index finger, ready to give her the ass-chewing of a lifetime, just as soon as he was able to speak again.

"Pa, you gonna stay in there all day?"

Chastising himself for being a negligent father, Cole brushed past Jackie and peered out the door. He breathed a sigh of relief when he spotted Todd happily currying Ruth. "Be right out, son," he called, amazed he sounded so normal.

He spun around, pointing his finger at the woman again. "You . . . you . . ."

"What?" She batted her lashes again as she had at Merriweather.

"That won't work with me." He kept shaking his finger.

"It's not nice to point, cowboy."

He dropped his hand to his side, clenched his fists and relaxed them repeatedly, then reached up to straighten his hat. He blinked three times, then met her laughing gaze again. *Damn.* "You'd best remember one thing, Lolita-Jackie-Clarke-Belle."

"Just Jackie will do." She tilted her head and smiled, her lashes fluttering so fast he wondered if they might never stop. "What would you like l'il old, empty-headed me to remember . . . sir?"

The southern accent was outrageous enough to break the spell she'd cast on him. He drew a deep, calming breath. "Remember that I am not a cowboy."

Her laughter followed him as he pivoted on his heel and stomped out the door with what little remained of his dignity. Maybe he'd better visit the waterfall again this morning. He could use another icy dousing. That might help him think straight again, though the frigid water's effect sure as hell hadn't lasted long last night.

Todd had stopped currying Ruth and stood staring at both adults as if they'd lost their minds. Well, the boy was a lot smarter than his pa. Cole smacked his fist into his palm, never breaking his pace as he approached Todd.

No doubt about it—Cole was being punished for breaking the law. For kidnapping. He never should've agreed to do Merriweather's dirty work. *Too late for regrets.* He couldn't undo what he'd done. The sooner he collected his gold and sent Lolita-Jackie packing, the sooner he could take his son to Oregon.

Hesitating, he remembered his plans to raise cattle in Oregon and called back over his shoulder, "I am not a cowboy *yet.*"

The crazy woman laughed even louder.

Jackie watched Cole and Todd walk into the woods without telling her where they were going, let alone when they'd be back. *Men.* With a sigh, she went back inside and slumped into the rocking chair, her knees trembling.

That kiss. A hot flush crept up her neck and into her cheeks. Jeez, that man could kiss. She fanned herself, allowing her head to fall back against the chair.

After Blade, she'd believed herself uninterested in any relationship, let alone one based on simple lust. *Who are you kidding, Clarke?* Her attraction to Cole was a lot more than lust, and there was nothing simple about it.

And that was the part that terrified her. Without a doubt, she was unable to have a physical relationship with a man and keep her heart out of it. *Damn shame, too.* Life would be a lot simpler that way.

She wanted Cole Morrison in a bad way. He could reduce her to a quivering mass of hormones and molecules with a glance. Her response to Blade had never been anything like this. Oh, it had been good—damned good—but not . . . soul shattering.

Soul shattering, Clarke? Why didn't she throw *heart-breaking* into the equation, too? No, Cole hadn't broken her heart. Yet.

But he would . . . just like every other man she'd ever cared about.

Reminded of his cowboy remark, a smile tugged at the corners of her mouth. There was nothing boyish about Cole Morrison except his grin. She envisioned him the way he'd looked this morning asleep in bed, with his shaggy hair tousled, morning beard stubble darkening his jaw, and that hunky torso barely covered.

He'd looked good enough to eat. With seconds.

And that kiss . . . "Oh, Lord, you've got it bad, girl." Jackie rose, trying to shake off the last vestiges of the awakening she'd experienced in Cole's embrace.

Unfortunately, the man's kiss was potent enough to linger long after he'd fled the scene.

She paused at the table, pressing her fingertips to her lips. No one had ever kissed her quite like that before. Like he wanted to consume her. Own her. Love her.

Love? A bitter laugh tumbled from her lips, and she busied herself clearing away the breakfast dishes. She'd learned her lesson about love after her marriage and Blade. Enough of that foolishness.

It wasn't that she didn't like sex. The problem was—and always would be—keeping her heart and her hormones separate. Divided and conquered, so to speak.

Could she learn to separate sex and emotions? Men did it all the time. A shudder rippled through her. It wasn't as if she had to worry about contraception, at least not for a while. She'd had her Depo-Provera injection just two weeks ago. With any luck, she'd be home before she was due for another one.

Then again, maybe she wouldn't need any contraception. She should just join a nineteenth-century convent and end this nightmare once and for all. She could be the official hairdresser for the Holy Sisters of Quantum Theory.

No, even if she never made love again, Jackie Clarke couldn't qualify as nun material. Besides, she wasn't even Catholic.

"You're hopeless," she muttered, attacking the crumbs on the table with an angry swipe. When she straightened, she stared through the open door at the rugged mountains in the distance. Some of the peaks looked familiar even in this century, though she certainly couldn't name them.

Amazing. If she hadn't accompanied Blade into

these mountains, she wouldn't be here now. In a way, her ill-fated affair with Blade had brought her here to this place.

And this time.

Everything happens for a reason, dear, Aunt Pearl had always said.

Maybe the old biddy had been right all along. Jackie walked out onto the porch and tossed the crumbs to the ground. No man had ever made her feel the way Cole did, and she was crazy about Todd, too. *Was* she here in 1891 for a reason?

Her heart fluttered and pressed upward against her throat, and lust had nothing to do with that. Here came the terrifying part again. With a sigh, she wiped her suddenly sweaty palms on the borrowed apron and swallowed the lump in her throat.

Foolish dreams had led her down the aisle right out of high school, and that had been a disaster. But after a lifetime of Great-Aunt Pearl's ridicule, she probably would've married the man in the moon if he'd asked. On the other hand, if her mother had lived . . .

Enough. "End of stroll down Memory Lane. Eject tape now." She squeezed her eyes shut, then blinked until her vision cleared.

Needing to keep busy, she grabbed the broom and made several passes across the porch, then paused to gaze into the distance again. A cloud of dust rose just beyond the boulder that marked the trail leading to the Morrisons' cabin. Curious, she stared until a man on horseback emerged. He rode steadily toward the cabin.

And her.

"Oh, nuts." She should hide or something. . . . Shouldn't she? But the guy must've seen her by now, though not closely enough to recognize her. Yes, he raised his hand and waved, never halting his steady progress.

She didn't want Cole to have any trouble with the law because of her. But who would recognize her as the famous Lolita Belle in this Ma Ingalls getup? Her thoughts went immediately to her hair, and she hurried into the cabin and donned the sunbonnet she'd found among Elizabeth's things, tucking every strand of neon red inside. Once the ribbons were tied securely beneath her chin, Jackie stepped back onto the porch and drew a deep breath. *Look cool.* Considering her archaic attire, cool was impossible, so she settled for calm.

The rider brought his horse to a stop several yards in front of the cabin and sat staring at her. Who was he? Was he dangerous? What did he want?

And where the hell was Cole?

Drawing a deep breath, Jackie squared her shoulders, grabbed the broom handle again, and resumed her sweeping. If the stranger made one threatening move against her, she'd ram that broom right where it counted. It wouldn't kill him, but he'd wish it had.

She glanced at him from beneath her lashes and saw him nudge his horse into a walk. He advanced slowly, his features gradually taking shape.

Beneath the brim of a black cowboy hat, his face was mostly a shadowy blur. Even so, there was something unsettling about the angle of his jaw, the way he held his shoulders.

Blade.

Her heart slammed into her breastbone and she clutched the broom in a death grip, pivoting to face the intruder. She had nothing to fear from Blade, but—she dug her nails into the wooden handle of the broom—he'd be smart to avoid her at all costs. Yet here he was. Or was he? Come to think of it, did Blade know how to ride a horse?

She looked at his face again, and her heart did a somersault. If this guy wasn't Blade Smith, he was his exact twin. An ancestor? It almost made sense, in a sick sort of way.

"Mornin'." The man brought his horse to a stop again a few feet from the porch step. "I'm lookin' for a fella named Cole Morrison. He around?"

Blade with a Texas drawl? Jackie would've laughed, but common sense prevailed. For a change. "Mr. Morrison isn't available right now." She smiled in what she hoped was an appropriately demure manner for a Victorian lady.

"Available?" The man made a snorting—and very un-Blade-like—sound. "Well, does that mean he's here or not, ma'am?"

"Was Mr. Morrison expecting you?" Jackie fluttered her lashes. "I didn't catch your name, sir."

The man shifted uncomfortably in the saddle.

He was hiding something. She peered intently into his dark eyes. Was he Blade? A little rougher around the edges, not as immaculately groomed by a long shot, but still Blade . . . ? With an accent?

"Name's Smith." He stared at her as if checking for her reaction.

And Jackie forced herself not to react, though her heart rate tripled.

"Rock Smith," he added with a smile.

Smith. Rock? She regained control and drew a shaky breath. "Rock?" She cleared her throat and sniffled. "Really?"

The muscles in his jaw rippled, and she knew he was clenching his teeth. Just like Blade.

"Yes, ma'am. Really." He heaved a weary sigh. "My pa had to deliver me durin' the War between the States, and he dropped me on my head." Smith flashed her a smarmy grin reminiscent of the Blade she'd left in her time.

"I see," she said, trying to resolve the man's identity as someone other than Blade, but he did have the same last name. The most common name in the English language, she reminded herself. Even so, this Rock Smith persona was outrageous enough to be one of Blade's cons.

"So my ma said my head was hard as a rock." He gave a shrug. "Folks in east Texas are queer that way, so, naturally, my name's Rock."

Queer east Texans? Gee, that's reassuring. She cleared her throat again. "Naturally. All right, Mr. Smith." There was no way she'd call any man "Rock." She tightened both hands around the handle of her broom and held it in front of her, though her visitor hardly seemed threatening. Still . . . "I'll tell Mr. Morrison you called."

"Beg pardon, ma'am, but when do you expect he'll be . . . available?" He grinned again.

A con artist, just like his descendant. And there was no way she'd believe this man wasn't Blade's ancestor. She squinted. Though she still couldn't be totally certain this wasn't Blade himself playing an evil game.

It sure as hell wouldn't be the first time.

"I'm not certain," she said carefully. "If you'd care to leave a message, I'll be sure he gets it."

"Y'all do that." He tilted his head to one side, then his gaze plunged to her not-so-heaving bosom. Chuckling, he shook his head.

Heat crept up Jackie's neck to her cheeks, but she tried to pretend she hadn't noticed his affront. However, one thing was now perfectly clear—this man was looking for Lolita. Didn't he recognize her from the Silver Spur? And how had he known to look here? Cole had seemed certain he didn't recognize anyone in the saloon that day.

Maybe Cole's baggy shirt had hidden her then and the bonnet was doing it now. She glanced at the huge brim. Thank goodness. Concealing her hair and being less voluptuous than Lolita might have saved her. Twice.

"What message do you wish to leave for Mr. Morrison, sir?"

"Who are you anyway, ma'am?"

Jackie watched him carefully for any reaction, then released a slow sigh. "I'm Miss Clarke, the governess."

Smith guffawed—that was the only term to describe the sound he made. Then his expression changed as he shifted his weight in the saddle. Even so, no trace of recognition appeared in his dark eyes.

"Makes a man curious to know how a struggling miner can afford to hire a, uh, governess." He arched a brow. "Y'all tell Morrison I know what he did." Leaning closer, Smith said, "Goodfellow will double Merriweather's offer. I'll be back in two days for your answer."

"*My* answer?" Jackie's blood turned cold. "What do you mean?"

"I got me a feeling you know exactly what I mean." The man's smile was malicious. "If you don't have the right answer, then I'll just have to keep Goodfellow's gold for myself. Y'all have a real nice day, ma'am." He tipped his hat and whirled the horse around, galloping away in a cloud of dust.

She fanned the air and coughed. Maybe this was the solution. She'd be returned to Devil's Gulch, Cole would get his precious gold, she'd finish posing for that wretched portrait, then touch it like she had during the fire . . . .

And pray.

The same miracle—or disaster—that had brought her here could just as easily return her. Right? Weren't time portals always two-way? *Jeez, Clarke, this isn't Star Trek.*

Well, if time portals weren't two-way, they damned well should be. Once back in her own time, she could get back to work, visit Aunt Pearl for a reminder of what a loser she was—as if she could forget—and return to her little apartment.

Alone.

She trudged to the front step as if each leg weighed a ton and sat with an undignified plop. She let the broom fall with a clatter at her side.

Home. That was what she wanted, after all. Her own bathroom with running water and a flushing toilet, cable television, video rentals, blow-dryers and curling irons . . .

No adorable little boy asking her to read stories.

No little boy's daddy turning her hormones topsy-turvy.

No more soul-shattering kisses.

Cole and Todd took their time bathing in the icy waterfall. The longer Cole could postpone facing Jackie again, the better. She was driving him crazy.

And, Lord help him, he *liked* it.

"Damn," Cole muttered, remembering this morning's kiss. Then last night's kiss. While his son scrambled into his clothing, Cole turned around and headed back under the waterfall for another cold shower.

As things were, by the time he was scheduled to return Lolita to the Silver Spur, Cole would have to consider moving to the falls permanently. The woman didn't actually have to touch him to set him on fire. Hell, he didn't even have to lay eyes on her—let alone hands or lips—to become as fired up as a rutting bull at spring thaw. Then again, bulls rutted in the fall.

Damnation, now he was starting to think like a cowboy.

"I am not a cowboy," he muttered, swaggering out of the water and grabbing his shirt.

"I never said you was." Todd looked at him thoughtfully, his eyes wide and filled with questions.

Cole buttoned his shirt, then pulled on his jeans. He sat on a boulder and stretched his legs out to let his feet dry. "I hate putting socks and boots on wet feet."

Todd imitated his father's actions, his smaller feet reaching Cole's knees as they sat side by side in the morning sun. "I like Miss Jackie," Todd said, staring out across the small stream. A moment later, he turned his head and pinned his father with that look that said he was about to ask one of *those* questions.

Not now. If he asks me where babies come from, I'll curl up and die right here and now. Cole gnashed his teeth and nodded, reaching over to ruffle his son's dark blond hair. "Yeah, I like her, too."

"I can tell." Todd's eyes twinkled.

Cole loosened the top button of his shirt. "Getting warm fast today."

"Yep."

Rubbing the back of his neck, Cole tried to summon

an indifferent expression. "Now, just what do you mean, 'I can tell'?"

"About Miss Jackie?" Todd shrugged and tossed a pebble into the stream. "I just can. That's all."

Cole remained silent for several moments, pondering just how much his son had noticed. But Todd was only nine. *Almost ten.* Sure, he could tell his father liked someone, but not . . . how much. Could he?

"All right, if you say so." Cole drew a deep breath and decided to change the subject. "I've been doing a lot of thinking." He sent his son a sidelong glance, noting the boy's sudden rapt attention.

"About what?"

"Oregon." Cole released a long sigh.

"You mean we ain't—aren't—going to St. Louis?" Todd's eyes were as round as saucers. "Honest?"

Cole chuckled quietly. "You didn't like it much the one time we went back to visit, huh?"

The boy's cheeks pinkened, but his expression remained thoughtful and solemn. "Well, Grandma and Grandpa were real nice," he said, "but there were too many people."

"You remember it pretty well." Cole smiled at his son, his heart swelling with pride. "But you were still little then."

"I was six." Todd lifted his chin a notch.

"So you were." Cole drew a deep breath, knowing how much worse it would've been to lose Elizabeth if he didn't have Todd. "I'm sure glad you're my son."

Todd beamed. "Me, too." He tossed another pebble into the water. "Is Miss Jackie goin' to Oregon with us?"

Cole's heart slammed into his ribs. "Well, no, of course not." He gave a nervous chuckle. "Whatever gave you that idea?"

"Well . . ." The boy looked down at his hands folded in his lap.

"Well, what?" Cole kept his tone gentle, though the way his blood was roaring through his head, that was no small feat.

"Like I said before, I . . . I like her." Todd lifted one shoulder. "She's fun."

Fun? A hot flush crept over Cole's body. "I, uh, believe she has another job lined up after she's finished, uh, teaching you." *And tormenting me.*

Todd's face fell and his disappointment permeated the air around them. "Oh," he said.

"You like her that much, huh?"

The boy nodded without looking at his father. "Chief Byron likes her, too."

Woman with Fire in Her Hair—and mouth—will make a good squaw. She will warm your bed when the snow covers the mountains, and give you many fine sons.

"Yes." Cole drew a quick breath. It didn't help. Chief Byron had no idea how much fire that woman's mouth was capable of igniting.

Todd faced his father. "What's wrong, Pa?"

"Wrong?" Cole stood and unbuttoned his shirt.

"You look sorta . . . strange. Feverish, maybe." Todd rose and reached up on tiptoe to press his hand to his father's forehead.

Feverish was one way to put it. "No fever." *Not that kind, anyway.* "I'm fine," Cole lied, turning his back on his son to peel off his dungarees.

"Then what's wrong?"

"Someday you'll understand, son," Cole said, dropping his breeches and heading toward the falls. He kept his back to his son until after the frigid waterfall did its job.

And soothed the wild beast again.

Chapter Ten

Jackie sat on the boulder where Cole had kissed her the night before. In the bright midday sun, she didn't worry about cougars or other beasts that might be roaming the hills. Maybe she should have, but in this case, ignorance was bliss. Or so she convinced herself.

She had a decision to make. More than one, actually. Extricating herself from Cole Morrison's life would be the kindest thing she could do for him and his son. On the other hand, if she simply ran away—and managed to get lost in the mountains again, no doubt—he wouldn't receive the promised gold from either Merriweather or Goodfellow.

Goodfellow was willing to pay more, and that was also where Jackie would find her unfinished portrait. She had to get to that portrait before the real Lolita showed up and cost Cole the gold and Jackie her time portal.

But as long as it was completed, did it really matter whether the portrait was of Jackie or Lolita? Her time-portal painting had been of the real Lolita, after all. Now that Jackie thought about it, though, she remembered the way the face in the painting had transformed from Lolita's to Jackie's.

Dammit, Clarke—get back to that portrait before it's too late.

She rolled her eyes skyward. *Damn.* Did the way Lolita's face had changed to hers mean Jackie's current fate was to *be* Lolita Belle? A sudden consideration made her flesh turn cold, and she stiffened. Bracing herself with her arms extended behind her, Jackie considered the impossible. Of course, much of her life seemed impossible these days. Even so, she had to consider it.

When she'd fallen back in time, had the real Lolita gone forward? This was all starting to sound like a low-budget science-fiction movie. Question was, how would the movie end? Swallowing the lump in her throat, she drew a deep breath and watched a hawk sail by, mocking her with its serene appearance.

Could it be true? Was the real Lolita in Jackie's time trying to figure out modern technology and the nuances of dating and the modern single woman? Another thought made Jackie laugh out loud and sit up straight.

Was Lolita educating Great-Aunt Pearl?

Poor Aunt Pearl. Jackie bit her lower lip, remembering the last time she'd seen her aunt, then revised her concern. *Poor Lolita.* Either way, Jackie knew Lolita and Pearl would be worthy adversaries. Hell, Aunt Pearl would probably prefer having Lolita to ridicule instead of Jackie. Lolita's life had to be a lot more interesting than Jackie's.

In any century.

With a sigh, she slid off the boulder and trudged slowly toward the cabin, pondering the whole mess. *If* she and Lolita had actually traded centuries, then didn't they both have to trade again to set things right? What if Lolita liked modern times, indoor plumbing, and the feminist movement? Could they both be in the same time together?

Jackie froze. She was in big trouble. Then again, maybe she was borrowing trouble. She had absolutely no proof that she and Lolita had traded places, other than the fact that she was here and Lolita wasn't. On the other hand, Goodfellow had said Lolita—er, Jackie—was earlier than expected. She threw her hands up in surrender, her mind and emotions dueling inside her body.

And how could she be certain Rock Smith wasn't Blade trying to con her again with that dumb cowboy routine?

Damn. She needed to release some major stress. At home, she would've gone to Jazzercize, then seen Dom for a massage. The thought of her favorite massage therapist's magical hands made her moan and rub the kink in the back of her neck.

"Face it, Jackie, you aren't Dom." Maybe she couldn't get a massage, but she could do some aerobic exercise to relieve her stress. Besides, Todd's fatty cooking would go straight to her thighs in no time, so exercise would serve a dual purpose. Triple. Relieve stress, burn fat and calories, and . . . take her mind off Cole.

No, be honest, Clarke. Not just Cole—sex with Cole.

Too risky, because she couldn't keep her heart out of it. Sex was one thing—lovemaking was another.

"Why can't you be a wanton, Clarke?" She had to stop thinking about sex. Exercise was the answer.

There was no such thing as spandex in 1891, so she would have to improvise. She was completely alone in the wilderness, for heaven's sake. No one would see her. At any rate, she certainly couldn't exercise in this Little Bo Peep regalia.

Looking over her shoulder to ensure she was still alone, she removed the sunbonnet as she stepped into the cabin and unbuttoned Elizabeth's dress. She squirmed out of it, then folded it over the back of the rocking chair. For a moment, Jackie stared at the rocker. Elizabeth would've rocked Todd to sleep in that chair.

All the grief Cole and Todd must've felt since Elizabeth's death washed over Jackie, and she pressed the heel of her hand to her breastbone and bit the knuckles of her other hand. She wanted—needed—to form a picture of Elizabeth in her mind. What had Cole's wife looked like? Did he have a photo or a painting? Jackie made a mental note to go through more of the books and journals on Cole's shelves after her workout. Maybe there was a wedding album or something.

She looked around the cramped cabin. There simply wasn't room in here for a decent workout, so she shrugged and peered through the open door again. No one around but a few birds and a squirrel staring at her as if she had suddenly grown two heads.

Laughing at her own foolishness, she stepped outside and onto the bare ground in front of the cabin. "You ain't seen nothing yet," she said to the surrounding wildlife. She paused with her hands on her hips and drew a deep breath, then glanced down at her attire. The lace-trimmed chemise and pantalets—

or were they pantaloons?—were far less revealing than her usual tights and leotard.

"Get over it, Clarke." She reached over her head, then leaned far to each side, stretching her stiff muscles. Placing her palms flat on the ground, she felt the muscles in the backs of her legs pull and elongate. Yes, exercise was just what she needed.

Sex is exercise.

No, Clarke. Get over it.

After stretching for several minutes, she started with some simple jumping jacks, then segued into a jazz routine she'd learned in class. The familiar music played through her head, and she gradually gave herself over to her endorphins.

Time and place forgotten, Jackie worked hard. Stress became a distant memory, and her body relished the familiar activity and the endorphin high. Her routine had been shot all to hell with this time-travel gig, so anything familiar was a welcome change at this point.

A strange rhythm joined the music in her brain, and she stopped abruptly to stare at the man seated on the front step. With a small drum wedged between his knees, Chief Byron gave her a toothless grin and an approving nod, and kept right on beating his drum.

Oh. My. God. The old man must think this was some sort of rain dance. Well, come to think of it, aerobic exercise *was* a ritual. And she wasn't doing anything wrong, after all.

Feeling her flesh begin to cool and her pulse rate slow too soon, Jackie gave a shrug and returned to her workout, adjusting her mental music to match Chief Byron's. Several more minutes passed before she'd had enough. Reaching over her head, she stretched, then bent forward to repeat the process.

She didn't want to wake up sore in the morning in any century.

"Thanks, Chief," she said, straightening. "You play a mean tom—"

The direction of the chief's gaze made Jackie bite off her words as she swung around to survey her unexpected audience. Todd stood by the paddock fence, his eyes wide and jaw slack. Allowing her gaze to drift slightly to the right, Jackie found a much longer pair of legs and followed them up past slim hips, taut abdomen, broad chest, sinewy neck. . . . Cole's jaw twitched and his lips were set in a thin line, with his nostrils slightly flared, his eyes narrowed to twin slits of disapproval.

Jackie's mouth went dry, and she shoved her hair back from her face. "Hey, guys." She waggled her fingers in their direction, refusing to be embarrassed. These Victorian men needed some enlightenment. And then some.

"What the devil are you . . . ?" Cole walked slowly toward her, his son at his side. "What . . . ?" Again he faltered, unable or unwilling to complete his question.

Damn. He probably thinks this is part of Lolita's act. Jackie gave a shrug and kept smiling, forcing herself to meet his gaze. "Exercising, and Chief Byron was good enough to play my, uh, accompaniment."

Cole shook his head, but his gaze dropped to her breasts. *Uh-oh.* Jackie realized the thin cotton chemise probably outlined every detail.

She held her breath, and her nipples stiffened in response to the heat of his gaze. Liquid fire slowly unfurled through her core like tendrils of smoke.

Jeez, she wanted this man. A shiver of anticipation

skittered down her spine. Her breasts rose and fell with each breath, and Cole seemed mesmerized.

Couldn't she set aside her emotions and morals just this once for a wild, lurid affair with Cole Morrison? Maybe it would be good for her to let go, to forget about her heart and her hang-ups. What would it take out of her to seduce this man? Regardless of what the future held, she knew one thing for certain.

She'd go crazy if she didn't have Cole Morrison at least once—she licked her lips—or twice.

Don't forget the kid, Clarke.

She should cover herself. Self-disgust oozed through her, and after a few tense moments, Cole also seemed to drag himself from the spell he'd cast over them both and rolled his eyes heavenward. His cheeks reddened and he shifted his gaze to the chief.

"What's going on here, Chief?"

The old man appeared nonplused, looking from Cole to Jackie, then back to Cole as if their inability to grasp the obvious were absurd. He grinned again. "The maidens in my tribe never danced this way." His dark eyes twinkled, and he directed a longing glance in Jackie's direction. "Sadly."

Jackie smiled at her elderly friend. "You're a treasure, Chief." She'd better get her butt inside and back into her dress.

"I like this dance," the chief said with conviction.

"Thanks, Chief." A niggling worry eased through Jackie as she inched her way toward the steps. She'd just squeeze by the old boy and grab her clothes. . . .

"The custom is obvious," the chief continued. "Do you not see it, Pale Eyes?"

Uh-oh. Jackie had no idea what sort of custom the old man thought she'd been practicing, but she knew trouble when she heard it. *Well, sometimes.*

Cole chuckled without a hint of humor, yanking his hat off to slap his thigh. "Custom?" He shook his head. "It might be obvious to you, Chief, but all I saw was a half-naked woman prancing around like she had ants in her drawers."

"I was exercising." Jackie's cheeks warmed, and she grabbed the post beside the steps, ready to vault over the railing if the chief didn't clear the steps for her retreat. But another part of her squared her shoulders and stood her ground. "There's nothing indecent about it, Cole Morrison, so—"

"Oh, really?" He quirked a brow.

"Really." She put her fists on her hips and glowered.

"The dance, Pale Eyes," Chief Byron repeated, rising to stand beside Jackie, his drum clutched under his arm. "You understand."

"No, Chief, I don't understand much of anything these days." Cole barked a derisive laugh and raked his fingers through his hair. "Why don't you enlighten me?"

Chief Byron straightened, his chin high and his expression deadly serious. "Woman with hair like fire was doing her tribal mating dance."

Jackie choked. *Mating dance?* And what tribe did he think she belonged to—the Redheaded Floozies?

Cole's face turned so red it was nearly purple. Todd's eyes widened even more.

The chief pointed one bony finger at Cole and said, "For you."

All the air rushed out of Jackie's lungs, and she nudged past the chief and ran inside. She grabbed her dress and pulled it on, her hands trembling.

The thought of mating with Cole Morrison undid all the good her exercise had done.

Another type of exercise would be far more satisfying about now.

Clarke, you're in major *trouble.*

Somehow Cole managed to sit at the table for a cold dinner with a now fully clothed Jackie, his son, and Chief Byron. Stunned silence had been their only response to the chief's description of Jackie's dance.

Mating dance, my behind.

Of course, his rear end wasn't the part of him that had responded to her little performance. What in the hell had she been trying to prove, parading around outside in her unmentionables? *Even if she looked damn good in her unmentionables.*

Remembering the sight of her pert bosom outlined beneath clinging white cotton made Cole's throat close too soon around a lump of corn bread, and he washed it down with lukewarm coffee. Since he and Todd had been gone all morning, no one had prepared anything for their midday meal. Cole peered at the woman who'd occupied his mind far too much in the last few days as he spooned honey onto cold corn bread. She probably couldn't cook anyway.

A woman like Lolita didn't have to cook. He took a vicious bite of corn bread and managed to find the edge of his tongue, too. "Shit."

"Now who has a potty mouth?" Jackie asked tauntingly.

Todd and Chief Byron both snickered, but a glower from Cole shut them both up, and he set aside his corn bread, his appetite gone. "I apologize for my language," he said stiffly, reaching for his cup again. "I'll be more careful in the future."

Jackie's eyes twinkled mischievously. A second later,

something brushed against his ankle. And again. He started to look under the table to see if a critter had found its way into the cabin, but the expression on Jackie's face stayed him. He swallowed hard and an inferno settled right between his legs.

The critter was a woman with flame-red hair.

Judging from his body's response, she might have been rubbing another appendage—one a little higher and a whole lot harder.

She was killing him. Little by little, she was wearing him down to a poor excuse for a man who couldn't think beyond his privates. She worked her toe beneath the edge of his dungarees and found the top of his boot, then bare skin.

Time ceased. His privates throbbed. Any second now, the buttons at his fly would give and shoot across the room like stray bullets. Then everybody'd see his sorry state.

Pitiful, Morrison. Just pitiful.

Sweat formed all over his body. A breeze wafted through the open door. He shuddered and raked his fingers through his hair. The falls were calling to him again, screaming his name.

Jackie stroked the inside of his calf with her toe, sending rivulets of warmth up his leg to fortify his aroused state. Lord help him, but he didn't need any fortification. He needed to break a commandment real damned fast. *Fornication*—not fortification. He needed a woman.

He met her gaze and she licked her lips.

God help him, but not just any woman. Her. Only her.

Dangerous thinking, Morrison. His gut clenched and he drew a shaky breath. "I need some air." He slid off the bench and stood, trying to ignore the nagging throb as the seams and buttons at his fly gouged his eager flesh.

"You okay, Pa?"

"Yeah," he lied. He walked slowly and grabbed his hat. "I'm going to the mine. Be back before dark."

"But I thought you weren't going today," Jackie said, her voice too pretty. Too seductive. Too . . . *too.*

"I know what I said." He didn't look back, nor did he have any intention of going to the mine. He had a date with a waterfall, and at the rate he was going, he'd be permanently waterlogged. "A man's got a right to change his mind. Besides, I need to go."

And *that* was no lie.

Shoving his hat onto his head, he trudged out the door and toward the trail leading to the mine. He'd keep right on walking, though, until he found that icy waterfall. Another shudder rippled through him as the mountain air dried the sweat from his skin. He drew deep gulps of fresh air, and by the time he reached the falls, he felt almost in control again. Almost.

He stripped and placed his clothes and boots neatly on the boulder where he and Todd had sat this morning. Stonily, he marched into the water's steady flow and gasped as the icy sting met his bare skin.

This constant state of arousal and deliberately freezing himself couldn't be good for a man. It violated the laws of nature. Man was supposed to go forth and be fruitful. Propagate the species. Sow his wild oats.

Shit.

He stood with the water pouring over his head and down the length of his body, his arms braced against the sheer rock wall behind the falls. Motionless, he welcomed the abatement of his lustful side.

His fingers and toes tingled, and he knew better

than to stay in the near-freezing water any longer. He'd warm himself in the sun, then dress after his skin dried. Maybe he'd douse himself another time before he dressed. It was worth a try if it would help keep these constant urges under control a mite longer.

He sat naked on the boulder beside his clothing, confident of his privacy. Farther downstream where the water met a beaver dam, he would've had many visitors, but all of the four-legged variety. Here only an occasional bird flew overhead. He was completely alone.

The sun warmed his skin despite the coolness of the breeze. The scent of pine mingled with the air and tickled his senses. What a glorious day. He should have brought his journal along, but he'd been too danged desperate to think straight.

Maybe if he spent some time jotting down his feelings, he might be more successful at combating his crude urges. Then again, if he wrote down all the thoughts coursing through his mind, the words wouldn't be fit for anyone to read. Especially his son. No, that wasn't a good idea, since Todd loved to read Cole's stories.

A real man didn't sit around sunning himself when he should be working. Shame slithered through him. He never would have wasted a day like this before Jackie came into his life. No, sir.

"Enough lazing around, Morrison," he muttered, rising and stretching. The sun had made him drowsy and dulled his senses, but he knew what would fix that straightaway, and headed for the water again.

His dash into the frigid water was different this time—less desperate and more playful. He hooted like Todd had this morning, and lifted his face up to let the water revive him. No trace of his sun-induced lethargy remained.

It was too late for him to accomplish much at the mine now, but there were some chores he could do at home. Outside. Away from Lolita-Jackie.

The image of her flushed face, disheveled hair, and slender curves flashed through his mind, but he forcibly banished them. No more of that. He had plans to make for the future. At last.

He hooted again and raised both hands in the air, turning slowly in the water. They were going to Oregon. The dream he and Elizabeth had planned would happen. He closed his eyes for a moment, wishing she could be here to share this, but he figured she knew somehow.

But he sure as hell hoped she didn't know about the kidnapping. Or Lolita-Jackie . . .

Cole winced, pushing the thought aside. He couldn't undo what had been done. *Live with it, Morrison.* Everything would be all right as soon as he had Todd out of Colorado and on the road to Oregon. Then Cole could leave his short-lived crime spree behind.

And Lolita Belle.

His gut clenched as he stood where the water barely hit one arm and his hip, thinking. He wouldn't miss Lolita, but Todd's "Miss Jackie" was another matter. Cole's Lolita-Jackie . . .

No, not his.

He turned toward the water again, dousing himself thoroughly and expelling such thoughts. *Think about the future.*

Since Elizabeth's death, he hadn't even opened the book they'd bought about Oregon. Now was the time. He'd haul out that book and show Todd the illustrations he and the boy's mother had dreamed over for years.

Whistling, Cole stepped out of the water's flow and shook himself like a wet dog, droplets flying from his hair. He wiped his eyes until his vision cleared, then turned toward where he'd left his clothes.

And froze.

Jackie stood beside the boulder wearing a prim and proper brown dress. Cole couldn't breathe. All he could do was count the buttons at the front of her basque, one at a time, pondering what lay hidden behind them.

The water's alleviation of his rutting state expired in a single, powerful thud of his heart. His body responded before he could form any rational thought.

Hard. Fast. Prominent . . .

"What," he croaked, forcing his gaze from her bosom to her face, "are you doing here?"

She licked her lips. "I think you know the answer to that question"—her gaze dropped and her eyes widened—"big guy."

He crossed his hands in front of his impudent and not-so-private privates. Watching her watch him, he dragged in a shaky breath. A gentleman would grab his clothes and get the hell out of here while the getting was good.

And Cole Morrison was a gentleman. *Damnation.*

"Where's Todd?"

"He and Chief Byron are reading *Huckleberry Finn.* It's a long book." She shrugged and flashed a grin that turned his blood molten. "So I decided to come and finish what we started before." Tilting her head to one side, she smiled again. "And here you are."

"Yeah," was all he could manage. His arousal

flinched and throbbed, reminding him how long it had been since he'd felt a woman's body rise against his in the throes of passion. Gentleman or not, he couldn't drag his gaze from her luscious mouth. Her tongue slipped between her lips and glided smoothly across them again, leaving a rosy luster in its wake.

He should be angry at this invasion of his privacy, but he couldn't summon the gumption. Only one thing could possibly spur him to action now, and that wasn't about to happen in reality.

But he could imagine plenty.

She continued to stare at him, and he returned the favor, envisioning the endless row of buttons popping open one at a time until her dress pooled at her feet. Underneath, she probably wore the thin white chemise and drawers—Lord help him—he'd seen her cavorting in earlier.

If the expression in her eyes was any indication, she was every bit as aroused as he. Were the tawny peaks of her breasts taut and straining against the confines of her clothing? Did her insides feel hot and all aquiver, as did his? Was she hankering to kiss him as desperately as he was to kiss her—he swallowed hard—all over?

Damnation.

If he remembered correctly, the narrow ribbon at the front of her chemise was buttery yellow. In his mind, he untied it and slowly opened the soft white fabric until it gaped, revealing the tops of her full, firm breasts.

"Jackie," he whispered, barely able to breathe, let alone talk. His voice held a warning note, he hoped. One she'd best heed if she expected him to remember much longer that he was a gentleman. He forced himself to look at her face again, forsaking the delectable thoughts of how she would look disrobed.

She bit her lower lip and a flush crept across her cheeks, almost as if she could read his thoughts. Her eyes were moist and wide. Innocent.

Lolita, innocent? What was he thinking? But it didn't matter. Nothing mattered except the ache in his loins and the hunger in his very soul.

"I came to give you what we didn't get to last night," she said, her voice taking on a sultry quality he hadn't noticed before. "Whether you want it or not."

Oh, he wanted it all right.

She smiled and looked pointedly to where his hands still tried to hide his blatant arousal from her hungry gaze. "It's easy to forget things. I'd be willing to bet neither of us has been getting much sleep."

"Well . . . but . . . I . . . " How the hell did she know he hadn't been sleeping well? "You want to . . . ?"

"Oh, yeah, I definitely want to. In fact, I've been looking forward to this." She smiled and opened the top two buttons of her dress. "Warm today."

"Hot," he whispered, struggling for every breath. His gaze lingered again at her breasts—full, round, perfect. *Don't think about those.* He definitely had a powerful weakness for her bosom. A man could never get enough of a woman like her.

And she came here to finish what they'd started last night.

A roar commenced in his ears as his heart pounded wildly. He couldn't fight her again. If she so much as touched him, he'd ravish her right here on the ground like the wild beast she'd created in him.

Surrendering, he let his hands fall to his sides, unable to shield himself from her any longer. Naked, vulnerable, he whispered her name again.

She stared at his throbbing manhood, and Cole was powerless to stop her. At this point, he couldn't deny her anything she wanted.

And he hoped she wanted plenty.

"My, but you are an impressive specimen." She sighed. "Just a sec," she said, then reached into her deep pocket and withdrew something long and shiny.

What the hell was that and what was the woman up to now? Her dallying would be the death of him. His mouth went dry. Yes, he wanted her. Desperately. *Damn.* He didn't feel like a gentleman now. *Rutting boar* seemed far more appropriate, and there was nothing he wanted to do more than rut at this particular moment.

He'd transformed from a single father with a worthless mine to a kidnapper and a lecherous monster. A beast. The thought gave him pause, reminding him of a French fairy tale his mother had loved. Swallowing the lump in his throat, he took a step toward Jackie—no longer Lolita-Jackie to him.

She advanced a step and held out one hand. "You might want to get dressed first."

He paused, blinking as her words reached his addled mind. "What? I thought . . . "

"What did you think, big guy?" The corners of her luscious lips curved in a mischievous grin, and her gaze dropped again. "It seems a shame to cover such a, uh, magnificent specimen, but the hair will make you itch like mad."

"Hair?" What the devil was the woman jabbering about now? "What hair?" The only thoughts he had of hair were too crass to mention.

He stared at her outstretched hand, then back to her breasts, following a thin blue vein up the side of her neck until it disappeared behind her curls. Finally he met her gaze, forcing himself to pay attention to her words instead of his lust.

She held the long silver object up in one hand and made a snipping motion. "I promised Todd he could watch, but since you wormed your way out of your haircut last night, I—"

Cole roared and pivoted on his heel, marching right back into the waterfall, her laughter following him all the way. She'd played him for a fool and he'd fallen right into her little game. No more.

His lust waned beneath the sting of humiliation and the icy water. He'd make her turn around while he dressed, then he'd let her cut his damned hair. And if—when—his body decided to rise to her bait again, well, he'd just ignore it. He glanced down at his now-flaccid privates. "You hear that?" he whispered through the running water.

No answer.

Good thing his privates couldn't answer, because the answer he needed to hear would've been a lie anyway. Disappointment pressed down on him as he forced himself to admit the truth, at least to himself.

Though he knew it was wrong, during those few moments when he'd believed she meant to have her way with him . . .

He'd felt more alive than he had in years.

Chapter Eleven

Jackie watched Cole stomp back into the waterfall, and she laughed even though she felt more like crying. She'd seen the naked desire in his eyes and the even more naked state of his body.

And what a body. Cole Morrison was one well-endowed man. He couldn't have been more beautiful if Michelangelo had risen from the dead to create him. But it was much more than his looks that drew her to him. He was a good man—kind, generous, a loving father.

And a kidnapper. Don't forget that.

Tonight, by God, she would find out why he'd been willing to abduct her for pay. He'd promised, and she wouldn't let him weasel out of telling her again. Cougars, bears—nothing would stand in her way tonight.

Then after his confession . . . maybe they'd get back to that other unfinished matter between them. Of course, there were really two unfinished matters between them, but until Henri's broken finger was healed . . .

She cleared her throat. After having seen Cole's blatant erection she couldn't call their attraction a *small* matter by any stretch of the imagination. Not that she had before.

Somehow she'd known exactly where he was going when he'd stormed out of the cabin earlier. Todd had been only too eager to tell her how to find the falls, though she'd worried the whole time that she might become lost again in the mountains. But she'd found the falls. And Cole.

Whoa. She fanned herself and released a long, slow breath.

Of course, she probably should fill him in on the visitor she'd had this morning. Rock Smith. The name made her cringe, but was it really any worse than Blade? *Yep.*

But *he* couldn't be any worse than Blade. Unless he *was* Blade . . .

Should she tell Cole about Smith's visit and Goodfellow's offer? What if it was really Blade setting a trap for her again? She had to be careful and think this through first.

And *if* she decided to tell Cole about Smith, should she do it before or after they made love . . . ? Could she keep her emotions disengaged long enough to have casual sex?

No. Get real, Clarke.

She cared about Cole Morrison even more than she wanted him.

The thought of lying naked in his arms made her tingle all over, and her nipples stiffened against her clothing. She glanced down, wondering if he'd be able to see through the brown fabric. *No. Darn it.*

In all seriousness, urging Cole to return her to the Gold Mine Saloon and the unfinished portrait was the right thing. He'd get paid, and maybe she could go home, and stop thinking about seducing him with every breath she took.

Unless Lolita Belle was living Jackie's life. *Stop that.* She couldn't think straight as it was without adding more confusion.

As it had this morning, the thought of going home left her feeling sort of empty and confused. A lump formed in her throat. *Get over it.* She wasn't the kind of woman a man like Cole Morrison wanted as a stepmother for his son. Besides, he thought Jackie was a notorious saloon singer. Hardly mother material.

Of course, in truth, she *wasn't* a saloon singer. She was just a foolish hairdresser from another century, trapped in the past because of her own stupidity.

So she should sleep with him, have her jollies, and be done with it. Get him out of her system. Wasn't that how a man would handle it? *Slam, bam, thank you, ma'am?* That was the ticket.

Sure, Clarke. Stop lying to yourself.

There was no way she could engage her hormones without engaging her heart. Those caring torpedoes were total duds, and she was in deep doo-doo.

And while she was fulfilling her quest for truth and great sex—which she *really* needed to forget about—should she also tell him how she'd ended up in Devil's Gulch in the first place? Could a nineteenth-century man believe in time travel? Well, considering she was still having trouble accepting it herself, that was doubtful.

But *should* she tell him?

"Turn around and give a man some privacy," Cole said from the edge of the falls, jarring her from her troublesome thoughts.

"Too late. I've already seen you." She grinned and waggled her brows. "And I must say you looked *real* good. Big guy."

"Would you quit calling me that and just mind your manners for a change? I'm freezing in here." His face reddened, but the steady streams flowing over his shoulders and down the front of his body shrouded his more interesting attributes from her roving gaze.

"You blush nicely, too." She laughed when he scowled. "All right, I'm turning around now."

"No peeking."

"Promise."

"Behave," he said from much closer behind her.

"I'm not peeking."

"But you want to."

"Yes, but I won't." *This time.* She heard the rustle of fabric and knew his jeans were in place again. *Darn.* No more voyeurism today. "You finished yet?"

"Yep."

She turned around just as he was buttoning his blue chambray shirt. "Pity to cover all that." She gave an exaggerated sigh and his scowl deepened. "Careful, your face might stay that way."

"Ha. Ha." He pulled his sexy red suspenders over his shoulders and sat on the edge of the boulder. "Since you insist, go ahead and cut my hair. That's what caused all this trouble in the first place."

Not exactly. Jackie kept her thoughts to herself as she went to work on Cole's damp hair. The dark curls were sleek between her fingers, and she had to lean across his shoulders to do the back, her breasts brushing against him. She felt him shudder and smiled to herself.

She could've had him this afternoon—right here in the Rocky Mountain sunshine. Her heart raced, and his warmth radiated through his damp shirt, narrowing the distance between them. This man had some kind of power over her, and it both frightened and thrilled her at the same time.

Cole Morrison simply stole her breath without even trying. Even more disconcerting, he'd made her *care* about him and his son.

She chewed her lower lip as she snipped and layered his wavy hair into a neat, collar-length style. "There. Hmm. I wish I had a little gel. Your hair is perfect for the messy look." She finger-combed the strands around his face. "Very sexy."

His Adam's apple traveled down, then back up his throat, then he reached behind him and felt his hair. "You left it kind of long back here," he said, his voice rough and smooth, like good whiskey—so Blade had claimed. She wouldn't know good whiskey from bad.

"I couldn't bring myself to take off all your curls." She reached up and brushed a strand back from his forehead. "They're too pretty to cut."

"I don't *want* to be pretty."

"Okay, handsome." Her voice fell to a husky whisper, and she rested her hand on his shoulder, his warmth filling her with need.

And promise.

Should she tell him about Goodfellow's proposition now? No, not until Cole told her why he needed money badly enough to kidnap her. Then she'd tell him.

But maybe she'd seduce him first.

Listen to yourself, Clarke. Aunt Pearl would have a

heart attack if she knew what Jackie was thinking. Cole looked up at her, his expression pensive, but the hunger still burned in his blue eyes.

She gulped, massaging his shoulder. *To hell with not-so-Great-Aunt Pearl.*

But she had to be honest with herself. Aunt Pearl's conscience wasn't really what prevented Jackie from throwing herself at Cole right here and now. It was hers. She couldn't do it without falling for him completely, and that was out of the question.

Back on topic, Clarke. Maybe he would tell her why he'd kidnapped her now. She slid the scissors into her pocket and sat beside him on the boulder. "Cole?"

"Hmm?" He looked at her again, and his eyes darkened. "What is it? You already cut my hair."

"Not that." She drew a deep breath, then released it very slowly. "Tell me now."

He appeared confused. "Tell you what?"

"Why you kidnapped me."

The light in his eyes faded and his jaw twitched.

"Don't grind your teeth."

His eyes narrowed and his jaw twitched again. "I don't want to tell you, but I reckon you have a right to know." He looked up at the sky and shook his head. "Like any man, I like to keep my failures secret—only for my own musing and misery." He released a ragged sigh. "I'll tell you tonight, like we agreed."

"Hold on there, cowboy—"

"I asked you not to call me that anymore."

"Big guy—"

"Or that."

He made a move to rise and she swung her legs onto his lap. "Don't you dare walk away from me."

Staring at her skirt and legs draped across his lap,

he asked, "What the hell kind of game are you playing with me, Lolita?"

"Jackie." She leaped to her feet and walked in circles around the clearing, then spun around to face him, her fists resting on her hips. "How many times do I have to tell you my name is Jackie?"

He rose, towering over her, his broad shoulders casting a shadow across the clearing. "Right now you're acting more like a Lolita than a Jackie. That's why."

That stung. A lot. Jackie's lower lip trembled and her throat clogged. She wouldn't cry, but, dammit, he was right. Drawing a shaky breath, she knew what she had to do. "You're right, Cole. I am, and I'm sorry."

He tilted his head to one side, clearly skeptical. "You are?"

"Yes." She lifted her chin and met his gaze. "I'm sorry, because I don't want you to believe I'm Lolita Belle. I'm *not.*"

He shook his head and slapped his thigh. "Here we go with that nonsense again."

"Truth, Cole." She stood her ground, refusing to look away. "God's honest truth."

He rubbed his chin for a few minutes, his expression studious. "Then I'd say you're the one who's got some explaining to do." He arched a brow. "Wouldn't you?"

"Yes. I . . . I'll tell you tonight, but you'll tell me the truth first. Like you promised." She drew several gulps of air, mustering all the courage she could. "Have you read all those Jules Verne novels in your collection, Cole?"

"Yep, more than once." His brow furrowed. "Why?"

"Because truth *is* stranger than fiction."

Chuckling, he shook his head and cocked one eyebrow. "Are you trying to tell me you came here in a spaceship?"

Her breath caught. "Something like that."

He didn't laugh at her and his expression grew sober. "I don't know why, but I'm really looking forward to hearing your story."

"I know why." She grinned.

"Oh, you do, huh?" His lips twitched and he almost smiled.

"Because you like me." Her voice lowered and softened as the heat of desire washed through her again. "And you want me." *And you're being a terrible tease, Clarke.*

His jaw flinched again and his eyes darkened. "Yes, ma'am," he said, his voice rumbling around inside her and hitting every nerve ending, "but I was raised knowing I can't have everything I want."

She reached for the buttons at the front of her dress and released them very quickly. "Well, I don't do self-deprivation very well myself." She eased her dress over her shoulders. "It's unhealthy."

Both his brows shot upward and his mouth gaped open. "What are you doing, woman?"

"Since you're determined to make us wait until later—to talk, I mean . . . " She let the dress drop to the ground, then retrieved it and placed it on the boulder.

"But . . . "

"Relax," she said in her sexiest voice, then she leaned forward and kissed him hard on the mouth. "I'm just going to have myself a little shower, big guy."

"But . . . "

She reached for the ribbons at the front of her antiquated underwear. "You going to watch, or turn your back and stand guard like a good boy?"

A visible shudder rippled through him and he turned his back, folding his arms and standing at attention. "Hurry up about it."

Laughing, she stripped and left her undies with her dress and hiking boots, then darted into the falls. The shock of the frigid water made her shriek. After a few moments, she grew somewhat used to the icy shower and peered through the sheet of running water at the man who still stood with his back to her.

"Damn," she muttered. "I was really hoping you'd want to be very, *very* bad."

Jackie closed the book she'd been reading to Todd and gazed down at his face. Asleep, he appeared even younger. She struggled against the sudden urge to gather him into her arms and hold him close. But he wasn't a baby. He wasn't even her son.

Unexpected tears gathered in the corners of her eyes, but she blinked them away. She wasn't allowed to cry. Great-Aunt Pearl had always said so . . . .

Cole was out feeding Ruth and putting her in the stable for the night, so Jackie sat with the leather-bound copy of *Huckleberry Finn* clutched to her chest and watched Todd sleep. And remembered . . .

Her mother had always read her bedtime stories. Jackie had been only a year older than Todd was now when her mother died. Old enough to read her own stories, Great-Aunt Pearl had said. Even that first night after the police officer had come to tell them about her mother's car accident, Jackie hadn't been allowed to cry. Only the weak and wicked cried, Great-Aunt Pearl had insisted.

So Jackie had shed her tears alone in her room with only an old doll to share her grief. She'd learned very quickly to keep her feelings to herself. No affection, no tears, no emotions whatsoever.

No wonder she'd eloped with her high-school sweetheart the night of her eighteenth birthday. They had been very much in love, but both so immature that the marriage was doomed from the start.

Jackie the idealist had wanted the perfect little house with flowers and a picket fence. And she wanted babies. Lots of babies. If she ever had a daughter, she would name her Sandra, after her mother.

She'd almost had a baby. Jackie had conceived shortly after the wedding, but a miscarriage shattered that dream along with all the others. Great-Aunt Pearl had called it a sign from God. Jackie and her husband had buried their grief, rather than facing it, and that had signaled the beginning of the end.

After the divorce, Jackie'd had no choice but to move back in with her aunt—a nightmare from the first day. As an adult, Jackie wasn't about to play by the old woman's rules any longer. She paid rent and kept to herself, trying to ignore her aunt's constant criticism.

Jackie smiled to herself, remembering the day she had received the small-business loan for her beauty shop. The old house she and her partner converted had an unused apartment upstairs, so Jackie had moved in while the downstairs was still under construction.

She shook her head. No more rules. No more hiding. No more Great-Aunt Pearl.

Of course, she'd still felt obliged to pay a weekly

visit to her aging aunt, and the criticism only grew worse over time. So Jackie had immersed herself in the business. She worked long hours, scrimped and saved, reinvested every dime into the shop, and had practically no social life, let alone a love life.

Then Blade had come along. . . .

And the rest, so they say, is history. She stifled a giggle when she considered how accurately that described her current situation.

Jackie rose slowly and placed the book on the shelf, realizing Cole was probably finished with the horse by now. A sense of doom pressed down on her. Why? She was about to learn the truth Cole had promised her.

And tell him the truth about herself as well.

Oh, God. Would he call her mad and send her away? She drew a deep breath and lifted her chin a notch, pulling the shawl Cole had given her around her shoulders. Whatever happened, she'd deal with it.

After all, only the weak and wicked ever cried. She might be a tad wicked, but Jackie was *never* weak.

Remind yourself of that later, Clarke.

The front door was closed, because this evening was cooler than any since Jackie's arrival. She opened it and stepped quietly onto the porch, pulling the door firmly shut behind her. Cole definitely wouldn't want his son to overhear them.

For that matter, neither did Jackie. She didn't want Todd to think she was crazy, and she certainly didn't want him to believe his father was a kidnapper.

Cole Morrison hadn't really abducted her. He'd saved her.

A cool breeze swept up the pass and made her shiver. She glanced upward, noticing the nearly full moon shining through a small break in the otherwise overcast sky. Silver bathed the small clearing, giving the area a surreal appearance.

Appropriate backdrop for her *Twilight Zone* tale.

She pulled the shawl closer and gazed toward the paddock. She saw movement and squinted. A tall figure closed the gate, then headed toward the cabin.

Cole.

His powerful, long-legged stride brought him toward her quickly. Perspiration coated her palms and she wiped them on her skirt. Her throat constricted, her breath quickened, and her heart thudded against the wall of her chest. Fluttering butterflies did a dance in her stomach. It had been years, but she recognized the symptoms.

She was in love with Cole Morrison.

A moment of terror seized her and she couldn't breathe. She should run away. Far away. Very fast. Now. Before it was too late . . .

Too late for what, Clarke? She had no Great-Aunt Pearl here to criticize her behavior. She had no one to answer to in 1891 but herself.

She was already lost.

Suddenly the thought of seducing him took on an entirely different meaning. She could no longer pretend she was interested in casual sex. *You're a fool, Clarke.* She'd never been interested in casual sex with Cole or any other man.

For Jackie Clarke, there had never been anything remotely similar to casual sex. She was challenged in the separation of emotions and lust department. An outright failure. Hell, she wasn't even trainable.

She still wanted Cole—more than ever—but now she had to face facts. She couldn't sleep with Cole without giving him everything she had.

Whether he wanted it or not.

Making love.

"Todd asleep?"

Jackie gasped and squeezed her eyes shut. "Yes, he's asleep."

"I'm sorry I startled you." He stepped up onto the porch and stood facing her.

She tilted her head back and looked up at his face, barely visible in the moonlight. How could she have allowed herself to fall in love with this man? A man who was good and kind and so very sexy?

All right, *how* was easy. *Why* was more difficult. She should have seen it coming. Who did she think she was fooling with that lust stuff anyway? It had been love all along, but she was too much of a dweeb to recognize the danger signs. She should have stopped herself.

She . . . was being ridiculous.

"Cat got your tongue?" he quipped, and his teeth flashed silvery white with his smile.

"I . . . I was just having what Aunt Pearl would call a 'Come to Jesus' meeting."

"Meeting with who?" He glanced quickly over his shoulder.

"Me, myself, and I."

He sighed and placed both hands on the porch rail. "About my reasons for doing what I did?"

"Um, among other things." She struggled to keep her voice sounding as calm as possible. The last thing she needed was for him to suspect her true feelings. "Are you ready to tell me?"

"I reckon now's as good a time as any." He glanced toward the cabin and Todd, then straightened and took her hand. "Let's walk."

Jackie stared at her hand swallowed by his larger

one and barely halted the shudder of longing that began from her very core. "All right."

They stepped off the porch and headed toward the paddock. Stopping at the fence, he turned to face her. She stared up at him, wishing she could see his eyes. Cole had very expressive eyes. Then again, perhaps she was better off not seeing them right now. Considering.

"I'm listening," she said, hoping her voice didn't reflect her state of mind, let alone heart. And why was he still holding her hand? He rubbed the callused pad of his thumb against her knuckles and she shivered.

"You cold?"

"Uh, a little." She tried to smile, but her lips quivered instead.

He released her hand, but just as she started to sigh in relief and regret, he slid his arm around her shoulders. "That better?"

His voice was rich and vibrant in the chilly night air, and the weight of his arm provided welcome and not-so-welcome warmth. She could handle this. Resist temptation. She was a strong woman. Everybody always said so. Everybody except Great-Aunt Pearl. "Thanks," she finally managed.

He absently rubbed her upper arm through her shawl and dress. Didn't he have a clue what he was doing to her? Her insides knotted into a tight fist of longing low in her middle, the pressure and emptiness mounting with every breath she took, every thump of her foolish heart.

He gave her shoulder a squeeze and cleared his throat. "All right, I've been thinking on this, and I decided you have a right to know why I . . . did what I did."

"Kidnapped me," she corrected.

"Yeah, that." He cleared his throat. "Because you've been so cooperative. Otherwise, I wouldn't feel obliged to tell you."

Somehow she supposed there was logic in that, but it managed to escape her. "Go on, I'm listening."

"When Elizabeth and I first came to Colorado, we had big plans." He raked his free hand through his hair and stared toward the cabin. "Miners were getting rich all over the place, and we figured we could find enough gold to finance our future. We didn't care much about being rich, but our dream was important."

She sensed that his thoughts were on his wife right now, and not on the woman he had his arm around, but that was all right. Elizabeth would always be a part of Cole and Todd, as she should be. Jackie, on the other hand, had no right to that claim at all.

"Tell me about those plans, Cole," she urged. Once upon a time, she'd had plans and dreams herself. Her throat constricted and burned, but she managed to suppress another shudder before it began.

He sighed and looked down at her, then off toward the shadow of the mountains, a dark smudge against the clouds and moonlight. "Oregon. We were going to Oregon once we had enough gold to buy a place."

"But you didn't go."

"Never eked out more than enough low-grade ore from that mine to keep food on the table." He made a sound of self-disgust. "Toward the end, when Elizabeth . . . "

Jackie remained silent, though she wanted to beg him to finish the story. She sensed his pain and hoped this served as a catharsis for him. Cole Morrison had been carrying a mountain of guilt on his shoulders.

"Before Elizabeth died, she asked . . . " He faced the cabin again. "No, she *begged* me to take Todd home."

"Home?"

"St. Louis." He shook his head and sighed. "I didn't promise her that, but I did promise I'd take Todd away from here, where he'd have a chance at a decent life and real schooling."

"I see." And she did see. Cole had made a promise he hadn't kept, and that was tearing him apart. "So why don't you just go back to St. Louis?"

He made a snorting sound and dropped his arm. The sudden absence of his warmth left her bereft, emotionally and physically. Shoving his hands into his pockets, he faced her again.

"Elizabeth's father owns a mercantile there," he continued, his voice quiet and edged with bitterness. "He wanted to pay mine and Todd's way back after Elizabeth died, and offered me a job. Hell, a partnership."

Jackie couldn't imagine Cole Morrison taking charity from anyone, and she certainly couldn't picture him working in a store the rest of his life, partner or not. "So why didn't you go?" He needed to say the words so he could forgive himself.

"I took Todd back there to visit, and I seriously considered it, but . . ." He jammed his fingers through his hair and turned away again. "I just couldn't give up on our dream. Mine and Elizabeth's. I figured I could keep digging, and sooner or later the gold would come." He dropped his hands to his sides. "But it didn't. And now I know it won't."

"Then Merriweather came along and offered you gold to take Lolita Belle to the Silver Spur." *So Cole can have his dream.* Jackie drew a shaky breath. If anybody discovered she wasn't the real Lolita, Cole would never have his gold or his dream.

"That's it. The whole pitiful story." He held his hands out to his sides, palms turned up. "I'm a failure, Jackie. There you have it. I saw this as my last chance to take Todd to Oregon instead of back to St. Louis with my tail between my legs. Foolish pride, I suppose."

She remained silent for several moments, pondering the irony of the entire situation. Cole had done something that violated his personal code of honor by kidnapping Lolita. But fate had chosen this particular time and place to throw Jackie into his path instead. Why? Was she here for a reason?

Get over it, Clarke. She knew better than to paint such grandiose schemes for herself. This, like most of her life, had been just one more piece of rotten luck.

Yet how could she call it rotten luck to land right here and now with the man she loved? *Really* loved? This wasn't puppy love, as she'd had with her ex-husband, or a foolish fling like Blade. This was real, genuine, to-die-for love. And right now, the man she loved was in pain.

Slowly she raised her trembling hand and touched his cheek. The initial contact of her sensitive palm with his rough whiskers sent a jolt of longing through her. She squeezed her eyes closed and bit her lower lip. Why did love have to hurt?

He covered her hand with his, holding it pressed against his cheek. After a moment, he turned and planted a kiss in her palm, then squeezed her hand and drew it down in front of him. "I'm sorry I dragged you into this mess."

"Don't be sorry," she said. "There's no need."

Now he'd want to know why she insisted she wasn't Lolita, but telling him would sentence Cole to never having his dream. But if she didn't tell him, he'd go on believing she was a notorious saloon singer.

Jackie had to sacrifice herself for the sake of Cole's dream. If at all possible, the portrait would return her to her own time, then all this would become nothing but a memory. She'd return to her work, her salon . . . and Great-Aunt Pearl.

"Now it's your turn. Tell me about your, uh, spaceship." His lips twitched in the moonlight.

"I . . . " She pulled her hand free and turned her back on him. "I was just pulling your leg, Cole. Didn't you realize that?" She gave a nervous laugh that died on a stiff, chilly breeze.

He put his hands on her shoulders and she ached to turn into his embrace, to bury her face against his shoulder, to hold him so close she could feel their two hearts beat as one.

But she didn't.

"Jackie, you promised." He massaged her shoulders. "I get the feeling something's changed," he said. "Do you hate me for what I did to you?"

She whirled around and stared up at him, her mouth agape. "No, not that. It's me, you big oaf. *Me.*"

"What about you?" His voice was surprisingly calm. "Tell me, Jackie. Trust me."

Trust me.

She hadn't trusted anyone since her mother. And her mother had died and left Jackie. Releasing a long, slow breath, she said, "I want to trust you, Cole. But it isn't that simple."

"You told me you aren't Lolita." He tilted his head to one side. "Are you saying now that you are?"

Jackie's heart slammed into her ribs. Pressure built in her throat and she tried to speak and failed. *Tell him you're Lolita.* She tried again.

She couldn't.

"*Are* you Lolita Belle?"

She clenched her teeth, struggled to form the words. . . .

"Jackie?" He sounded worried now. "Are you feeling all right?"

She shook her head.

"Are you cold?"

She shook her head again.

He grabbed her and gave her a gentle shake. "Damnation, woman, will you just tell me the truth? You're making me crazy."

"You make me crazy, too," she finally said. She couldn't tell him she was Lolita, but she wouldn't tell him who she was or where she was from either. A lie of omission only—as if that made it all right. "You make me crazy, Cole, because I *want* you." *Because I love you.*

"Jackie . . . " His voice held a note of warning.

"When I saw you naked down by that waterfall, I thought I was going to die if I couldn't touch you. Kiss you. Have you . . . "

"Don't." He sounded hoarse, as if struggling to keep himself under control.

"I behaved horribly—playing the tease and all. I'm sorry for that." She forced herself to breathe slowly, steadily. "So sorry."

That was the secret. She had to revert to her original plan to seduce him, then tell him about Goodfellow's counteroffer—let him have his gold and his dream, then send him on his way. Perfect solution.

And this way, only *her* heart would get broken.

But she would have this one night with Cole. This one memory of making love—*real* love—to cherish in whichever century she spent the rest of her life.

He'd be free and she could give him his dream. Great sex and a dream. He'd be fine.

And so would she.

Chapter Twelve

With a groan, he claimed her mouth, and a torrent of yearning seized her.

Her response and redirection were astonishing, considering how confused she'd been only a moment ago. His lips were blistering yet pleasing. Velvet yet strong. Tender yet wild.

And exactly what she needed right now. Glorying in the power of his kiss, she threw her arms around his neck and clung to him, returning his kiss with equal fervor. He was hers.

For tonight.

He hauled her in closer, and the heat of his desire scorched her through the worn fabric of her *Little Women* dress. Her shawl fell open, no longer needed as a new and insistent warmth took control.

She whimpered—an alien sound Jackie was certain she'd never made before—a faint echo of the low growl that rumbled through him.

All the "I am Woman, Hear Me Roar" lessons her mother had shared during those early years fell aside like ashes in the wind. Jackie's senses emerged screaming from the dark place where she'd hidden them, unveiling her mind and soul and—God help her—her heart. Just when she thought she was safe—that her caring torpedoes had done their job at last and that she had all this in perfect perspective—hormonal hell broke loose.

He ravished and claimed, and she imagined herself standing on a rocky, mist-shrouded cliff in Scotland, overlooking a stormy sea. A castle loomed in the distance, a ship on the horizon, and she was a damsel in distress being rescued by her handsome and oh-so-virile knight in shining armor.

She was, simply, losing it.

He fueled her senses with his unique, musky man scent. The coarse grain of his stubbled chin abraded her face, but she didn't care. She feared only that he might stop, leaving her breathless and empty and alone again.

His arms were like steel around her, and he lifted her upward, tugging her hard against his full, magnificent length. His mouth never left hers as another beastly rumble left him and filled her with an unbearable ache. She'd never known such longing, such need.

Jackie Clarke had met her match in Cole Morrison. He was too much man for her to control with her feminine wiles, such as they were. He was infinitely more dangerous than any con artist could ever be. . . .

Because he was real. Vulnerable. Honest.

And because she loved him with all her heart.

It didn't help matters that he was the sexiest hunk of male flesh she'd ever encountered or hoped to encounter again in any century. He provoked within her a starving demand that exceeded any tangible, logical need she'd ever known. She would drop dead on the spot if he stopped. Even more terrifying—without him, she feared she would never be whole again.

He wove his fingers through her hair and tilted his head, his mouth insatiable, granting and demanding more with every desperate breath they shared. She slumped against him, incapable of supporting her own weight, her legs disintegrating beneath her like the Wicked Witch of the West after the proverbial bucket of water.

Yes, she was melting, melting—her body into his. Her breasts swelled and flowed against the hard planes and muscles of his chest, throbbing from the gentle massage of her clothing, the rough texture of his shirt. Her nipples thrust forward, hardening, dragging a muffled sob of need from her throat.

He stopped, tearing his mouth from hers, observing her with gleaming, feral, passion-lit eyes. Their mutual raspy panting reverberated like thunder in the moonlight. She curled her fingers into his shirt, her grasp fierce. He wouldn't end this here. She couldn't bear it. She'd rather die. Tonight was all she had. . . .

"Love me, Cole," she whispered. "Just for tonight."

Then, suddenly, their mouths fused together again, breaths, longing, need merging, uniting as one. She clutched him to her frantically, and his fingers tangled through her hair, increasing the insistence of his kiss, urging her to open to him.

She parted her lips, inviting his thrusting, seeking tongue into the warmth of her mouth. Renewed longing ricocheted through her body, tightening every muscle like a ponytail holder about to snap.

A groan reverberated through him, feeding her, driving her mad with wanting. She echoed the sound as he deepened the kiss. His tongue slid over hers, surveying, raiding with sleek strokes that left her trembling. She needed another part of his body inside her, mimicking these same movements. She wanted to hold him fast and tight and deep.

Pretend this could last forever . . .

She savored the molten heat of his kiss. Nothing else mattered but him holding her, kissing her, wanting her. Nothing. She wouldn't let anything else matter.

There was only this moment in time. Only this night. Only this man who held her as if his life depended on it. Only this . . .

Persistent warmth gathered low in her belly, insisting that she see this through. Tonight.

He dragged his mouth from hers, and she gasped in protest. "No, please," she whispered, trying to summon some of the teasing persona she'd portrayed so well earlier. "We aren't finished yet, big guy."

"This will never be finished, because I can never have enough of you." Voraciously, he blazed a trail of kisses down the side of her neck to the curve of her shoulder, easing his hand between their bodies to cup her breast. She smiled, urging him to do more. Much more.

Lowering his head, he covered her nipple with his lips. The layers of fabric separating them seemed to melt away beneath the sudden heat of his mouth. Her breath caught and her head rolled backward. The clouds parted and she saw stars—both real and surreal.

Through her thin gown, he drew her nipple into his mouth. A low, fierce tone tore from her. He leaned her back against his strong arm, lifting her upward to meet his ravenous lips.

He held her fast with mouth and arms as he teased and tantalized her erect and sensitized nipples, soaking the fabric and brushing over it again and again. A river of lust flowed through her.

"Cole," she whispered breathlessly, clutching him to her. "I want you."

He released the buttons at the front of her dress, then shoved the layers of damp fabric aside, baring her to the cool night air and to his red-hot kisses.

"I want you," he murmured, alternating between murmured words and hot, wet strokes of his tongue. "You're so beautiful. So perfect."

Jackie sobbed with longing as he drew her deeply into his mouth. A shudder rippled through her and she pressed herself greedily against him. "I need you now, Cole." She could make love with him on the ground, if necessary. Nothing mattered but having him.

All of him.

Wordlessly he swept her into his arms and kicked open the paddock gate, allowing it to swing shut behind them. He ducked as he entered the stable. The scents of hay, horse, and leather surrounded them as he found his way through the darkness. He eased Jackie to her feet and slipped the shawl from her shoulders, spreading it across a pile of clean straw in the corner.

Moonlight filled the small shelter, bathing Cole in silver. Jackie's breath caught as she saw the eager expression in his eyes. "I want you, Cole. Now."

He put his arms on her shoulders and peered

intently into her eyes. "Be sure, because"—he drew a ragged breath—"I can't stand not having you another minute."

"Thank God." She gave him a shaky smile and eased her open dress and chemise from her shoulders, allowing the garments to puddle at her feet. His eyes widened and he reached for her.

"Patience." She grinned more openly now and bit her lower lip, bending over to untie her hiking boots and kick them off. She eased her Scarlett O'Hara underwear over her hips and kicked them aside. Holding her hands out to her sides, she said, "All right, I'm all yours, big guy."

He sucked in a breath. "Do that again."

She laughed. "Undress?"

"No, the bending-over part."

She laughed and moved closer. "Are you a butt man, Cole Morrison?"

"Butt man?" He stroked her upper arms, sending rivulets of desire trickling through her. "What's a butt man?"

"Uh, a man who likes a woman's butt best." She released the buttons at the front of his shirt and eased her hands against the magnificent muscles of his chest. "God, Cole, I want you so much I'm going crazy."

"I went crazy that first day," he breathed, shrugging out of his suspenders and shirt.

Remembering how he'd looked when she'd caught him naked at the waterfall, Jackie held her breath and opened his belt buckle, frantically working on the fly of his jeans. "You didn't answer me." She eased his jeans down over his slim hips, gently releasing his impressive erection. Her insides turned molten in anticipation. Heat radiated from his magnificent anatomy, spanning the distance between them.

"Answer . . . what?" he croaked, kicking off his boots and stepping out of his jeans.

"Are you a butt man?" she repeated, barely able to breathe, let alone speak coherently. "Speaking of butts . . . " Breathlessly, she kneaded the flesh of his bare buttocks, itching to bring her hands forward, to wrap them around his rock-hard length.

He cradled her breasts in his hands, brushing his callused thumbs against their rigid peaks. "Your butt is wonderful, ma'am," he whispered thickly, "but *these* beauties drive me insane."

"All of you drives me loco." She bit her lower lip and allowed her hands to follow her burning desire slowly around his hips. Pausing just shy of her goal, she massaged his groin with her thumbs, her hands trembling.

"Lord, woman." He dipped his head and took her nipple into his mouth, grazing it with his teeth.

Fire kindled inside her, a liquid inferno created deep within her, sizzling until she wanted to scream. Dying with need, Jackie eased both hands around his throbbing erection, stunned all over again by the size of him. "Have mercy." Great-Aunt Pearl would have fainted to hear her most frequently used phrase voiced in this situation. But it fit.

Oh, yes. Jackie couldn't wait to discover just how well he fit. Glancing down at her hands wrapped around him in the moonlight, she sucked in a sharp breath.

"Now?" she asked, stroking the length of him.

A guttural growl erupted from deep in his chest and he swooped her into his arms, placing her on the waiting shawl. Hovering over her, he devoured her with his eyes, then lowered himself slowly to cover her nakedness with his own.

"Beauty, meet the Beast," he whispered.

Cole gazed down at her, feasting on the beauty spread out before him like a rare and precious gift. Once more, he saw her nipples draw tight, reminding him she shared his eagerness.

From the moment he'd pulled her from the street that day back in Devil's Gulch, he had wanted her. Craved her. Hungered for her.

Her and only her.

This time he was the one who trembled, overcome by the power of his desire for this strange woman with hair so red it rivaled the brightest cardinal. As Adam must have when he'd tasted the forbidden fruit, Cole smiled.

"What's so funny?"

"I'm not laughing." He wanted to touch, to taste, to savor every perfect moment of this night. He lowered his head and sampled one honeyed nipple, his lips gliding across it, followed by his tongue.

Her moan washed over him, compounding his own need. He wanted to thrust himself into her, take her hot and fast and fierce. But this was too perfect to rush, too wanted to waste.

He hungered to watch her need blossom into womanly ecstasy while he was buried deep inside her. The only thing that could make this more perfect would be if the sun were shining and they were outside where he could see every detail, every expression, every curve and hollow of her slender body.

She buried her fingers in his hair as he teased and nibbled at her breasts. "Sweet," he whispered, drawing her nipple deeply into his mouth while he brushed the other peak with his thumb.

Another soft moan came from her lips and she gripped his shoulders, her nails digging into his bare flesh. "Now, Cole," she whispered, panting. "I can't . . . wait."

Her words sent blistering, bright bursts of hunger through his veins. He kissed her other breast, teasing her with the tip of his tongue, drawing and sucking until her breathing came shallow and quick and she squirmed beneath him.

He stroked one hand along her flat belly, resting at the curling hair between her thighs. She was hot, as he'd known she would be, and for a moment he reminded himself that she most certainly wasn't a virgin. That knowledge didn't sadden him, though. In fact, her experience and boldness were part of what he loved most about her.

Loved?

He froze for a moment, lingering over her, lifting his face to gaze down into her eyes. If he could have seen her expression clearly, would he find love in her eyes? Or merely desire?

Don't think, Morrison.

She pressed her mound against the heel of his hand and moaned again—a sound he echoed from deep in his own throat. Now wasn't the time for thinking. Only action would do.

He found her womanly folds and paused again. She was hot and wet and ready. Holding his breath, he parted her with thick, trembling fingers, groaning aloud at her response. She gasped and tilted her hips, granting him entrance. The womanly scent of her wafted up to him, spicy and sweet.

"Oh, Lord," he murmured, feeling her feminine

core tighten around his probing fingers. "I don't think I can . . . wait."

"Don't wait." She urged him back up the length of her, capturing his engorged body in her hands. "Have mercy." Brushing her thumb over his throbbing tip, she slid her other hand down his full length. "I want you. Every . . . blessed . . . inch."

That did it.

Cole allowed her to guide him against her womanhood, positioning his throbbing tip. He closed his eyes, drawing deep breaths to regain control of his spiraling need. He wanted this to last a good long while, but he was so aroused he feared he might explode on contact.

With a trembling sigh, she wrapped her arms and legs around him. He'd never been more aware of himself as a man in the very physical sense as he was at this moment. She empowered him, and that was both thrilling and terrifying.

He was a big man—he'd always known that. She was tall for a woman, but delicate of bone and with just enough flesh in all the right places. Beneath his hulking form, she seemed tiny. Even so, he knew he couldn't hurt her. She was too ready, too willing, too wild with wanting.

A feeling he understood too damned well.

The friction of her body against his set him on fire. Her breasts were delicate and soft compared to the unyielding planes of his chest, her nipples hard and tantalizing against him.

He couldn't wait another moment. Pressing himself steadily inward, he held his breath, savoring every life-threatening inch. She closed around him even as she drew him deeper and deeper into her tight sheath.

"Have mercy," he whispered, repeating her earlier declaration. "Easy, don't move, woman."

"In your dreams . . . big guy," she breathed, kneading his buttocks and urging him deeper.

She squeezed him tighter, held him as if she would never let him go. God save him if she changed her mind now.

Moaning, she eased her knees higher, locking her heels around his waist. He couldn't hold back any longer and buried himself swift and hard, pausing to gasp as she held him fast with velvet promise. She shuddered beneath him.

"Did I hurt you?" He gazed down at her face, bathed in shadows now as the moon no longer shone through the door. "Are you all right?"

"No, you didn't hurt me." She squeezed him hard and angled her hips more fully against him. "But I'm not all right. Yet."

He chuckled low and deep, then she moved against him again and his laughter died on a groan of exquisite agony. If he didn't move inside her right now, it would soon be too late.

Vowing to take her with him on this shattering journey, he withdrew until only his throbbing tip remained within her, then plunged into her receptive body. Again and again, slowly, he drove into her, feeling her clench and swallow his full length.

She met him thrust for thrust, matching his movements, increasing the depth of their union. He gritted his teeth, praying he could last long enough to show her the pleasure he so desperately wanted to give.

Every muscle in his body trembled as he moved urgently with her. They rose and fell together in perfect rhythm—laboring, battling, mastering. Hot, bright, and dazzling, lightning struck and he lost control, taking her on a frenzied, wild voyage from which he knew neither of them would return unchanged.

Faster, harder, he lunged to the depths of a scorching explosion as she arched upward, contorting around him. He came into her, filled her with his seed and his very essence. Everything he had, everything he was, melded into this moment in time.

Her body convulsed and she cried out her own completion. She clutched his shoulders, rocked with him, and they remained locked together as intimately as a man and woman could possibly be.

He caught a fistful of her hair and kissed her soundly, passionately, tenderly. This had been much, much more than a man relieving himself with an available woman. He couldn't think right now about what had just happened. His mind was foggy, his body drained.

Showering her face with tiny kisses, he shivered as she stroked his sweaty back, massaging his muscles and easing his return to the mortal world. This woman gave and took with an appetite that stunned him and left him shaken.

And confused.

All he knew for certain was that what he'd said earlier was true. He could never get enough of this perplexing woman. Already he felt his body hardening with desire, still buried deep within her.

"You were . . . "

She pressed her fingertip to his lips. "Not now," she whispered. "Don't spoil it."

He cupped her face and felt her tears. She tried to turn away, but he held her fast. "Did I hurt you?"

"You were wonderful," she said. "Much too wonderful to be real."

He wondered about the hint of sadness in her voice.

A hot flush crept over his face as he remembered his powerful explosion. It had been such a long time since . . .

There could be a child. Could that worry be the cause of her tears? He would never let her give birth to his child out of wedlock, and having seen the way she treated Todd, he couldn't imagine his Jackie being sad about the possibility of a child.

Lolita, on the other hand . . .

Swallowing hard, he raised himself up on his elbows and gazed down at her shadowy form. Their two hearts slowed, hammering together as one to the cadence of the ancient dance between man and woman.

Dance? He tensed, wondering and remembering Chief Byron's words.

Woman with Hair Like Fire was doing her tribal mating dance.

For you.

And it had worked.

Chapter Thirteen

Jackie slept like the dead, exhausted from keeping pace with the greatest lover of the nineteenth *and* twentieth centuries. *What a man!* She rolled out of bed with every muscle aching, reminding her of all the ways he'd touched her.

A smile curved her lips as she washed and dressed, eager to see him, yet dreading it at the same time. They'd talked very little after that first time, mutually eager to make love again.

And again.

She waved her hand in front of her face as heat crept to her cheeks. For an old-fashioned guy, Cole Morrison was very creative in the hay. Literally.

But now she had to tell him about Goodfellow's offer. Sadness gripped her heart, and her stomach lurched. Why had fate thrown her back here to fall in love and have her heart broken? It was too cruel. Too gut-wrenching.

Too damned typical of Jackie Clarke's life.

Dragging in a shaky breath, she climbed down the ladder to find Todd and his father seated at the rough wooden table, eating breakfast. "Good morning," she said quietly.

"Miss Jackie," Todd said, "we're going to Oregon."

Her heart constricted again. "Oregon?" When were they leaving? She poured herself a cup of coffee and sat woodenly at the table, avoiding Cole's gaze. She couldn't look at him right now, knowing they would soon be separated forever.

"Jackie?" Cole asked quietly. "Are you . . . feeling all right?"

She blinked and shot him a sidelong glance. "Of course. When are you going to Oregon?" So Cole had decided that dream was going to happen, after all. *Good for him.* Not so good for her.

"That depends . . . on a lot of things," Cole said, his tone sober.

She felt his gaze on her, but she couldn't look at him just now. Did he pity her? The fallen woman who'd been fun for a night, and who'd soon be out of his life for good?

Oh, cut it—

A soft knock at the door made her jerk, sloshing hot coffee over the rim of her cup and across the back of her hand. She dried it on her skirt, then blew on the reddened skin while Cole answered the door. *Don't let it be Smith or Goodfellow or Merriweather.* Should she hide? Her heart vaulted into her throat and she gripped the edge of the table, prepared to make a dash for the loft.

"Chief Byron, come on in," Cole said as he swung open the door. "There's some mush on the fire."

The chief shuddered visibly. "Thank you, no."

Todd chuckled, and Jackie couldn't suppress her own small grin. The chief was definitely a welcome visitor just now, distracting her from her dismal thoughts. Later she would find Cole alone and tell him all she had to tell.

And destroy everything once and for all.

He had a right to the truth, and she had to make sure he took Todd to Oregon. Her dreams were dead, but there was still hope for his. Closing her eyes, she drew a deep breath and took a sip of Cole's bitter coffee. *A girl's gotta do what a girl's gotta do.* She'd be all right. She was tough. Strong.

Right.

"An eagle told me it is a good day for fish." The chief's dark eyes twinkled. "I thought Son of Pale Eyes might like to catch fish."

"Can I, Pa?" Todd leaped to his feet, his enthusiasm unmistakable.

"I could be mistaken, but I'd say that's a boy who definitely wants to go fishing," Cole said, chuckling. "Where were you planning to go?"

"Near beaver dam, down the pass." The chief nodded. "Good fishing there."

Cole rubbed his chin thoughtfully. "That'll take most of the day."

"Please, Pa?" Todd tugged on his father's sleeve.

Cole chuckled again and tousled his son's hair. "Sure, but take a dinner pail for you both."

"We will eat fish," Chief Byron insisted, straightening.

Cole winked at his son. "Probably, but take something along just in case."

Jackie's mind worked overtime. She would be alone with Cole all day. Alone. She could spend more time in his arms before shattering any feelings he might have for her. Okay, so maybe it was selfish of her to want to make love with him again before telling him the truth, but she felt like being selfish. *Dammit.*

"And be back *well* before dark," Cole said as his son threw together a noon meal for two.

"Thanks, Pa."

"Don't forget your fishing pole, Huck."

"Pole." Chief Byron snorted. "I will use only hands and spear, and we will see who catches more fish."

Todd's little-boy giggle warmed Jackie, but it was a bittersweet warmth. Soon both Todd and his handsome father would be out of her life.

The boy raced out the door ahead of his elderly companion, who lingered and looked back over his shoulder, his dark eyes glittering with mischief. "Pale Eyes will not go to the mine today." With a knowing smile and a nod, the chief followed Todd.

And left Jackie alone with Cole.

The morning after was always awkward, she reminded herself, and took a sip of coffee. She watched the play of rippling muscles through Cole's shirt as he cleared the table.

"You want some mush?" he asked, holding the black iron pot by its handle.

"Get serious." Jackie made a face and he laughed. That eased the tension between them, and she flashed him her biggest smile.

He set the mush aside and stood staring at her. "You should do that more often," he said, his voice warm and vibrant.

She shivered as the rich timbre washed over her. "Do what?" She rose and walked toward him.

"Smile."

She slid her arms around his waist and pressed her

cheek against his shoulder. "Good morning," she said in a husky whisper.

"I think you already said that." He wrapped his arms around her waist, though she sensed some fleeting—*thank goodness*—reluctance.

She gazed up at him, then stood on tiptoe and kissed him very softly. He responded and she relaxed in his embrace. "It bears repeating." She held his gaze with hers, carefully studying his reactions. "Cole, let's have a picnic."

His dark brows arched in surprise. "Today?"

"Sure, why not?"

"I really should go to the mine."

"Why?" She kissed his chin, his jaw, the lobe of his ear.

He sucked in a sharp breath. "Mine? What mine?"

Capturing her chin in his hand, he claimed her mouth in a breathtaking kiss that left her dizzy with desire. She wanted him every bit as much now as she had yesterday.

As their lips parted, she sighed. "A picnic, Pale Eyes."

He chuckled and lifted her off her feet, spinning her around the room. "You're turning me into an outright lazybones, woman."

"Nothing lazy about you, big guy." She rubbed herself against him in what she hoped was an invitation—or maybe a command performance. She should have watched more Mae West movies.

"You're makin' me crazy again."

"Good." She rubbed the heel of her hand along the hard ridge at his fly. "Is that a pistol in your pocket, big guy, or are you just happy to see me?" He turned crimson and she laughed.

"I'm *very* happy to see you." He kissed her again.

Sighing as their lips parted, she asked, "How far is the waterfall from this beaver dam the chief mentioned?" She licked her lips and watched Cole's eyes widen and his nostrils flare.

"Far enough." His deep voice rumbled through her and zeroed in on her hormones. "Are you really going to make me wait that long?"

"Wait for what?" She pursed her lips and tried to pull an innocent look, but she'd never felt less innocent in her life. She bit her lower lip.

"That 'pistol' in my pocket is loaded." He growled low in his throat and threw her over his shoulder. "You still want a picnic?"

"Yes." She laughed and pounded on his back, pretending —unconvincingly, she hoped—to resist his Neanderthal approach. Who would have thought that Victorian men liked sex games?

"Then we'll have us a picnic," he said, throwing the bolt, then heading toward his bunk. He dropped her onto the bunk and unbuttoned his shirt.

Jackie smiled up at him. "I thought you said we were going on a picnic, big guy."

He slipped off his suspenders and peeled off his shirt, then fell down beside her. "Later," he growled.

Hand in hand, Cole and Jackie walked slowly to the waterfall. The purpose of his last few visits was nothing but a memory now. Today he and Jackie would bathe in the falls together and make love on the quilt he'd stashed in the basket of food he carried in his free hand.

Make love.

He swallowed the lump in his throat. How would she react to his plans? Giving her hand a squeeze, he glanced at her profile, and his determination renewed itself. He was doing the right thing. Now if only she agreed . . .

Last night's cool rain had bathed the air with freshness. It really felt like spring now—not the unusual drought they'd been having. He chuckled to himself. Springtime in the Rocky Mountains typically brought snow, snow, and more snow. The unusually dry weather had seemed more like late summer than late spring.

He'd lost track of time since Jackie came into his life. Was it June yet? He shook his head and pushed a branch aside and held it until she passed safely, then ducked through behind her.

The waterfall came into view and they paused to admire it. "Spring thaw is what feeds this creek, but the snow in the high country is almost gone now," he said. "Pity."

"That can change pretty fast up here." A distant expression entered Jackie's eyes.

"Have you spent a lot of your life in the mountains?" He knew very little about her, yet he felt so close to her. And he was looking forward to getting a *lot* closer again today.

She shook her head. "No, but I got caught in a June blizzard. Once."

"You've probably been all over the world," he said, leading her to the boulder where he usually put his clothes. He set the basket on it and leaned against it, facing her. "Have you?"

"Have I what?"

He touched her shoulder and she turned toward him. "Jackie, something's bothering you."

She gave a quick shrug, but her eyes clearly revealed her anxiety. "Nothing important," she said.

"All right, if you say so." He massaged her shoulder and placed his other hand on her tiny waist. "I asked if you've traveled all over the world."

"Not hardly." She gave a short laugh. "Great-Aunt Pearl considered a Sunday drive in her old Caddie the equivalent of a trip to Europe."

"What's a Caddie? And did you live with your great-aunt?"

"A, uh, Caddie is a type of carriage." Her cheeks turned crimson. "My mother died when I was about Todd's age, and my great-aunt raised me. So to speak." Jackie rolled her eyes and released a ragged sigh. "Enough about me." She reached for the buttons of his shirt and waggled her eyebrows. "Let's frolic like wood nymphs."

Cole laughed and shrugged out of his shirt, then reached for the buttons on her dress. "You be the nymph and I'll be the satyr, thank you very much. My mother would've loved talking to you."

Jackie's expression changed again, her gray eyes solemn. "Really? Even though I'm corrupting her son?"

He eased her dress from her shoulders. "I'm thirty-four years old, Jackie." Resting his hands on her bare shoulders, he massaged her soft flesh with his thumbs. "Way too old for corruption."

"I wouldn't be too sure of that." She flashed him an impish grin and bent over to untie her strange shoes. After stepping out of them, she placed them on the boulder with her dress. "I bent over for you again, big guy," she said, facing him.

"I definitely noticed." He'd been hard since they left the cabin. And ready. Seeing her standing here in her unmentionables made him want to ravish her without delay. But he also wanted to take this slow and easy. Maybe if he could learn more about her, he would have better luck predicting her reaction to his announcement. Maybe.

"Yes, my mother would've really liked you, Jackie. Why is that so hard for you to believe?"

She shrugged again. "I don't know. It just is." She tilted her head to one side and gave him a quizzical look. "What was she like, Cole? And your father?"

"You keep changing the subject." He smiled and placed his hands on her upper arms again, remembering that the only thing separating him from her beautiful breasts was a thin piece of cotton.

"I'm curious about you, too." She opened his belt buckle and released the top button.

His breath caught and he tried not to think about the throbbing between his legs. "My father was a professor at the University of Missouri in Columbia."

Another button popped open.

"A professor? Wow." She eased her cool fingers beneath his waistband and gently massaged his lower abdomen. "So," she continued, her breathing ragged, "that's why you like books."

"Yeah, I suppose." He flinched, pulsing with rising hunger as her fingers grew closer and closer to the part of him that screamed for release. "My . . . "

She released another button and rested her cheek against his chest, her warm breath fanning his bare flesh, leaving goose bumps in its wake. "What was I saying?" he asked, so aroused he could barely put words together, much less think coherently.

"You were telling me about your parents." She opened the last two buttons and slid her hands inside the waistband, slipping them lower on his hips. "What about your mother?" Gazing up at him, she bit her lower lip and pressed her full length against him, cradling his throbbing arousal against her soft, flat belly.

"My . . . mother? Oh, yeah." He wrapped his arms around Jackie and held her against him, relishing the feel of her softness against his hardness. Knowing what it was like to be buried deep inside her made him want it all the more. There was no such thing as being sated where this woman was concerned. He would always want more.

"Your mother what?" She traced a line of fire with her tongue across his chest, drawing torturous circles around his nipples.

He shuddered, trying to remember what they were discussing, what he needed to tell her, the questions she'd asked him. *Oh, yes.* "My mother was a teacher before I was . . . born." He sucked in a breath as his dungarees fell to his knees, freeing him to her explorations.

And explore she did.

She cupped him in both hands and nipped his nipple with her teeth. "What was she like?" Jackie whispered, wrapping her hands around him. "Hmm?"

"Uh, she loved books, too. Read to me all the time, like you do to Todd." Cole grabbed her shoulders and set her away, untying the ribbons that kept her gorgeous breasts hidden. "She taught me to love books." He spoke very fast now, eager to finish this and give all his attention over to making Jackie writhe and moan beneath him again. "She especially loved fairy tales and mythology." He eased the camisole over her head, revealing her full, perfect breasts and tawny, erect nipples to his starving senses. "God, you're so beautiful."

"So are you." Jackie came closer, wrapping her

hands around his swollen organ again. Her nipples brushed against his chest, and he reached behind her to release the drawstring at her waist. As the fabric fell away, she gave him a playful little shove and he fell back against the sun-warmed boulder.

She slithered out of her underthings and tossed them carelessly onto the boulder, then bent over—Lord, he loved it when she did that—and removed his boots and dungarees. He started to stand up straight, but she giggled and shoved him down again.

She wanted to play games and was killing him with the delay. His gaze traveled the length of her—down her silken throat, along the curve of her shoulder, lingering at her breasts to watch her nipples tighten even more. With his gaze, he worshiped her, savoring the way her small waist flared to her hips.

And those legs . . . Long, supple, strong. Very strong. She'd wrapped those beauties around him last night and there'd been no escape. Of course, escape had never even crossed his mind. Eager to have her in his arms again, he pushed himself to his feet, only to have her shove him down again.

"Why'd you do that?"

She closed the small distance that separated them, her hips swaying, her breasts jutting forward invitingly. "I aim to have my way with you, big guy."

Her gaze rested between his legs and he hardened even more beneath her ardent scrutiny. Anticipating. "Woman, you can have anything you want," he breathed, "as long as you get to it before this hankering kills me."

"Hankering?" She made a wicked little sound in her throat that sent shivers down his spine.

And other places.

"I'll show you hankering." She covered him with her lovely body and kissed him fiercely.

Lips, tongue, mouth—she threw everything into that kiss, and he gave in turn. He reached for her breasts, but she slithered lower, eluding him, laving and nibbling his nipples until he groaned and shuddered.

He'd never had a woman do that to him before, though he supposed it made sense for it to please him, since it pleased a woman when he did it to her. Right now there was only one woman whose breasts he wanted to taste, and he aimed to taste every exquisite inch of her before this day ended.

This woman was even more powerful in the light of day than she had been last night. He wanted and needed her more than he'd ever imagined possible. The thought gave him pause, made him wonder about the significance of these feelings, and how she would fit into his plans for the future.

And, heaven help him, he wanted her to be a part of that future. He considered stopping her so they could talk, but she slithered against him again and rational thought fled. There was no stopping this now.

She draped herself across him, and he wanted only to roll her over and bury himself inside her. He knew she wanted him, too. In fact, he'd never made love to a more responsive woman than Jackie Clarke.

If she were any more responsive, he'd be dead by now.

She kissed her way lower, sliding her silken legs between his as the velvet peaks of her breasts brushed against the tense muscles of his abdomen, teasing and enticing. Realization slammed into him like a runaway train and Cole groaned—yearning blended with apprehension. He wasn't sure if he was worried she would continue or worried she might change her mind and leave him wondering. The only certainty in his life right now was that he was incapable of preventing her from doing anything she wanted. Anything at all.

And he liked that feeling. A lot.

She kissed the responsive skin of his inner thighs, teased every inch of him except that one part—the part of him that thrust upward from his body, throbbing and burning like a lit fuse.

She nuzzled the base of his engorgement. He'd never seen such an incredible sight, and he stared, transfixed, reveling in her purposeful explorations. Mesmerized, he couldn't have looked away for anything.

She tormented him with kisses along the entire length of his rigid member. He couldn't take any more. She was driving him crazier than she already had. "Jackie . . ." But rather than push her away, he laced his fingers through her fiery locks, telling himself he could coax her into ceasing this bedevilment for the sake of shared ecstasy. There was also the matter of his questionable survival if she continued much longer.

But continue she did.

She'd said she would have her way with him, but she should've warned him that it might be dangerous. Her tongue slid higher and higher until he believed he might expire right here. Right now.

But just as he convinced himself he had the strength and fortitude to stop her, she claimed his aching tip and he was as defenseless as a pine in a forest fire. He made a choking sound and gnashed his teeth, praying he could maintain enough control to delay the inevitable.

She glanced up at him, her gray eyes sparkling like silver in the dappled sunlight. Cole's composure steadily crumbled, dragging him closer and closer to gratification. He should make her stop.

I'm weak. Barely breathing, he endured her special brand of persecution. Soon he would pass his breaking point. But just a few more minutes . . .

He couldn't stop staring at her and what she was doing to his extremely eager body. Her lashes were long and black, her cheeks pink. Her naked breasts caressed his thighs, reminding him how desperately he wanted to touch and taste her.

Remembering the intensity of her response to him last night, he surged toward the point of no return. Dangerously close. His breathing sounded raspy and he closed his eyes. Her technique grew more reckless, shaking him back to reality. He couldn't wait another minute.

He gripped her shoulders and pulled her away from him, firmly but gently. Drawing huge gulps of air, he grappled for command. Grinning, she ran her tongue along her lower lip.

She really was trying to kill him. "Now it's *my* turn," he muttered, rising from the hard boulder with one arm wrapped around her waist. He grabbed the quilt and tossed it to the ground on a bed of pine needles, then kicked one corner until it was relatively flat.

He fell to the quilt, tugging her down with him. She covered his mouth with hers, kissing him wildly. Growling, he rolled until she was beneath him, and he found her breast, brushing his thumb against her puckered nipple. She shuddered and moaned and he dragged his mouth from hers, fastening his lips to her breast.

Ravenous, he consumed her. She writhed and arched against him, driving him to drink more deeply. More, always more. Raw, savage need pierced him, burning deep within Cole.

Pushing himself up onto his elbows, he gazed into her passion-glazed eyes. She looked like a beautiful, wild creature. Her firm breasts rose and fell enticingly with her ragged breathing.

He reclaimed her mouth, parting her lips with his tongue. Jackie's tongue probed his in return, converting his blood to molten ore. Desperation coursed through him. She'd unleashed a wild yearning from deep within him—something he'd never known before.

And the spirit of his flesh—and hers—would rule.

He tore his mouth from hers, gasping for air. She pressed her hand to the back of his neck, urging him toward her breasts again. Without delay, he hungrily claimed one swollen nipple.

She moaned and writhed with need as his onslaught continued. Her sweet breasts swelled and filled his mouth. He needed her, wanted her, had to have her. But he was hell-bent on giving her as much torture and pleasure as she'd shown him.

Jackie realized she'd unleashed a dangerous animal. This was the same man she'd made love with last night, but he was far less reserved today.

And she *liked* it.

He stroked her belly with his hand and found the concentration of nerves between her thighs, caressing her until she quivered. Releasing her nipple, he moved up her body again, covering her mouth with his.

Flames claimed her as he mercilessly brought her body to the brink of orgasm. She whimpered again—he was the only man who'd ever reduced her to whimpering—and contorted beneath his skillful touch.

She clung to him as his mouth possessed hers and his talented fingers invaded her most private place. Every cell in her body became his toy, his possession. For an interminable twinkling, the world ceased to exist. She wanted *him.* Nothing more. Nothing less.

Again he broke their kiss, then licked his way back down her throat, lingering at her collarbone as his hand continued to inflict mounting pleasure. He reclaimed her sensitive nipples, torturing her beyond any reasonable level of endurance.

"Please, Cole?"

"Not yet," he murmured against her. Ruthlessly he possessed her breasts—first one, then the other—with his tongue and teeth.

Her only defense against his delicious ravishment was to give in turn. She reached for his erection, finding him still hard and ready. Her insides clenched as he filled her with his thick fingers and her hips came off the quilt.

Hungrily she wrapped her hand around him. "So hot," she whispered. "Hot."

"Mmm."

Swollen, starving flesh pressed against flesh. She coiled into a tense spring, on the verge of snapping. Reality ceased. Every curve, every hollow, every nerve of Jackie's body sprang to life in a new, raw version of its former self. Cole staked his claim with his mouth and hands. Kissing his way down her belly, he replaced his fingers with his hot, wet mouth.

"Have mercy," she whispered, and he chuckled against her, the vibration zeroing in on her hormones with amazing accuracy.

She was on fire. This was a primal, basic, and undeniable hunger. He forced her to yield to her most carnal and animalistic desires. She left the ground as her senses coalesced and erupted.

Unintelligible moans of torment, bliss, and desire bubbled up from her. She groaned, growled, cried out, but he persisted. Only he could end this madness, and she knew he wanted her as desperately as she wanted him.

She'd never known that something that felt so wonderful could actually become torture. But this was indeed torture. Someone had to give. She sensed his mounting frustration, his inner battle to maintain control.

As her spasms subsided, he released her and crept up her body again, pinning her beneath him. She couldn't think of anyplace she'd rather be.

"I want you inside me," she whispered, tilting her hips toward his. "All of you."

With a low growl, he came into her hot and fast and fierce, filling her. Claiming her.

"Have mercy," she muttered, shocked all over again by the size of this man.

Whoever said "size doesn't matter" lied.

The depth and completeness of his possession stole her breath. She took every delicious inch of him, wrapping her legs around his waist, angling her hips to allow even more thorough penetration.

Their bodies brutalized each other in their quest, striving to give and to take. Their hunger possessed them like a glorious, unrelenting madness.

Love-lust aflame, the crashing of swells against the

seashore. This was everything—the only thing. Swept away to another world—a place where time ceased to exist—they rocked against each other. Seeking. Giving. Taking.

She'd never felt so full, so complete. Jackie grew hotter, her muscles constricted, her body craved more yet could take no more. Cole's movements became more urgent, almost punishing, and she was a glutton for his method of punishment.

A kaleidoscope of colors burst before her eyes with yet another wondrous explosion. After Cole Morrison, she would be ruined for any other man.

But she would never want another man.

He tensed and exploded within her. His blistering heat filled her, claimed her.

And God help her, she knew she would never be the same.

Chapter Fourteen

Cole held her in his arms for what seemed an eternity, the sun beating down on his backside, burning skin unaccustomed to the light of day. A smile tugged at his lips and he inhaled the scent of woman beneath him.

He kissed the top of her head and rolled to his side, noticing the stripe where her hair parted. "Your hair is really brown," he whispered.

She nodded against his shoulder. "Very dark. Are you just now noticing that?"

"I was, uh, too busy to, uh . . . "

Giggling, she pushed onto her elbow and lay on her side, facing him. Her expression sobered and she reached up to shove a stray curl off his forehead. "You're a beautiful man, Cole Morrison."

"I'm not sure 'beautiful' is the right word." He flashed her a grin.

"Handsome on the outside," she said with a sigh,

"and beautiful in here." She rested her hand over his heart. "Where it matters."

His gut clenched and he cupped her cheek in his hand. Was now the time to tell her his plans? "Jackie, what are you doing to me?" he asked instead, kissing her softly. "You make me think about poetry and the fairy tales my mother read to me as a child." He glanced down at her bare bosom. "And you make me want you. Constantly."

She arched a brow, and a wicked smile curved her kiss-swollen lips. "Constantly?"

"Constantly." He hardened against her thigh. "See for yourself."

She laughed and kissed him soundly. "So what's wrong with that?"

"A man's gotta work once in a while." He chuckled, enjoying the way she combined play with the far more serious matters of the flesh. "Not to mention eat and raise children."

Her laughter died and the sparkle in her eyes dimmed. "Todd says you're going to Oregon."

"I thought a lot about what you said last night about dreams." He stroked her bare shoulder, struggling against the burning hunger growing within him all over again. Now they needed to talk and the other would have to wait. His body flinched in disagreement and he glanced downward. *Yes, you can wait.*

"I'm glad you're going to Oregon," she said, though sadness tinged her voice, and her eyes glittered dangerously. "Really."

"So am I." He cupped her rosy cheek again, brushing his thumb along her temple. "And we want you to come with us."

Genuine shock flared in her eyes. *"What?"* She pulled from his embrace and leaped to her feet, standing over him in all her naked splendor. "I'm imagining things. I couldn't possibly have heard you right."

He rose slowly and faced her. "I'm serious, Jackie," he said, stroking her upper arms. "We both want you to come with us to Oregon. Is that too horrible for you to even consider?"

She turned her back on him and he saw a tremor race through her slender body. He ached to gather her in his arms, but common sense commanded him to give her a few moments to consider his offer. "Jackie?"

"What?"

Her voice sounded thick, oddly muffled.

"Are you crying?" He hadn't meant to make her cry. She was a strong woman and he doubted that tears came easily to her. "Please don't—"

"Please don't say anything." She spun around to face him, her eyes moist, her face stained with tears. "Just . . . don't."

He stood there helplessly, his arms hanging limply at his sides when all he wanted was to gather her against him and beg her to go with them. "We have to talk about this. It's important."

An odd gleam entered her gray eyes, and she tilted her chin a notch. "More important than your gold? More important than Lolita Belle's opening night?"

"Yes, more important than both." His voice fell to a ragged whisper. He needed answers, and she was the only person who had them. "Who *are* you? Really?"

She sniffled and shoved her hair back from her face. "You mean, you don't think I'm Lolita Belle anymore?"

He shook his head slowly. "Who are you?"

"I told you." She started toward the falls. "My real name is Jackie Clarke."

He followed her into the water, allowing the frigid stream to purge his mind and quiet the fire in his body. Unfortunately, it did nothing to ease the riot in his heart and soul. After a few minutes, she shook herself and stepped out, taking a seat on the smooth stones a few feet from the water's edge.

Cole watched her for several moments. She looked like one of those wood nymphs she'd mentioned earlier. He remembered illustrations from one of his mother's books. There'd been a beautiful, slender female being with wings. With a start, he realized how very much Jackie resembled that being.

"Jackie," he whispered, taking a seat at her side. He glanced at her and saw her shiver. "You're freezing." Immediately he slid his arm around her shoulders and pulled her close. "Maybe we should get dressed now and head back to—"

"No." She turned and faced him. "I want—*need*—to have all this settled in my mind today." With a tremulous smile, she touched his cheek. "And . . . I want to make love with you one last time."

"Jackie . . ." What did she mean by that?

"You told me you need the gold Merriweather promised you in order to go to Oregon," she said matter-of-factly, pinning him with a no-nonsense look. "Do you or don't you, Cole? Which is it?"

He released a deep sigh and combed his fingers through his hair. "Well, the only new homesteads I've heard of recently are down in Oklahoma Territory, but that's not Oregon. I'm afraid all the homesteads in Oregon are gone. I'll have to buy land."

"No, Oklahoma is a far cry from Oregon." She chuckled quietly. "I can't picture you and Todd as Okies."

"Okies?"

"Never mind." She tilted her head to one side, her expression unreadable. "So you *do* need the gold."

He clenched his teeth, afraid to answer. "We have enough to get to Oregon."

"And . . . ?" She waited a few seconds, then added, "But not enough to buy a ranch. Right?"

"We'll be all right. I'll get work and start saving, then—"

"So you do need the gold to have your dream." She held her hand up to silence him when he started to speak. "Admit it, Cole. The money Merriweather promised you is enough to *really* have that dream. Isn't it?"

He shrugged, but she narrowed her eyes. "Sure, it would be enough, but there are some things that are more important than gold."

"But *not* more important than dreams, Cole." Her eyes grew misty again. "Don't let go of your dreams. I did that once."

"I'm not letting go. Not ever." He kissed her forehead. "I'm holding on to you. Get used to it."

"Cole, your dreams . . . "

"Shh." He wished she would look at him so he could see her eyes. "Tell me about your dreams, Jackie." He pulled her closer, wanting to comfort her, to keep her safe. "Share them with me."

"Waste of breath."

He cupped her chin, tilted her face up to meet his gaze, then covered her mouth with his. "Tell me," he murmured against her lips. "Tell me."

"A home. A family." Her face crumpled and he watched her fight the tears. "Don't make me . . . talk about this. It hurts too much."

She'd already said enough to help him begin to understand. He rose, pulling her up to stand before him. "We want you to come with us to Oregon, Jackie." He buried his fingers in her tangled hair, lowering his face so close to hers he could taste the warmth of her breath. "Share our dream."

Before she could answer, he pulled her against him and kissed her, seeking answers from her response. She melted against him, trembling and warming in his embrace.

And he knew.

Jackie fished the bar of mystery soap out of the basket and gave Cole a shampoo massage, then they played in the falls some more, made love again. And again.

Exhausted and sated, they ate their picnic and Cole realized it was already late afternoon. "We'd better head back before Todd and Chief Byron beat us home." True regret sounded in his voice. "Though . . . I'd like to keep you naked indefinitely." He waggled his eyebrows suggestively.

Jackie laughed. "You're insatiable." She wrapped herself around him and kissed him. "I like that."

"The kiss or the insatiable part?" He grabbed her when she tried to pull away. "You promise to think about going to Oregon with us?"

"Don't spoil this." She freed herself and shook out her chemise, then pulled it over her head. "Ouch, I got sunburned."

"There?" His eyes glittered with a feral light.

She glanced downward, noticing his erection immediately. It was impossible to miss. "I wonder if you got sunburned . . . *there.*" *That's right. Keep changing the subject, Clarke.*

He glanced down, then shot her a wicked grin that

made her bones melt. "Hmm. Maybe we ought to test it and make sure."

"Like I said, you're insatiable." She pulled on her undies and tied them at the waist, then donned her dress. "And it's one of the things I like best about you, of course."

Keep 'em laughing, Clarke. She knew what she had to do, and no matter how much it hurt, she couldn't let him talk her out of it.

Sure, he'd asked her to go with him to Oregon, but it was what he *hadn't* said that hurt. *Why* did he want her to go? In what capacity? As Todd's teacher and Cole's mistress?

Or as his wife?

Did he love her as she loved him?

No, men like Cole Morrison didn't marry women like Lolita Belle, and for all intents and purposes, that was who and what she was in 1891. She paused while tying her boots. At least, until the real Lolita showed up. *If* she showed up . . .

Cole dressed and packed the picnic basket, then shook out and folded their quilt. "I'm glad you talked me out of going to the mine today," he said, flashing her another killer smile.

"Yeah, it was *real* tough, too." She laughed when he tossed the blanket aside and spun her in a circle. He lowered his mouth to claim hers and she clung to him, cherishing this last day.

That thought made her throat clog with unshed tears, but she resolutely banished any visible tears. The burning and tightening persisted, but she wouldn't cry. Not yet anyway. She had to stay tough and do the right thing.

Jackie didn't belong here. Some freak accident had thrown her back in time, and she had to get her butt back to the right century ASAP. Enough of screwing up Cole's life and hers. Life had to go on, as they said.

Yeah, right. She cradled his cheek in her palm as they separated, memorizing the way he practically made love to her with his eyes. No man had ever looked at her the way he did, and no man had ever made her completely lose control the way he had.

She would miss that. She would miss *him.*

Her heart squeezed and she drew a deep breath, reminding herself of Aunt Pearl's insistence that she never show her feelings. *Big girls don't cry, Jacqueline Marie.*

"You are going with us," Cole said, his voice gruff, his body hard and compelling against hers. "Don't deny it, Jackie. I know you want to."

It would be so easy to say yes. What if she stayed in Devil's Gulch waiting for the miracle that would return her to her own time and it never came? What if she was stuck here in the nineteenth century for the rest of her life?

Shouldn't she be with the man she loved? Would the last few pages of that script have told her what would happen next? Right now she'd pay any amount of money to have that script in front of her. Or a crystal ball . . .

"I . . . I'm confused," she said, and that was no lie. "I need some time to think about it." She sighed and met his gaze, dying to tell him she loved him, and to hear him utter those same words in turn. But he wouldn't. She was a notorious saloon singer, unfit for the roles of wife and mother.

And since when did Jackie Clarke give a damn about propriety?

She smiled to herself. Since she'd found someone

else she cared more about than herself. Two someones. Her reputation had never mattered to her, except in business, of course. But if she went to Oregon with Cole and Todd, there would always be that ugly Lolita thing between them. Right or wrong . . .

"Take time, then," he said. "Think about it." A furrow creased his brow. "I'll need more time to raise the money anyway."

Time, time, time. Suddenly realizing what he'd said, she leaned away from him and watched his fluctuating expression. "What is it, Cole?"

He shrugged and tried to turn away, but she held him fast.

"Cole Morrison, if you expect me to consider your offer, then you have to be honest with me." *And tell me in what capacity you want me to go with you to Oregon while you're at it.*

He shoved his hand through his hair and sighed. "Well, it's just that . . . "

"Cole?" She placed her hand on his arm, felt his muscles bunch beneath her touch. Something was really bothering him. "What is it?"

"I'm in a quandary."

"You and me both." She smiled, but his brow remained furrowed, his eyes worried. "What is it, Cole?"

He held his hands out to his sides in a gesture of helplessness. "I'm damned if I do and damned if I don't."

Ditto. "Why?"

"Don't take this wrong," he said, "but I never should've gotten involved in this kidnapping business."

Had he changed his mind about wanting her to go with him to Oregon already? "Of course not."

"The only good thing about it was finding you." His expression softened, his blue eyes devouring her again.

Jackie's knees grew weak, but she drew a deep breath and squared her shoulders. "And the gold."

He winced.

"Color me confused," she said, rubbing his arm. "Enlighten me."

"Don't you see, Jackie?" He gripped her upper arms and held her gaze with his. "I have to return the gold Merriweather already paid me."

"The *hell* you do."

"It would be dishonest for me to keep it," he persisted. "I didn't finish the job."

"Whoa, hold on." With a nervous laugh, Jackie turned to look at the waterfall, then faced him again. He wasn't touching her now. Maybe she could think straight for a change. "Let me digest this. You think you have to return the money to Merriweather for the *first* part of your, uh, mission?"

"Of course." He shrugged and gave her a sheepish and endearing grin. "I'm keeping you."

His words warmed her, but she filed the good feeling aside for later. She was sure she'd need it by the time this mess was finished. "But you delivered me once, as ordered, and he paid you for that part of the job. If you don't deliver me for my opening night, you don't get the extra gold he promised."

"Well . . ." His brow furrowed again. "I guess that's one way to look at it, but it still feels dishonest to me."

She knew in that moment that "straight arrow" Cole Morrison wouldn't agree to Goodfellow's counteroffer in a million years. Of course not. Why hadn't she realized that when Smith had first pitched it to her?

Goodfellow will double Merriweather's offer. I'll be back in two days for your answer.

Two days. That meant Smith would be back tomorrow. She either had to turn herself over to Goodfellow, or go public—so to speak—with her true identity before then.

Oh, boy.

She could play the martyr in a really big way and deliver herself to Goodfellow, then send the gold to Cole, but she knew he wouldn't accept it. Sighing, she tried to concentrate, to think logically. *What a joke. Logic and Jackie Clarke!*

She had to think, and she was running out of time. *Time. There it was again—the joke of two centuries.*

But she wasn't laughing.

"Tell me something, Cole," she said, her mind mulling over all the gory details. She placed her hand on his arm again and faced him.

"What?"

"If you give Merriweather back his precious gold, will you forgive yourself for ever getting involved in his schemes?"

Cole's jaw flinched several times, then he gave a quick nod. "I haven't spent any of it, so I reckon. Why do you ask?"

"Because I want you to forgive yourself, Cole. It's important to me." She paced, rubbing her chin and chewing her lower lip, then stopped to meet his curious gaze again. "*I* forgive you."

His Adam's apple traveled the length of his throat and back. "You do?"

She nodded and stepped toward him. "I . . . I care about you and Todd." God, how she wanted to tell him she loved him. "I want you to forgive yourself, and if giving back the money will do that, then do it."

He gave a quick nod. "Done."

She rested her cheek on his shoulder and slid her arms around his waist, then leaned back to gaze up into his beautiful blue eyes. She had to make sure he followed through with his dreams, no matter what happened to her. "I want you to promise me something else, Cole."

"What?" He rubbed her back and waist with his strong hands. "What do you want me to promise you, Jackie?"

"That you'll go to Oregon."

"But—"

"No buts." She drew a shaky breath. "No matter what it takes, live your dream, Cole. Yours and Elizabeth's."

His eyes darkened and she watched his internal struggle play across his features. Finally he drew a deep breath. "You're a good woman, Jackie Clarke."

She smiled, though her heart was breaking.

"Elizabeth's dead, and it's high time I got on with the rest of our lives."

"A part of Elizabeth lives on in you and Todd." A strange peace settled over Jackie's heart as she spoke, then she realized why with a start.

Her mother lived on through Jackie.

By letting Aunt Pearl's vindictive nature destroy Jackie's spirit, she'd betrayed her mother. But no more. Regardless of how this adventure ended, she'd never let Aunt Pearl—or anyone—destroy that again. She straightened and met Cole's smoldering gaze with another smile—a real one this time.

"The people we love always live in our hearts,

Cole." True conviction entered her voice and her heart.

"That's so." He pulled her against him and held her in silence.

She allowed herself a few silent tears—for her mother, the baby Jackie'd miscarried, and for herself. Now that she had things in perspective again, she had to help Cole find his dream. Maybe—just maybe—she could become a part of his dream.

And stay in the nineteenth century?

He tilted her chin upward and covered her lips in a kiss so tender it almost made her weep. She clung to him, savoring this moment. Somehow she had to tell him about Rock Smith and Goodfellow's offer, help him return Merriweather's gold, and clear his conscience. And help him find a way to get to Oregon.

After a delicious, lingering moment, he pulled back and smiled. "I just want to make sure you really understand that invitation to Oregon."

Her heart skipped a beat and she held her breath. "What about it, Cole?"

"I wasn't asking you to do anything . . . improper." Redness flooded his face.

"Ah, rats." She rubbed herself against him. "Are you sure about that, big guy? We've been properly improper already. Several times."

He drew a sharp breath and pressed the evidence of his desire against her belly. "I had something a lot more . . . permanent in mind."

It was her turn to stare in numb silence. Her blood pumped so loudly through her head, she could barely hear herself, let alone him. "Cole, what are you saying?" But she *had* to hear his words.

"Dang it all, Jackie, do I have to spell it out?"

His discomfort endeared him to her all the more.

"Yes, Cole," she said, blinking and afraid to believe. To hope. "Yes, you do." *So I can make damn sure I'm not dreaming this. Please, God, don't let me screw this up.*

Much to her amazement, he dropped to one knee, holding both her hands in his. Her head swam and she held her breath.

"Marry me," he whispered.

Chapter Fifteen

"I . . . " Jackie bit her lower lip. The man was on his knees *proposing* to her. "I . . . " He grinned and she couldn't contain her nervous laughter.

"What's so funny?" He placed his hand over his heart. "My pride may suffer a mortal wound, woman."

"Stand up, Cole," she whispered, then tugged on his hand, no longer laughing. "Please? I can't think with you . . . like that."

"On my knees, you mean?" He rose and pulled her hard against him. "Is this better?"

"Oh, yeah." She kissed him, twining her fingers through the soft hair at his nape. "I like this a lot."

"Mmm, so do I." He pulled back and his expression grew sober. Intense. "Will you marry me, Jackie? Be my wife? Help me raise Todd? Go with us to Oregon as soon as I save enough money?"

And never return to my own time?

The thought both terrified and thrilled her. She couldn't imagine anything better than being Cole Morrison's wife and having a son like Todd. And maybe more babies—a little girl named Sandra.

The man was offering her the world. His dream. Her dream. How could she refuse?

Yet how could she agree?

"Cole, do you really believe I'm not Lolita?" She had to know once and for all.

A moment's uncertainty flashed in his eyes, and a stabbing pain pierced her moment of joy. She couldn't marry him if he still believed she was Lolita. "Cole?" she repeated, waiting.

And hoping.

"I don't believe you're Lolita," he said. "At least, not anymore."

Her fairy tale shattered, her dreams died. A sinking feeling washed over her and her head pounded. "What do you mean by 'not anymore?' "

He shifted his weight from foot to foot. "Jackie, what am I supposed to think? You showed up in Devil's Gulch just before everybody was expecting Lolita, and your hair's that unnatural shade of red like hers."

She drew a deep breath and clenched her fists at her sides. In her heart and gut, she realized he still didn't believe her. *Damn.* "Then maybe you should just deliver me to Merriweather and collect your gold, cowboy." Her lower lip trembled and she bit it, but she banished the nasal drone of Great-Aunt Pearl's voice from the back of her mind.

"Jackie, don't. I—"

"I'm tired, Cole," she whispered. "We'd better get back." She met his gaze and her heart pressed upward against her throat, a tight fist of anguish. He looked like a man who'd lost everything, which wasn't true, of course. She was the big loser in this scenario. "Please don't look at me that way."

"What way?" One corner of his mouth turned upward and he raked his fingers through his hair. "Like a man who wants to kiss you, to hold you, to make you his wife?"

But not like a man who loves me and who believes me. She shook her head. "You don't have to marry me, Cole, just because we had sex."

He grabbed her upper arms and gave her a gentle shake. "Jackie, there could be a *child.* Lord knows we did everything right to make one."

Ah, so that's it. How could she explain contraception to a Victorian man? "Wrong time of month," she said.

"Huh?"

"It's just . . . *very* unlikely. Trust me." At least now she knew why he'd proposed to her. This wasn't about love or dreams. Mr. Straight Arrow was simply an honorable man doing the "right thing." *Well, to hell with this.*

"I won't let a child of mine be branded a bastard." His voice was intense and his eyes flashed angrily. "I can't believe you would risk that either."

She could've said something flippant, but the pain of the child she'd conceived and lost so many years ago stabbed through her anew. "If there's a child, I promise I'll let you know," she whispered. "Let's not borrow trouble."

"Trouble?" He let his arms fall to his sides, an expression of shock and disappointment marring his handsome features. "Children aren't trouble, Jackie. They're a blessing."

"I didn't mean it . . . that way." Her head ached and pounded and she rubbed her temples. She'd really blown things with Cole now, but it never would've worked anyway. Her eyes burned and she cleared her throat.

"My proposal still stands," he said stoically, closing his eyes before looking directly at her again. "And I meant what I said about not having a child of mine raised a bastard."

"I know you did, Cole." She held her breath, wishing she could tell him everything—who she was, where she was from, why she couldn't be pregnant. He already didn't believe the truth she'd told him about not being Lolita, so why would he believe time travel?

Because it was the truth.

"Damn," she muttered, dragging in a deep breath.

"What?" His jaw twitched again.

"Don't grit your teeth, Cole." She flashed him a smile. "I have something to tell you, but it's going to be hard for you to believe. Even harder than the fact that I'm not Lolita. Which I'm not and never have been."

"Are you . . . already married?" His brow furrowed and genuine worry entered his eyes. "No matter how much I want you, I never would've—"

"I'm *not* married, Cole." She stepped closer and touched his cheek, watching relief wash through him. "Dear, sweet Cole." She smiled up at him. "No, it's something much more bizarre, but it's the truth."

"Truth is good." He gave her a shy grin. "And you not being married is even better."

She threw back her head and laughed, feeling much better about everything. "Ready or not, Cole Morrison," she said with genuine conviction, "you're getting the truth, the whole truth, and nothing but the truth." She placed her right hand over her heart. "So help me God."

He sobered. "All right, I'm ready."

She glanced at the sun's angle. "I think we'd better save this until after supper."

"Jackie . . . "

"Really, it's a very long and amazing story." She stood on tiptoe and kissed his cheek.

"All right, as soon as Todd's asleep." Mischief and a familiar fire danced in his blue eyes. "That pile of straw's still there."

She laughed again and threw her arms around him, sighing with relief when he gathered her close. The thought of never feeling his arms embracing her again made a tight band of fear clutch her heart, and she held him tighter.

"There, now," he said, kissing the top of her head. "Everything's going to be fine. You'll see."

She leaned back and met his gaze. "I want it to be fine, Cole. More than anything." Drawing a deep breath, she added, "And once I've told you everything, we'll talk again about . . . what you asked me."

He smiled and kissed her forehead. "The word is marriage," he whispered.

There she went changing her mind again. Cole was offering her a dream—a dream she wanted more than anything, but only because she loved this man with all her heart and soul.

Marriage to a man I really love. Great sex whenever I want with Mel-Gibson-only-better. Children.

Love? Did he love her? Could he love her?

Dared she dream again . . . ?

* * *

Cole could easily make a habit of these evening meetings with Jackie. A smile tugged at the corners of his mouth as he tucked his son in bed and kissed him on the forehead.

"Did you and Miss Jackie finish *Huckleberry Finn*?" he asked, squatting beside Todd's narrow bunk.

"Almost." The boy yawned, then smiled, his eyes drooping. "I like Miss Jackie."

"So do I, son." Cole drew a deep breath and rose. "So do I."

"I want her to go with us to Oregon."

A pang of regret stabbed through Cole. He never should've mentioned Oregon to Todd. Now they'd have to wait. "We'll see what she has to say about that when the time comes."

"Good night, Pa."

"Sleep tight."

"Mama always said . . . that." The boy's eyes fluttered shut, and his even breathing indicated he was sound asleep.

Todd had very few memories of his mother, because he'd been only five when she died. Cole smiled to himself, then glanced at the rocking chair near the hearth. Remembering. . . .

He could picture her there, nursing Todd at her breast, humming softly. A lump formed in Cole's throat and he drew another huge breath. Memories of Elizabeth always led to the same place.

His unkept promise.

He walked slowly toward the door, trying to banish the images of his wife on her deathbed, and the sound of her shaky voice begging him. . . .

Damnation, Elizabeth . . . I'm sorry. So sorry.

Trying to keep that promise had driven him to

break the law. But if he hadn't agreed to do Merriweather's dirty work, he never would have met Jackie.

Elizabeth would want him to be happy. She'd said as much before her death—told him to remarry one day, and to give Todd a new mother. Elizabeth would always be Todd's mother, but Jackie loved him, too, whether she was ready to admit it or not.

Cole shoved aside his memories, deciding to deal with one woman and one truth at a time. His brain was downright overcrowded with worries and promises and dreams as it was.

Pity his dreams and promises were so damned contrary.

He opened the door and stepped outside, pulling it shut behind him. Jackie turned slowly toward him, pulling her shawl closer against the evening chill.

She'd promised him the truth, but for some reason he feared it. Truth was good, he reminded himself, gazing out at the last smudges of twilight.

"Todd's asleep," he said, sliding his arm around Jackie and pulling her against him. "Chilly this evening."

"Yes." She rested her cheek on his shoulder. "Well, are you ready for this?"

"I'm . . . not sure."

"Get ready, because it's show time, big guy." She sighed and pulled out of his embrace, taking his hand. "Let's sit here. Okay?"

He allowed her to lead him to the porch step, where they sat side by side, their thighs and hips touching. Everything about this woman aroused him. He couldn't remember being so randy all the time before, but he must have been as a younger man. Damnation, but Jackie made him *feel* young again.

And alive.

"All right," he said, watching the stars appear across the clear black sky, twinkling like diamonds. He wished he could grab one of them and put it on her ring finger. *Damn.* He'd spent far too much time lately remembering his mother's poetry and fairy tales. "I'm listening."

She kept his hand. "Promise to listen to it all?"

"Every word."

"No matter how, uh, crazy it sounds?"

He looked at her, though he couldn't see her clearly in the darkness. "No matter how crazy. I promise." Giving her hand a reassuring squeeze, he added, "Honest."

"Okay." She released a slow sigh. "First things first. I'm not from around here."

"I figured that." He smiled through the darkness, but sensed she wasn't in the mood for jokes. "Go on."

"I was born in Texas and raised in a small town in Arizona with my great-aunt."

"Pearl?"

"Right. Good old not-so-Great-Aunt Pearl." She shuddered against his side.

"I gather that isn't a good memory?"

"No, though I think she believed she was doing a good job, which is really scary now that I think about it."

"Sometimes you talk so strangely." He shook his head. "I'm sorry, go on."

"I talk strangely for a reason, Cole." She half turned toward him. "Here comes the part that will be hard for you to believe."

"I'm ready." He narrowed his eyes, wishing he could see hers, but it was too dark.

"Growing up in Arizona isn't why I sound strange to

you." She sighed again, then gave his hand a squeeze. "Cole, I was born in the year 1967."

"That makes you a year younger than—" He gulped, realization making gooseflesh pop out all over him. "Wait, did you say . . . what I think you did?"

"Yes. April eleventh, *19*67, Cole."

She was madder than a March hare. Nuttier than his mother-in-law's fruitcake. A raving lunatic. "Jackie, you feeling all right?"

She threw one hand up and stared at the sky. "See? I knew you'd do this."

"It's not poss—"

"Yes, it *is* possible, because it happened to me, Cole." A bitter laugh erupted from her, containing no humor at all. "It happened to *me*. One day I was hiking down a mountain in the month of June, and the next I was back in time over a hundred years."

"Jackie, I'm worried about—"

"Hey, don't worry about me. I've been vaccinated against half a dozen diseases that are common in this century. You're the one who should worry." Groaning, she pulled her hand free and leaped to her feet, pacing back and forth in front of him.

Cole rose slowly, trying to sort this through. "Jackie, traveling back in time isn't possible."

"Tell that to God or whoever sucked me into that painting and planted my pitiful ass in your lap, bucko."

"First of all, your ass is quite fine, ma'am, and I'm grateful to God for planting you in my lap." He took a step toward her, but she backed away. "And other places."

"But . . . ?" She stood with a fist perched on each hip and lifted her chin just as the moon rose, bathing the clearing in silver. "Go on, ask all those questions that are bouncing around in that brain of yours."

He took another step toward her, ready to grab her if she bolted. The woman wasn't well, and he cared too much about her to risk letting her wander off into the wilderness and get lost.

"I'm waiting, big guy. Fire those questions. Let her rip."

"All right." He stood less than a foot from her and watched the moonlight play across the planes and angles of her pretty face, wishing he could gather her in his arms and chase her demons away. But he'd promised to listen. "Assuming you really are from the future—God Almighty, will you listen to this?—how did you get here? And what painting?"

"Good questions." She started pacing again. "I'll spare you the Blade business and cut to the chase."

"Chase?"

"Yeah, me and about ten million snowflakes against the world."

"What?"

She paused in front of him, again placing her fists on her hips, lifting her chin as if daring him to doubt her. "Someone took me to a cabin in the mountains, not very far from here, I think, and left me there. He stole my car and all my money."

"Car?"

"Oh, I guess this is pre–Henry Ford, huh?" She shook her head and made a strange sound. "A car is a horseless carriage, runs with an engine instead of a horse."

Cole chuckled. "I reckon if we can have trains, we can have those, too." He tilted his head to one side. "Someday."

"Airplanes and space shuttles, too, Cole."

"You've been reading my Jules Verne novels."

"Nope, just Mark Twain." She folded her arms in front of her. "It's all true, Cole."

"You still haven't told me how it happened."

"Right." She paced again for a few minutes, then stopped, looking toward the mountains. "Like I told you, I was abandoned in the mountains, so I started walking down. I know nothing about the mountains, Cole."

"I noticed." He smiled. Crazy or not, this woman touched him in a way no one ever had. "I'm listening." He kept his tone gentle, trying to encourage her.

"I had no idea it could snow in June."

"Ah, yes, I remember you mentioned that."

"I was so cold, so frightened." Her voice fell to a whisper.

He believed her. Not the time travel part, but this part. No one could put this much emotion into a story that wasn't true. If only he'd been there to take care of her . . .

"I found a ghost town, but only one building was standing." She chuckled again, then looked right at him. "The Gold Mine Saloon in Devil's Gulch."

A shiver raced down his spine. "Devil's Gulch is a busy place, Jackie," he said gently. "Not a ghost—"

"It *will* be, though." She rubbed her arms and pulled the shawl closer. "Anyway, I took shelter in the saloon and found a few things I could use. A lamp, some food, matches . . ." Her voice trailed away.

"What happened next?" He stepped closer and put a hand on her shoulder, relieved that she didn't flinch away. "I want to know, Jackie. Tell me." *And get this sickness out of your mind before it destroys you.*

"A painting of Lolita Belle." Jackie laughed again,

a crazy, shrill sound. "Her name was on the painting, along with the year 1891."

"And I kidnapped you from that artist's place out on the edge of town."

"Exactly, so you *do* believe me."

He remained silent and felt her withdrawal. She shrugged his hand away and lifted her chin again. "Anyway, it was cold and I started a fire in the stove. There was an old movie script there to read, so I settled down in front of the stove to read."

"What happened?"

"Fire." The word was barely more than a strangled whisper in the night. "Fire."

"Ah, Jackie." He reached for her and pulled her into his arms, relieved when she came willingly. Trembling, she rested her cheek against his chest and he stroked her hair. "You're safe now."

She pulled back slightly, looking up at him. "No, not until you believe me, Cole."

She had to finish this. He sensed that. "What happened next?" Her body trembled in his arms and he rubbed her back, hoping to calm her.

"There was no way out, but I remembered a window behind the bar, near Lolita's painting." A small sob tore from her throat and she covered her mouth. "I was so afraid, Cole. So afraid . . . "

"I'm here now."

"I . . . I couldn't find the window. Something fell and knocked me down." She drew a shuddering breath. "Lolita's painting crashed to the floor with me. I knew I was going to die."

"You didn't die."

"No, and that's when the miracle happened."

Now certainly wasn't the time to tell her she was talking nonsense. He just held her and prayed that sharing her story would purge her of this madness. *God willing.* "What miracle, Jackie?"

"The painting started to glow and I touched her face. Lolita's face."

"Go on." A chill seeped into Cole's bones and he couldn't shake it. He swallowed hard, listening.

"Her face . . . became mine."

Cole's heart raced and his gut clenched. A thin coating of perspiration popped out all over his body. He held her tighter, suddenly afraid. Had the fire done this to her? Driven her mad?

But what did *he* fear? Her madness? *No.*

He feared for his own sanity.

Dear God, I almost believe her. He dragged in a shaky breath, still rubbing her back. She trembled against him, and he leaned back to gaze down at her shadowy face in the moonlight. "Then what happened?"

She lifted one shoulder in a shrug and sighed. "I woke up in the Gold Mine Saloon, but it was brand-new, like it is now." A nervous laugh bubbled up from her lips. "The Brothers Grime—"

"Grime? Who are they?"

"Goodfellow's henchmen, Zeb or Zeke or whatever his name is, and the other one."

"Ah, the pair who came here looking for you?" He was starting to understand why Jackie had become such an agreeable hostage. The word made him cringe. "I figured they came here because of the morning I dragged you out of the street and you asked me to help you." He shuddered. "I swear, I'll never forgive myself for not listening to you then."

"Please forgive yourself, Cole." She reached up and cradled his cheek in her palm. "I've forgiven you."

The urge—no, the *need*—to kiss her thundered

through him, and he lowered his head to claim her lips. She clung to him and he felt her quivering. Was he strong enough to help her through this madness?

Would she recover at all? She had to.

In his arms, she didn't feel insane at all. Did it really matter that she believed she was born in the future? After all, they'd been getting along quite well so far.

Yes, it mattered for her. He had to help her get well.

She ended their kiss and drew a quick breath. "I thought then that I should go back with them and let Henri finish Lolita's painting," she continued, her voice stronger now. "But I didn't want to get . . . "

"Get what?" he prodded.

"I didn't want to get you in trouble." She rested her cheek against his chest again and he massaged slow circles into her back. "Oh, Cole, I'm still afraid."

"Shh, I'm here." He lifted her chin and gazed down at her, wishing again that he could see her eyes. It warmed him to know she'd been trying to protect him, despite her obvious . . . problems. "Why were you worried about the painting being finished?" And how could she have touched it in the future if it didn't exist? The entire thing made no sense, but she couldn't see that.

"It's my time portal," she said matter-of-factly.

Inwardly, he groaned. "Time . . . portal?"

"Of course." A gentle breeze wrapped her skirts around his legs. "It pulled me back in time, so I figure it can just as easily send me forward."

"Do you . . . *want* to go back, Jackie?" He sounded as crazy as she did. "I don't want you to leave."

"I . . . I'm not sure, Cole." She sighed again. "Part

of me—a very big part—wants to stay here with you and Todd more than anything."

"I'll take care of you," he said. "I want to marry you, Jackie."

"Even knowing who and what I really am?"

"Yes." No matter what, he would take care of her. If she spent the rest of her life believing she'd traveled back in time, then so be it. She warmed his heart, filled his soul, made beautiful love to him, and she took good care of Todd. "Marry me, Jackie."

"Now that you know the truth . . . " She drew a shaky breath. "Yes."

What more could a man ask?

Jackie approached the moonlit outhouse with resolve. She'd be staying in the nineteenth century, so she'd better get used to the inconveniences and conveniences, such as they were.

She smiled, giddy in the knowledge that she would be staying here and marrying Cole Morrison. With a thumbs-up gesture, she whispered, "Yes," and did the Snoopy dance in front of the outhouse.

Laughing at herself, she entered it and took care of business, then stepped out and stood gazing up at the stars for a few wondrous moments. Cole would love and protect her. Funny, but she'd never thought she needed a man's protection before—but it was much more than that. Knowing someone cared enough to want the job made her heart swell with love.

Yes, love. Though he still hadn't spoken the words, she knew in her heart that Cole loved her. How could any man put up with her otherwise, let alone want to spend the rest of his life chained to her?

She had a lifetime of love, commitment, great sex, motherhood—even if she never gave birth, she'd have Todd—and joy ahead of her. Amazing what a little quantum leaping could do for a girl.

Speaking of great sex, she and Cole had a date with a pile of straw. Internal warmth settled low in her belly and unfurled through her like tendrils of smoke, focusing on her smoldering core. Turning in the direction of the stable and the man she loved, she hurried toward what promised to be a *very* memorable rendezvous.

Another thought filled her mind, and she paused. While it was true Cole hadn't professed his love for her, she was guilty of the same omission. *So much for honesty, Clarke.* Squaring her shoulders, she vowed to remedy that error in about two min—

"Oomph." A gloved hand clamped over her mouth, and an arm of steel hauled her toward the trees. She tried to scream, then twisted, bit, kicked, and struggled against the man, but he was too powerful. A familiar, sickeningly sweet scent touched her nostrils, demanding she remember something, but she failed.

All she could think of was that Cole was waiting for her. She leaned away from her abductor and stomped on his foot, straining to break free.

"You bitch," the man snapped, his hot breath scorching the side of her neck. An evil chuckle filled her ear. "I always was partial to redheads."

Blade. Rock.

She jabbed her elbow into his ribs and he wheezed, but his grip never faltered a bit.

"That's it," he said, throwing her to the ground and straddling her.

Jackie gasped, preparing to scream, but he shoved

a filthy rag into her mouth, then tied his bandanna over it. It happened so fast. *Damn.* She screamed anyway, but the muffled sound couldn't have traveled more than a few feet. A silent scream filled her brain, her heart, her soul.

Cole.

She gagged on the rag, and scalding tears streamed down her face. Breathing through her nose, she stopped gagging and vowed to find a way to escape. Smith obviously planned to collect Goodfellow's gold for himself.

The joke would be on him, though, because she wasn't about to play the role of Lolita Belle again. No matter what it took, she'd convince Goodfellow this time that she wasn't Lolita. She didn't *want* to see the painting finished now.

Fate couldn't be this cruel. Blade Smith had screwed up her life in the future, and his dropped-on-his-head ancestor was trying to finish the job now.

Just when she'd found happiness at last and Cole promised to take care of her.

Chapter Sixteen

Cole spread a quilt out on the pile of straw where he and Jackie had made love the first time and lay on his back to wait. He grew hard so fast it made him dizzy.

Jackie might be crazy, but she was his. That thought made him shake his head in bewilderment, even as it made his heart sing with joy. He'd take care of her, give her plenty of loving, and eventually she'd get better.

She had to.

The fact that he wanted her, crazy or not, was pretty telling. He couldn't deny any longer that he was in love with the woman. Thinking back, he realized he hadn't told her yet. At least, not with words. Women were strange that way. They liked to have everything spelled out.

Fine. He'd tell her tonight. And he'd tell her about

his stories, too—another dream she didn't know about. She'd find out sooner or later anyway.

He folded his hands behind his head, wondering what was taking her so long. Women were curious creatures, and it always seemed to take them twice as long as he thought necessary to answer the call of nature. He had a call of nature to take care of right here, but he didn't intend to rush it.

She'd be along shortly, and they'd make love, plan their wedding, then maybe they'd make love again. And again. He smiled to himself, his groin tightening with a longing ache—an itch he knew just how to scratch.

They were getting married. Todd would be happy about that. He'd wanted Jackie to go with them to Oregon, and now she would.

If they went.

Gnashing his teeth, Cole released a ragged sigh. He had to return Merriweather's gold, and that was all there was to it. Even Jackie agreed.

Cole thought back to their day by the waterfall, remembering how thoughtful and downright philosophical she'd been. She understood that Elizabeth would always be in Cole's heart, but there was room there for Jackie, too. It took a strong woman not to resent a man's past.

In fact, she was one of the strongest women he'd ever known, despite her strangeness. She made a lot of sense much of the time, and he enjoyed talking to her about things most women didn't want to think about at all.

But if Jackie was so strong, how could she be so crazy?

"Damn." While she'd told him her story about the blizzard, the ghost town, the fire, the portrait . . . Cole had actually caught himself *believing* her wild tale. He swallowed hard, the gooseflesh he'd experienced while she spoke returning with a vengeance.

A sense of dread suddenly swept through him, powerful and all-encompassing. He bolted upright, listening to the gentle breeze, the rustling of the aspen leaves, and . . .

Nothing.

Jackie should have returned by now. Had she gone to the cabin to check on Todd? No, he'd already done that, and she knew it. He rose and headed out into the stillness.

An eerie calm blanketed the clearing. Even the breeze had suddenly vanished, leaving him listening to nothing but the wild thunder of his own heart.

He pivoted toward the outhouse and started walking, quickening his pace as he grew closer, running by the time he skidded to a stop before the small structure. Clearing his throat, he lifted his hand, hesitated, then knocked. She'd probably laugh at his foolishness.

Nothing. He knocked louder, then softly called her name. Still nothing. Fear spiraled through him, and he opened the door, finding the small space empty.

He stood staring at the cabin, then looked toward the stable. Could she have fallen on her way to meet him? Maybe she was lying silent in the darkness. Frantic, he realized he needed light.

Cole ran to the cabin and slipped through the back door to check on Todd. The boy was sound asleep, curled on his side. Cole's heart skipped a beat, then raced out of control. He had to find Jackie for them both.

Quickly Cole climbed the ladder to make certain Jackie wasn't in the loft. Finding no evidence that she'd been there, he took the lamp with him and went through the front door. He searched the porch, the area directly in front of and all around the cabin, then covered the worn path between there and the stable.

Retracing his steps, he searched the outhouse again, then surveyed a wide area on both sides of the path between there and the paddock. Fear settled in his gut as he slipped into the stable again. Ruth nickered a greeting, but Cole found no indication that Jackie had been there.

She was gone.

Sick with worry and fear, Cole trudged back to the porch and sat there, placing the lamp at his side. Had she agreed to marry him merely to humor him so she could slip away in the night like a thief?

He remembered the way she'd felt in his arms, so alive, so giving, so passionate. That could not have been pretense. No woman was that talented an actress.

Except . . . maybe the legendary Lolita Belle.

His throat burned and his gut roiled. Clenching his fists, he rose, staring out at the mountains. Jackie wouldn't have wandered off alone at night. She wasn't *that* crazy.

Was she?

He held his breath. Should he go after her? She could be in trouble. Lost. Afraid.

But she left me.

She had told him to follow his dreams, and had even promised to share those dreams. Then simply walked out of his life?

"Think, Morrison. *Think.*"

Rubbing his temples, he thought back to that first day in Devil's Gulch, then to the day he'd kidnapped her from the artist's cabin. What had she said about the painting?

I thought then that I should go back with them and let the artist finish Lolita's painting.

Was she trying to find her way back to her imaginary time in the future? Was she *that* crazy?

Or that devious?

A sudden suspicion slithered through him, and his flesh turned icy cold. *The gold.* If she'd played him for a fool, then she would've taken Merriweather's gold.

No. She wouldn't have. She cared about him—had agreed to marry him. He remembered the way she treated Todd. Jackie couldn't have . . .

There's only one way to know for sure.

Carrying the lamp, he opened the cabin door and stepped inside. The golden light bathed the tiny cabin, and he went immediately to the loose stone in the hearth. He set the lantern on the mantel and worked the stone free with his fingers, then reached into the opening. His fingers touched the leather drawstring and he withdrew the pouch, testing its weight in his hand.

Relief coalesced into renewed worry. She hadn't taken the gold, but she was definitely gone. A woman out to deceive him would've found the gold first and taken it with her. That meant one of two things.

Either Jackie had become confused and wandered into the wilderness . . .

Or someone had dragged her away against her will.

The jarring motion of the horse jerked Jackie awake. Every muscle protested her slouched position, and she straightened, grappling for her bearings.

Where the hell was she?

Then she remembered and tried to call out Cole's name. Her captor had left the gag in place and she rearranged her tongue, but the effort was wasted. Smith had her bound and gagged and totally at his mercy.

Would Cole come after her? She squeezed her eyes shut, wondering if he would realize she'd been kidnapped. Again. The last thing she wanted was for him to think she'd left him by choice. Not after . . .

Bile rose in her throat, and for a moment she thought she might retch. That would finish her off quickly with this stupid rag stuffed in her mouth.

She breathed slowly through her nose. No, she wouldn't let this bastard win. Maybe she couldn't exact revenge from Blade personally for abandoning her and ripping her off, but she could fix his ancestor's butt.

And she would, too. Jackie was getting really sick of good-looking con artists doing her dirty. This victim scenario didn't suit her at all. In fact, it pissed her off royally.

The creep had tied her hands and was leading her horse down the pass. He sat tall and easy in the saddle of the horse in front of her, and she gave him what she hoped was the evil eye. If looks could kill . . .

A lone light in the sleepy town of Devil's Gulch flickered below. Remembering the first time she'd seen the town, a chill stole into the corners of her heart and soul. The Gold Mine Saloon had been her haven that day, saving her from certain death in a surprise blizzard. This time she dreaded passing through those doors.

Cole, please find me.

With nothing but moonlight guiding them, Smith

brought his horse to a stop and dismounted, then looped the reins over the branch of a young aspen. He wandered into the trees for a few minutes, then returned, buttoning his fly and scratching himself.

This guy looked like Blade's double, but he sure as hell didn't have his descendant's suave, sophisticated manner. Smith flashed her a grin that told her he knew she was watching, and maybe his bad manners had been deliberate.

And calculating?

He rubbed the back of his neck and stretched, then looked at her.

"Won't be much longer now," he said, rubbing his hands together. "I'll have enough gold to get all the way ba—Er, to California."

Back? Had he been about to say he wanted to get *back* to California? Blade was from California. *Clarke, you're imagining things.*

She tried to speak, and he looked at her as if surprised to see the gag. "I suppose we don't need that now." His voice sounded surprisingly gentle. He untied her hands and hauled her off the horse, all traces of gentleness nothing more than a fleeting memory.

Jackie's knees collapsed and her legs trembled. She remained on the ground, rubbing her wrists and waiting for her circulation to return.

Smith chuckled and she looked up at him, hating him.

His laughter died and he narrowed his eyes. "Don't even think about trying anything." He walked behind her and loosened the bandanna holding the rag in her mouth.

The offending gag fell away and she gasped for air, running her tongue along her cracked lips. "Water?"

she croaked, and he handed her a canteen. She took it, but didn't meet her captor's eyes, trying to think of some means of escape.

She took a long drink of tepid water, easing the burning sensation. Finally she passed it back to him and forced herself to stand. Facing the creep, she asked, "Why did you do this?"

Smith gave a quick shrug. "Gold."

"But why did you go to the cabin the other day if you planned to do this all along?"

His eyes twinkled and he rubbed his chin, then tapped his head with his index finger. "Pretty smart, huh?"

Jackie barely managed to suppress her laughter. "Gee, I guess I'm not as smart as you," she said, rotating her aching shoulders and making sure both arms still worked. "I don't get it."

"First of all, I had to make sure you were still there."

Who? Jackie or Lolita? "Ah, my disguise didn't work, huh?" She flashed him a grin, hoping to disarm the thug.

"Well, when I saw you at the Silver Spur, I wasn't sure you were really you. I could hardly believe it when Merriweather told me." Chuckling, he scratched his head and adjusted his hat. "Then I went back to Devil's Gulch and told old Goodfellow about the woman I'd seen—though I didn't tell him *where.* There aren't many women in these parts with hair that matches that particular description."

Was it Jackie's imagination, or was Rock's speech improving and his accent waning?

"Goodfellow offered me a fortune to bring you to him."

Good old Rupert. "How sweet of him." Jackie sighed and held her hands out to her sides. "So he offered the gold you told me about for my, uh, safe return. Is that it?"

"That's it."

"I still don't understand why you told me to give Cole—I mean, Morrison—that message."

Smith leaned closer and said, "See, *that's* the smart part."

"Uh, right." Jackie shook her head slowly, wondering how hard Rock's father had dropped him.

"Fooled you, huh?"

She gave a nervous laugh. "Yeah, I'd say *fool* is the right word for it."

"You still don't get it. Do you?"

A chill swept through her and she held her breath, waiting. "No, I don't get it."

"See, I figured you would hightail it down to claim Goodfellow's gold for yourself, so I waited and watched for you to start down the pass."

"But I didn't."

"So I grabbed you. Case closed."

Case closed? He didn't sound like a man of the nineteenth century now. "I guess you're smarter than you look then." She had to play along until she could be sure.

Smith straightened, practically preening his feathers. "You might be a little on the mouthy side, but I wouldn't mind having a little fun before we head to town." He waggled his eyebrows. "Know what I mean?"

Jackie's throat tightened and her belly revolted. "No, I'm afraid you're *way* too smart for me."

He moved closer and trailed his fingertip along the side of her neck to the top of her neckline. "You know, have a little fun."

Jackie swallowed the bile rising in her throat and

drew a deep breath. "No, we'd better not," she said, scanning her limited mental database of historical terms. "I've had the . . . the pox."

He threw his head back and roared. Obviously being overheard wasn't high on his list of worries now.

"Then I guess we'll go to town." He inclined his head toward her horse. "Saddle up."

She glanced over her shoulder. "I need to, uh . . ." She aimed a thumb over her shoulder.

He shook his head slowly. "No way. I'm not letting you out of my sight," he said. "Ma'am." He tipped his hat again and flashed a dazzling smile.

How many personalities did this guy have lurking behind his pretty face? *Just like Blade.* Jackie lifted her chin a notch and gathered her skirt into her hand. "Very well," she said with as much dignity as she could muster. "I hope the horse won't object when I pee my pants."

Smith chuckled and boosted her into the saddle. "The horse won't notice and neither will I." His smile held a warning. "You're the one who'll have to sit in it."

In that moment, Jackie realized the guy'd been playing dumb all along. *I'll bet his name isn't really Rock.* Then another thought made her look harder at his finely chiseled features, his glossy black hair, and his obsidian eyes.

Was he Blade? Had the dumb east Texan thing been another of Blade's cons? She had no idea how he could have gone back in time with her, but she intended to find out who he was once and for all.

He tied her hands to the saddle horn again, but left the gag off. At least that was progress. As he strolled toward his own horse and swung his leg over the beast's back, Jackie watched the way he moved.

Graceful—too graceful. Like Blade. But could Blade ride a horse? She scanned her memory, then remembered something about an uncle of Blade's who owned a dude ranch somewhere. Of course, that might have been a lie, too. Still . . .

A dull roar filled her ears as he led her horse down into town. She remained silent, studying the angle of his shoulders, the way he moved his head, everything about him.

She couldn't be sure, but her unease mutated until she realized she could probably never be happy knowing Blade might be running around loose in the same century. She *had* to know.

A plan formed in her mind, and she put things into perspective. She'd test him. That was it. But she knew better than to do it out here where there was no one to witness anything he chose to do to her. She'd wait until they were at the Gold Mine Saloon.

But what would she do if this Smith really was Blade? More importantly, what would *he* do to *her* if she discovered his identity?

She'd face that if and when it happened. Meanwhile, she had to face Goodfellow, Dottie, and the Brothers Grime again.

The streets of Devil's Gulch were deserted, but smoke rose from chimneys, and lights filled windows in the predawn hour. Soon the town would bustle with activity, as it had the morning she'd first met Cole.

Cole. Her heart squeezed, and she prayed he wouldn't assume she'd left him under her own power. Even though he hadn't said the words to her, she wished now that she'd told him she loved him.

Great-Aunt Pearl's oppression had a grip on her even here. No more. From now on, Jackie Clarke would let her feelings be known.

I love you, big guy. Believe that. Trust me, Cole. Trust me.

Cole combed the mountainside, left no boulder, no tree, nothing unsearched near the cabin. He returned to the cabin shortly after dawn, wanting to be there when Todd awoke. The boy realized immediately that something was terribly wrong.

Jackie was gone, and the miniature grown-up immediately seized control of Todd again. Cole saw it . . . and hated it.

No matter what it took, he'd find Jackie and bring her back. He loved her and wanted her, no matter who or what she was or had been. And his son needed her.

They barely touched their breakfast as Cole explained to his son that Miss Jackie was missing, and he needed to find her. A knock sounded at the door, and Cole tipped over the bench in his haste to answer it, but it wasn't Jackie.

Chief Byron stood framed in the open door wearing a frown. "I couldn't sleep," the old Indian said, stepping into the cabin and glancing around, then up the ladder. "She is gone."

"How did you know?"

"A dream."

Cole nodded, then glanced at his son. The boy looked so solemn. "I'm going to find her and bring her back, Todd."

The chief met and held Cole's gaze, a knowing look in his wise old eyes. "Yes," he said, then looked at Todd. "We will finish the book about the boy called Huck today. Then we will tell Woman with Fire in Her Hair—Miss Jackie—about it when she returns."

Todd brightened and nodded, but Cole saw the glitter of unshed tears in the boy's eyes.

Clenching his fist, Cole vowed to accomplish two things before the sun set today. He would find Jackie, and he would make the bastard who'd taken her pay.

Because he knew—knew it in his heart, his soul, and his gut—that she hadn't left here willingly. Someone had stolen her away. Just as he had not long ago.

But that had been fate. This was simply *wrong.*

And God help the bastard if he's harmed her in any way.

"Thank you, Chief," Cole said, struggling to keep his voice calm. "I'd appreciate it if you'd stay here, just in case she comes back before I find her."

"A herd of buffalo cannot move me from this place until I see her with these old eyes."

Cole squeezed the old man's shoulder as he righted the bench and took a seat across the table from Todd. The old man understood things no white man could possibly know. It was uncanny, and very welcome just now.

"I saw . . . marks on the earth," the chief said. "A struggle."

"Show me."

Cole followed the old Indian outside and saw the scuff marks it had been too dark for him to find earlier. "Somebody kidnapped her," he whispered, swallowing hard, then returning to the cabin with the chief.

Cole smashed his hat onto his head and strode toward the door, then hesitated. Gnashing his teeth, he retrieved his rifle and ammunition. He felt his son's gaze on him and met it.

"I'll be careful." He swallowed the lump in his throat and Todd flew into his arms. Cole rubbed the boy's shoulder and dragged in a shaky breath. "I promise."

Todd nodded against Cole's side. "Bring her home, Pa," the boy said.

Cole forcibly quelled his rising fear. Unable to speak, he nodded again, then wrenched open the door and stepped into the early morning light, closing the door behind him.

He glanced at the horizon, wondering which way to go. Common sense said he'd find her in one of two places—the Gold Mine Saloon in Devil's Gulch or the Silver Spur in Lost Creek.

But where should he look first?

Saddling Ruth, he weighed his options. Merriweather was expecting Cole to deliver Lolita. It stood to reason that Goodfellow would be turning the district topsy-turvy looking for her.

Cole led the mare into the sunlight and stroked her muzzle. Then he swung himself into the saddle and headed down the pass.

Toward Devil's Gulch.

After Smith pounded on the door for several minutes, the front door of the Gold Mine Saloon swung open and Jackie grimaced, waggling her fingers at Rupert and Dottie. "Hey, long time, no see."

They both surveyed her groggily, as the saloon wasn't due to open for hours yet. "What the hell?" Rupert finally asked, rubbing his eyes. He wore a silk robe tied at his waist, and Jackie strongly suspected the sawed-off, cocky runt wore nothing underneath.

Gag me.

Dottie looked as though she'd been up all night—entertaining Rupert, no doubt—without a hair out of place, and her fake beauty mark was glued on the opposite cheek from where Jackie'd first seen it. Jackie made a mental note to ask the buxom blonde about her migrating beauty mark.

"Well, I'll be damned," Rupert said, shoving the perpetually unlit cigar into the corner of his mouth.

Criminy, did the man sleep with that stupid cigar in his mouth? Suppressing a shudder, Jackie batted her lashes and forced a smile. "Top o' the mornin' to ye, Mr. Goodfellow."

"It's the middle of the damned night," he said, holding the lamp higher and staring at Jackie as he removed his cigar. "So you found her." He turned his attention to Smith, though the cigar still pointed at Jackie.

"Yep," Smith said.

Every time Jackie glanced at her captor, he looked more like Blade. *Damn.* She ran her fingers through her tangled hair and gulped.

It didn't change Smith's appearance one bit.

Rupert grinned, sending Jackie to new and dangerous levels of nausea. "Well, well, well, so the famous Lolita has returned, but still without all her attributes, I see." He heaved a mournful sigh.

Jackie shrugged, deciding to play along. For now.

"Dottie, show her to her room."

Jackie arched an eyebrow in the blonde's general direction. "I *know* the way."

Dottie yawned.

"Very well, tell Zeb to guard her door." Rupert shoved the cigar back into his mouth. "With his miserable little *life.*"

Jackie suspected the lowly Zeb was more honorable

than the high and mighty Rupert P. Goodfellow. And neither of them could hold a candle to Cole Morrison. She closed her eyes, praying again that he would believe in her enough to search.

She headed toward the stairs—those same stairs she'd been afraid to ascend in her time. No, she decided, *now* was her time. *Get used to it, Clarke.* That other life was a distant memory.

She glanced back over her shoulder, her hand on the banister. Except for Blade. Pausing, she met his gaze, and a slow, insidious smile spread across his handsome face.

Dammit, he is *Blade. Isn't he?*

Her flesh turned clammy as she stood staring at him, and listening to the exchange between Smith and Goodfellow.

"I'll take that gold now and be on my way," Smith said, no longer looking at Jackie.

"Let's be civilized about this," the weasely saloon owner said. "Dottie will show you to a room and we'll do business at a decent hour."

"Right now's decent enough for me." Smith hooked his thumb through a belt loop and cocked his hip at an angle.

Just like Blade.

Damn. Jackie just wanted him to go away and leave her alone. Getting revenge didn't even matter anymore. Why the hell had he followed her? She held her breath, reminding herself how ridiculous she was being. First of all, she had no way of knowing for certain that this guy was really Blade.

She looked again and he met her gaze. She narrowed her eyes, trying to read his mind, wondering, needing confirmation.

He winked.

Oh, God. All right, he was Blade and he obviously wanted to rub it in. Her belly burned and her heart slammed into it—not a good feeling by any stretch.

"Changed my mind, Rupert, old boy," Smith said. "I'll take that room." He stared at Jackie, who still stood on the stairs. "Put it *real* close to Lolita's."

"In your dreams, slimeball," she said, climbing the stairs to the hideous green velvet room and slamming the door.

Once inside, she leaned against the heavy door, willing her heartbeat to slow and her mind to function clearly. If she ever needed to use her head, it was now.

"All right, Clarke," she whispered, turning up the wick on the lamp, then pacing the room. "Think."

Someone tapped on the door. "I'll be right across the hall if you change your mind," Blade called through the door, chuckling.

She held her breath until she heard him walk away and close the door to his own room. If only she had a key for the lock. She'd never understand how she could've let that bastard touch her in the first place.

All she wanted now was Cole.

Swallowing the lump in her throat, she caught a glimpse of herself in the gilded mirror occupying most of the opposite wall and walked slowly toward it. "Clarke, you look like hell."

But there was something else in her reflection that drew her. A clue. An idea. An inkling.

What the hell was it?

She whirled around and grabbed the lamp, placed it on the dressing table, then leaned forward to stare at her shocking reflection. Her sunburned nose was peeling, new freckles had appeared across her cheeks, and her lips were chapped.

"Lovely." Grimacing, she lifted a hand to the tangled mass of red curls.

And froze.

A wicked cackle rose from her diaphragm, and she rushed to the wardrobe in the corner. She threw it open and selected the most demure gown in the Lolita collection and tossed it on the bed. A few moments later she opened the door, and a dozing Zeb fell into the room.

"What? Huh?" He scrambled to his feet, a dazed expression on his wrinkled face. "Miss Lolita."

Jackie flashed him what she hoped was a dazzling smile and touched his arm. He blushed. *Perfect.* "Zeb, how nice to see you again."

"It is?" Nonplused, he backed toward the open door. "I'll just get back to my post now, Miss Lolita. Ma'am."

"Don't be in such a hurry, Zeb," she said, touching his arm again. "I need a little favor."

His Adam's apple bobbed up and down the length of his skinny neck. "A . . . a favor?"

"Yes, dear." She gave a mournful sigh. "I want you to fetch me a nice tub of hot water and . . . " She leaned close and whispered in his ear.

"N-now?" he croaked.

"Now, Zeb." She smiled again and he blushed. "Right now."

"B-but I ain't supposed to leave my post." His eyes jerked back and forth between her and the door. "Mr. Goodfellow will cut off my whiskey for sure."

Ah, poor Zeb. What he needs is a good alcohol-treatment program.

"Lock me in, Zeb," she said, and his eyes widened. "I won't mind. Really. I just want a nice, warm bath soooo bad. But bring me those other items first, please?" She smiled and he looked as if he might croak. That would be damned inconvenient.

"Sure thing, Miss Lolita." He bobbed his head and backed out the door, pulling it shut behind him.

Jackie laughed quietly to herself, then went to the door and pressed her ear against it. After a few minutes, she twisted the knob and it gave easily. The fool had forgotten to lock it.

Fine, she'd get her answers first. Slipping out the door, she crossed the hall to the room they'd given Blade and turned the knob without knocking. A brunette let out a shriek and pulled the sheet over her head.

"You can't keep your wick dry in any century," Jackie goaded, closing the door behind her. The girl in Blade's bed couldn't be a day over sixteen. "Jail bait, Blade? Tsk, tsk."

He chuckled and shrugged, reaching for the whiskey bottle on his nightstand. "You remembered how good it was between us and came back for more, babe?"

"Only in your wettest dreams." She folded her arms and leaned against the door. He hadn't denied his identity. Well, at least now she knew. "I just want to know one more thing, Blade."

"What?"

"How the hell did you get here?"

He sat up and the sheet slipped down, revealing his tattoos and rippling muscles. The guy was still a looker, but she'd take Cole over fifty Blades.

"That piece of shit you call a car died, and I got lost in that frigging blizzard," he said, shaking his head. "I sneaked in the back door of this place." He looked around and snorted. "At least I think it was this place, and I saw you sitting there reading. It was warm and dry, so I hid behind the bar, figuring I'd, uh, surprise you in the morning. Next thing I knew, the place was on fire."

A shudder of remembrance swept through Jackie and she swallowed. "How'd you get here? I don't understand."

"When you disappeared in that painting, I dove in after you. It's fate, babe."

She wasn't crazy after all, and that painting really was a time portal. "So you woke up here, too?"

He nodded.

"In the gutter where you belong, I hope."

"In the kitchen, but I slipped out before anybody saw me." He chuckled and the brunette peered over the edge of the sheet. "This won't take much longer, sweetcakes." He turned his attention back to Jackie. "So . . . you going to help me spend Goodfellow's gold, babe?"

Jackie shook her head and gripped the doorknob. She'd heard enough. "Oh, I wouldn't spend what you don't have yet, if I were you. And—"

"Oh, I'll have it, and I'll enjoy every penny." He took a drink from his whiskey bottle, his dark eyes glittering as he swallowed. "And what?"

"I never want to see your sleazy ass again in any time or place." Ignoring his menacing chuckle, she slipped out the door and returned to her room.

She walked slowly to the mirror again, staring at her reflection. Her gray eyes snapped and her nostrils flared. A sense of power flowed through her, confirming that she was doing the right thing. She hoped Cole would agree.

With a longing sigh, she squeezed her eyes shut, picturing Cole as he'd looked during their picnic at the waterfall. And he'd been so patient and gentle while she'd told her story of time travel. Only a man who really loved a woman would've listened to every crazy word, as he had.

Her belly tightened with longing, and her heart swelled with love. She loved him so much. With renewed determination, she opened her eyes and gave herself an emphatic nod.

"Ready or not, world."

Chapter Seventeen

Cole rode into Devil's Gulch hours before the Gold Mine Saloon would open its doors. He tied Ruth to the hitching post and pounded on the double doors until they swung open with a squeak of protest.

"We ain't open yet," a woman's husky voice called. "Come back later."

Cole wedged his boot in the door as she tried to close it. "I'm looking for someone," he said, hoping he wouldn't need the rifle he held close against his leg, where it wouldn't be easily noticed. But he *would* use it if he had to.

The door opened a little farther and he saw Miss Dottie's big blond hair. "Mornin', ma'am." He tipped his hat. "I'm looking for . . . " He hesitated, then realized they would know her by only one name. "I'm looking for Lolita Belle."

"Why?" The woman sounded suspicious, but the

door creaked open even farther. "What do you want with that troublemaker?"

Cole shrugged and flashed Miss Dottie what he hoped was a charming smile, searching for the words that would win his entrance. "She, uh, took something that belongs to me, ma'am."

His heart.

"Oh?" Miss Dottie swung the door completely open and her eyes widened as they looked him over from head to toe, then back again. "You're Cole Morrison, ain't you?" She wore only a bright red robe tied at her waist, her voluptuous bosom spilling out and her legs bare.

"Yes, ma'am, I'm Cole Morrison, and I really need to see Miss Lolita." He smiled again.

Dottie pursed her lips and sneered, but stepped aside to allow Cole to enter. He didn't care who he had to charm or who he had to anger, as long as it led him to Jackie. At least now he knew she was here.

"Thank you," he said as Dottie closed and locked the door behind him. "Where—"

"Morrison, what in blazes are you doing here at this godforsaken hour?" Goodfellow grumbled from the bottom of the stairs.

"Morning, Goodfellow." Cole removed his hat and dropped it on a nearby table. The man's name seemed wrong. It should've been "Badfellow."

"Morning? The sun's barely up. What the hell do you want anyway?" Goodfellow rubbed his beady eyes and rolled his unlit cigar from one side of his mouth to the other. "Well?"

"I came to see Miss Lolita." Cole straightened, keeping the rifle close to his body. "And I aim to see her."

The saloon owner narrowed his eyes, then shifted

his gaze to Dottie. "Do you know anything about this?"

The woman shrugged and said, "Says Lolita took somethin' of his."

Goodfellow turned his gaze on Cole again. "I reckon that means you're the one who took her to Merriweather." The little man nodded as he spoke. "Makes sense, I suppose. Merriweather hired you for the job, because no one would ever expect it. Do you realize this makes you an outlaw, Morrison?"

Cole didn't bother to respond. The man spoke the truth, though he knew Jackie would never accuse him of kidnapping her now. "I came to see her." He swung the rifle up in front of him and leveled it toward Goodfellow's gut. "Show me to her room."

"Ah, hell. I know you aren't gonna use that thing, so don't bother pretending."

"Don't test me." Cole kept his voice low, his eyes hooded. "I'm a man on a mission, Goodfellow. Don't stand in my way."

Goodfellow chewed furiously on his unlit cigar, his eyes finally reflecting his comprehension that Cole meant business. "I swear, that woman is more trouble than she's worth," the smaller man muttered.

"That's what I been tryin' to tell you, Rupert, but—"

"Shut up, Dottie." Goodfellow turned and stomped up the stairs. "Come along, Morrison, but I'm locking you in with her."

Locked in with Jackie? Cole could think of worse fates, but right now rescuing her was uppermost on his mind. He lowered the rifle to his side again and started up the stairs.

"Goodfellow, I'll take my gold now," a male voice said from the top of the stairs.

Cole swung the rifle around again, and the newcomer's eyes widened in obvious surprise. The pretty boy wasn't even wearing a gun.

"Ah, hell," Goodfellow muttered, pivoting to face Cole again, finding himself looking down the barrel of a rifle. "Hell."

"I believe we were on our way to Miss Lolita's room?" Cole said, keeping one eye on Goodfellow and the other on the pretty boy.

The stranger chuckled. "You blew it, pal," the man said. "Now I get the gold."

"You're the one," Cole said, adjusting his aim. "*You* kidnapped Jackie."

"Who the hell's Jackie?" Goodfellow asked, rolling his eyes.

"I am."

Cole looked toward the familiar voice at the top of the stairs and his breath froze. Uncertainty stormed through him, but quieted as soon as he met her gaze. Her beautiful gray eyes didn't lie.

Assured it was her and that she was safe, he looked at her hair again. She'd taken the scissors to it, leaving what appeared to be less than an inch of dark brown hair all over her head. No trace of red remained.

"What the hell . . . ?" Rupert's cigar hung limply from one corner of his mouth. "You aren't Lolita Belle."

"Bingo, Einstein," Jackie said. "Like I tried to tell you before."

She aimed her gaze at the red-faced stranger. "So much for that gold." She gave a dramatic sigh. "Crime doesn't pay . . . Smith."

Cole spared Goodfellow only the briefest glance, then turned his attention back to the stranger who'd stolen Jackie. "Smith? Who the hell are you?"

One corner of the man's mouth lifted. He looked

back over his shoulder at Jackie, then shrugged and met Cole's gaze. "Rock. Rock Smith."

"Rock, my ass," Cole said, tightening his grip on the rifle. It didn't matter. He didn't give a damn who the stranger was, as long as he let them be. "You listen good, *Rock*. You ever go near the woman I'm going to marry again, and I'll turn you inside out."

Cole started up the stairs toward the stranger, and Goodfellow wisely slithered down and out of their way. "Did you understand what I said, pretty boy?"

Jackie laughed, but Cole didn't dare risk looking away just now. "*Did* you understand me?" he repeated.

The man narrowed his gaze menacingly, but he nodded once. "Roger, Houston. I copy."

Cole kept his gaze pinned on the stranger. "My name isn't Roger or Houston." He inclined his head toward the door. "Get the devil out of here before I change my mind and shoot your sorry ass."

"Yes, go." Jackie's voice surprised them all, and the pretty boy seemed downright perturbed when she started down the stairs toward them. She stopped two steps above the stranger and glowered at him.

Cole saw something in her expression as she stared at the man. She definitely knew him, but the hatred in her eyes assured Cole she hadn't left willingly with the bastard.

Jackie placed both fists on her hips, and Cole recognized the look on her face. Smith was in for it, and Jackie Clarke was just the woman to give him an earful he wouldn't forget.

An insistent pounding commenced on the front door, and Dottie threw it open with a huff. "You'd think it was noon already," she grumbled.

Two burly men dressed in fancy suits with brocade vests shoved their way through, and a third one held the door open for a woman. She swept into the saloon wearing an expensive-looking green traveling suit with a huge feather in her hat. Her face was powdered and her lips painted. Her flaming red hair hung in curls to her shoulders, and her breasts were so large she looked as if she might topple forward from their weight.

Every person in the room stared in shock at the newcomers. Every person except one. Rock Smith—or whoever he was—leaped over the banister and bolted for the door.

Cole aimed his rifle after the coward, but the red-headed woman gave a bored sigh and shook her head as she peeled off her gloves. "Put that thing away, gorgeous," she said in a voice like silk. "I didn't travel all the way up here to this hovel to get myself shot."

"Lolita," Jackie whispered from directly behind Cole.

He turned and caught her as she fainted.

Jackie heard voices and struggled to open her eyes. Finally she blinked several times and a colorful blur greeted her. "Where am I?" she whispered, trying to rise.

"Stay," Cole said gently, then a cool cloth touched her forehead. "How do you feel?"

"Like I got hit by a Mack truck." Jackie blinked several more times and he finally came into focus. "Where are we?"

"Goodfellow put you in a room upstairs. I think he feels guilty. And he damn well should. I sure do." Cole stroked her hair. "This'll take some getting used to, but it's an improvement."

Jackie gave him a weak smile. "It'll grow, but this

is the real me, Cole." She reached up and cradled his cheek in her palm. "I'm so happy to see you. I was afraid. . . ."

"Don't be afraid." He kissed her palm, then bent to press his lips to hers. "I promised to take care of you. Remember?"

Jackie nodded, then asked, "Where's Todd?"

"Chief Byron is with him, but I asked the sheriff to bring them both to town."

Jackie couldn't quite picture Chief Byron in town. "Why?"

"For our wedding."

She smiled, then remembered bits and pieces of what had happened. "Was that really Lolita Belle?"

"In the flesh," Cole said, chuckling. "And I'd say she's got more than her fair share of that."

"And then some." Jackie remembered the portrait and her initial reaction to the woman's Rubenesque figure. "Now you see why it was so ridiculous for everybody to think I was her."

Cole chuckled again, still stroking her hair. "I don't care who you are or how you got here, Jackie," he said, his voice low and rough at the same time, rumbling around in her belly and spiking straight to her bone marrow. "I just thank God you're here with me now, and that you're safe."

She bit her lower lip and a tear rolled unheeded down her cheek and the side of her neck. "Look at me." She laughed and cried simultaneously. "Great-Aunt Pearl can't stop me now."

Cole shook his head, obviously stymied by her words, but he gave her an indulgent smile anyway. "I want us to get married today, if you're feeling up to it."

"Are you . . . sure, Cole?" She grabbed his hand

and held it very tight. "I won't . . . won't hold you to it if you've changed your mind."

"Never." He kissed her again, the tenderness of it reaching into her soul and surrounding her aching heart. "We're getting married."

Jackie trembled and sighed when their lips parted. "I want that," she said. "Very much."

"Good, then it's settled."

She pushed herself up to a sitting position. "I've never fainted before in my life."

"Probably the shock of seeing Lolita." He placed an arm around her shoulders and slid onto the bed beside her.

"You really think Goodfellow's feeling guilty about mistreating me?" She chewed her lower lip. "And you're determined to return Merriweather's gold. Right?"

He gave her a solemn nod. "You'll be marrying a poor man, Jackie." He sighed. "Does that bother you?"

"We're rich in every way that matters."

He smiled down at her. "I was hoping you'd feel that way."

"I do." She kissed his cheek and sighed. "Cole, that . . . that man," she said, her voice sounding odd even to her ears. "I have to tell you about him."

Cole's nostrils flared, and she felt him tense at her side. "Don't be angry," she said. "He's from the future, too . . . and he stole something of mine."

Cole stared at her for several moments, then nodded. "I'll help you find him and get it back, but we're getting married first."

"I definitely *don't* want to find him."

"Good, because I'm not letting you out of my sight again."

"Cole, I—"

A knock sounded at the door, and Jackie's heart leaped into her throat. "Easy, now," Cole said, rising. "I'll get it."

He opened the door, and Dottie stuck her head around the corner. "Mind if I come in?" she asked.

Suspicious, Jackie scooted back to lean against the headboard. This definitely wasn't the green velvet room, but that was always meant for the real Lolita. "Sure, come on in," she said.

Dottie had a pair of leather pouches with her and wore an expression of total bewilderment. She shut the door behind her and approached the bed. "That Rock Smith left these in his room," she said, placing the leather pouches on the bed at Jackie's feet. "I don't read very well, but you said your name's Jackie. Right?"

"That's right. Jacqueline, actually." She glanced down at the pouches. "Why?"

"I went through these after he left," Dottie continued, her cheeks reddening. "I figured he owed us for the night's stay and the trouble he caused."

"Saddlebags. What did you find?" Cole asked, reaching for them.

"Like I said, I don't read too good, but I think Jackie's name is on some of the things in there." Dottie inclined her head toward the saddlebags.

Cole passed them to Jackie. "You'd better take a look."

"Thank you, Dottie." Jackie smiled at the woman, a dull roar beginning in her head.

"There ain't nothing valuable in there anyhow." Dottie turned and went to the door, pausing with her hand on the doorknob. "I gotta tell you, the real

Lolita's one hell of a lot more trouble than you ever was."

Jackie laughed. "How's that, Dottie?"

The buxom blonde rolled her eyes at the ceiling. "She's been givin' that poor artist hell all mornin' over her portrait, makin' him redo things he already painted. And Rupert ain't helpin' much, insistin' it be done before tonight."

Jackie held her breath. The roar between her ears intensified, and Cole reached down and put his hand on her shoulder.

"I'm sending a breakfast up for you two that's fit for kings and queens—or Lolita Belle." Dottie made a face. "Rupert had real maple syrup sent in for Lolita, but after seein' her for myself"—Dottie shook her head and sighed—"I don't reckon she needs it."

Cole and Jackie both laughed quietly as the woman opened the door and Zeb rolled in a cart bearing silver trays and steaming coffee.

They both thanked Dottie and Zeb; then Jackie and Cole were alone again. Jackie looked down at the saddlebags. "Will you . . . do this for me, please?" Her hands were shaking so badly she didn't trust herself.

"Sure." Cole hugged her, then sat beside her and opened the pouches. He pulled out a burgundy leather wallet. A woman's wallet.

Hers.

"Oh, my God." Her voice was barely more than a strangled whisper as she reached for the item and opened the snap. "It's mine. These are mine. It must've been in his pocket when . . . " She withdrew credit cards, her driver's license, frequent-flier cards, phone cards. . . . The irony of it all washed over her and she laughed, then cried again.

Cole held her and rubbed her back as she wept, twenty-three years' worth of tears soaking his shirt before she finally regained her composure. "I . . . I'm sorry."

"No, don't be sorry." He picked up her driver's license. "This says 1967. You . . . were telling the truth."

"Yes, Cole. The truth."

He drew a shaky breath and looked at the picture. "This is you."

"Yes, with my hair grown out." She cleared her throat. "Cole, now do you believe me about . . . where and when I'm from?"

He stared at her license for several moments, then met her gaze. "Your word and this are proof enough. Will you ever forgive me for not believing you?"

"Don't take advantage of this, big guy," she said, "but I'd probably forgive you anything."

Drawing a ragged breath, he cupped her cheek. "When you were born doesn't make a bit of difference, because we're still getting married." He tossed the license onto the bed and pulled her against him. "I don't care if you were born in 1967 or 1867, as long as you're right here, right now, with me."

A sob caught in her throat. "You're going to make me start b-blubbering again."

He shook his head slowly. "If you need to cry, you cry. If you need to laugh, you laugh. If you need to scream, you scream." Pulling slightly away, he stared down into her eyes. "I mean it, Jackie Clarke. You be whoever and whatever you are, because that's the woman I love."

She held her breath, staring into his beautiful blue eyes. "Cole, I . . . I never thought you'd say those words." Smiling, she touched her fingertips to his lips. "I love you, too. More than anything."

"Enough to be happy, married to a struggling miner?"

She nodded. "But I still insist we follow your dream and go to Oregon."

The joy drained from his face, and her heart broke. "We'll try," he said dismally.

"Oh, Cole, don't." She rested her cheek on his shoulder and held him. "Let's just be happy today."

"Our wedding day."

"Yes, our wedding day." The words sent a shiver of anticipation through her, and she lifted her head from Cole's shoulder to stare at the saddlebags. "I'd like to put all this behind us, Cole. I don't want to stay another night in this saloon."

"Thank heavens." He chuckled. "But let's eat Goodfellow's food before we go. I figure he owes you."

"That he does. I . . . I'm afraid of this place, Cole. I'm afraid of that portrait. It might . . . "

He turned back to her and pulled her against him. "Don't be. I'll take care of you. I promise."

"I know, and I love you for that, but I'm still afraid."

"Let's get some food in your belly and see if that makes you feel any better."

"All right." She watched Cole rise and roll the loaded cart closer to the bed. "Mmm, the coffee smells wonderful."

He poured them each a cup and she added cream to hers, sniffing appreciatively before she tasted it. "That's the one thing you don't do well," she said.

"Make coffee?" Cole grinned, spooning food onto a plate. "Ah, here's that maple syrup." He poured some over the pancakes on her plate and passed it to her.

Jackie took a bite of pancake dripping with syrup. "Oh, that's sinful." She took another forkful and savored the richness. "It's warm, too."

"Mmm." Cole ate in silence for several minutes, then set his plate aside. He rose and crossed the room, turning the key in the lock. When he faced her again, a wicked gleam flashed in his beautiful blue eyes.

And Jackie knew exactly what he was thinking. She set her plate on the cart, her mind definitely not on food now.

"I can think of something that tastes a whole lot sweeter than that syrup." Cole started unbuttoning his shirt as he crossed the room. By the time he reached her, Jackie had stripped, throwing her clothes onto the floor.

"You look good enough to eat, woman," he said, kicking off his boots and shedding his jeans. His erection was huge and filled with promise.

Jackie licked her lips, waiting for him. He put his knee on the bed. She smiled, shoving the saddlebags to the foot of the bed and dragging Cole down to lie beside her.

"None of that other stuff matters anymore." His voice was low and intense, sending her libido into overdrive.

"Show me what does matter," she invited.

"With pleasure."

He covered her mouth with his, branding her with his warmth, his possession, his promise. Jackie arched against him, savoring the feel and taste of this man she loved.

He broke the kiss and reached for something. A moment later, something warm trickled across her bare breasts. "Have mercy," she muttered as he licked syrup from her breasts, drawing her nipples deeply into his mouth.

When he shifted his weight, she seized the opportunity and rolled on top of him, shoving him back onto the mattress. She straddled him, lowering herself onto his erection. He completed her, filled a painful emptiness she hadn't recognized until she found him.

He reached for the pitcher, and his eyes darkened to cobalt as he drizzled more syrup across her breasts and pulled her toward the warmth of his mouth.

She came almost immediately with him buried deep inside her and his incredible mouth kissing and licking her breasts. But he was still hard and relentless inside her, and she soared toward orgasm again and again. He thrust himself upward and reached toward the cart again.

"Pass the syrup," she purred.

Chapter Eighteen

They spent most of the day making love while they waited for Chief Byron and Todd to reach town for the wedding. Cole sent word to the preacher that his services would be needed that evening, then turned all his efforts toward making sure Jackie was happy and untroubled on their wedding day.

As for himself, he was happier than he'd ever believed possible. This unusual, short-haired woman from another time and place made him whole again. She filled his heart and soul and made him laugh and smile. Todd adored her. The only thing that could make their new life any more perfect would have been planning their move to Oregon together, too.

His dream.

But he refused to allow that single failure to spoil this day with the woman he loved. Toward evening they bathed, and Dottie sent up new clothes for them both with a note saying it was her wedding present. Of course, Cole realized Goodfellow had unknowingly paid for his suit and Jackie's pretty pink dress.

With Smith's saddlebags in tow, Cole escorted Jackie down to Goodfellow's office, wondering why she insisted on talking to the unscrupulous little man before they left. They had to pass through the main part of the saloon to get there, and the place was packed. A sign sat on an easel near the door, announcing that Lolita Belle's opening performance would be held tonight.

Jackie froze partway through the room, clutching Cole's hand in a death grip. He glanced down at her, and her face was ghostly pale. "Jackie?" Leaning down, he repeated her name.

"There." She pointed toward the bar with a trembling finger. "There."

Cole looked and immediately saw the source of her terror: Lolita's portrait. The buxom beauty was depicted almost completely naked, and a small sign on the corner of the frame said *Wet Paint!*

"It can't hurt you now," Cole said. "I'm here."

She nodded and he urged her through to Goodfellow's office, and away from Lolita's portrait. The story she'd told him had described the portrait in explicit detail, right down to the frame. She'd even known where it would hang.

Yes, he had to believe Jackie's tale of time travel. She might have died in that fire if not for the portrait. Whatever miracle had brought her here to him, he was eternally grateful for it.

He glanced down at her short, dark hair. No one would ever mistake her for Lolita Belle again. Surprising relief eased through him. Jackie was all his, but Lolita would always belong to her public.

They paused outside the ornately carved mahogany door to Goodfellow's office, and Jackie squared her shoulders.

"I sure wish I knew what you had on your mind," he said, just as she knocked.

"Come in," Goodfellow called, and Jackie opened the door, pulling Cole in behind her. Dottie Elam stood beside her employer, who sat behind his fancy desk.

"Ah, I see you've recovered," Goodfellow said, rising. "I must say, it's still quite a shock to see your hair . . . this way."

Jackie clasped her hands in front of her and lifted her chin. "Mr. Goodfellow, I've come to collect what you owe me."

Goodfellow chomped down on his cigar. "What I *owe* you? For what?" he asked through clenched teeth.

"My time *and* mistreatment." She drew a deep breath and waited.

Cole didn't give a damn about Goodfellow's money, but he sure admired Jackie's backbone. He shook his head and rubbed his chin, risking a glance at Miss Dottie. The woman's lips twitched and she winked.

Goodfellow glowered at Cole. "I understand you're planning to marry this woman, Morrison?"

"That's a fact." Cole took Jackie's arm and looped it through his.

"Then it's your responsibility to control her behavior." Goodfellow chuckled, a low, cynical sound that permeated the small, stuffy room. "I gave you room and board. I believe that's adequate, Miss . . . ?"

"Clarke." Jackie inclined her head. "I'm willing to deduct the cost of room and board, Mr. Goodfellow, but the fact remains that you held me against my will upon my unfortunate arrival."

"But so did Morrison."

Jackie shook her head slowly. "I went willingly with Cole."

Goodfellow's face darkened. "But—"

"Furthermore, you forced me to pose for that ghastly portrait, even after I told you repeatedly that I was not Lolita Belle."

"Well, I . . . " Goodfellow's face turned as red as the plush carpeting at their feet. "But . . . "

"I'm afraid she's got you there." Cole fell silent, sensing that Jackie wanted—and needed—to handle this on her own. He loved her all the more for her courage.

"And you hired that no-account Smith fella to kidnap her, too," Miss Dottie added, earning a scowl from Goodfellow.

"That's a fact, too," Cole said, chuckling.

"According to my calculations, and based on current market value, you owe me a minimum of three hundred dollars, Mr. Goodfellow." Jackie batted her lashes.

Goodfellow's mouth gaped open and his cigar landed on his desk, rolling until it came to a stop against a fancy gold box. The man moved his mouth as if he intended to speak, but no intelligible sounds emerged.

"In gold," Jackie added.

Miss Dottie threw her head back and cackled.

"Remember yourself, Dottie," Goodfellow said, turning his glare back to Jackie. "Why should I bow to your demands, Miss Clarke?"

Jackie gave Goodfellow the nastiest smile she could summon. "Because I could tell the sheriff about your hiring Smith to kidnap me." She looked around the room. "There are witnesses in here who'll testify to what they heard Smith say about that."

"Unless you're willing to send Morrison here to jail with me, I don't think the sheriff will listen." Goodfellow folded his arms across his potbelly, a smug grin on his ugly face.

"I'm afraid you leave me no choice, Mr. Goodfellow," Jackie said with a sigh, then drew a deep breath and sang a song about some place over the rainbow.

"Stop." Goodfellow put his hands over his ears.

Jackie paused to draw another deep breath and heard Cole's groan. She shot him an apologetic smile, then forged ahead with another verse.

"All right. All right." Goodfellow held up his hands in surrender. "I'll do it. Anything to stop your caterwauling."

"Gee, and here you were going to pay me to sing for your customers." Jackie batted her lashes as Goodfellow spun around and stepped behind a screen.

"That's where he keeps his safe," Miss Dottie whispered.

Cole wanted to laugh, but he chewed the inside of his mouth instead. He'd underestimated Dottie Elam.

A few minutes later, Goodfellow returned with a pouch of gold, which he tossed unceremoniously onto the desk. "That should be about three hundred dollars," he said, glowering at Jackie. "In gold."

Cole reached down and peered into the bag, tested its weight, then handed it to Jackie. "I'd say that's about right," he said, continually amazed by the woman he was about to marry.

"Thank you, Mr. Goodfellow," Jackie said. "I believe that concludes our business."

"Thank God for that." The man slumped into his chair as Jackie and Cole turned to leave.

Jackie paused at the door and turned back. "One more thing."

"Oh, how fortuitous," Goodfellow said, rolling his eyes. "I can hardly wait. Don't keep us in suspense any longer, Miss Clarke."

"If you don't marry Dottie Elam, you're an even bigger fool than I thought."

With that, Jackie swung open the door and left the room. Cole paused long enough to wink at a grinning Dottie and shake his head at Goodfellow.

When they passed through the front room again, Chief Byron and Todd were waiting near the door. Cole and Jackie hurried toward them, and Jackie hugged them both.

"You're both invited to a wedding," Cole said, grinning at his son's wide eyes and open mouth.

Todd hugged Jackie again, then his pa. "I take it this means you approve," Cole said, winking at Chief Byron.

"I told you so," the old Indian said with a nod, enduring Jackie's second hug with admirable dignity and a toothless grin.

"I'd like you to give away the bride," Jackie said to Chief Byron. "Would you do that for me?"

"I'm not familiar with this white custom, but I'm willing to learn," the chief said.

"Well, let's get over to the church," Cole said, more eager than ever to put some distance between Jackie and that portrait. "The preacher's expecting us, and it isn't fitting for Todd to be here."

He took Jackie's arm, and the four of them turned to leave just as music sounded and a cheer erupted from the miners. Jackie turned slowly toward the stage.

A woman started singing as the curtain rose, and they all stared. Dressed in silk and feathers, Lolita Belle belted a ballad that had every man in the place mesmerized. Except for her voice and the piano, the place was dead silent.

"So *that's* what all the fuss was about," Cole whispered. "I reckon she is talented."

"Yes," Jackie whispered, taking a step toward the bar as if in a trance.

"Are you . . . all right?" Cole stared at her. Dear God, she wouldn't leave now. Would she?

Jackie's eyes were wide and her lips set in a thin line. "Look," she whispered, pointing again.

Lolita's portrait glowed with an orange light, almost like flames. The same flames that had brought Jackie back in time?

Jackie knew, somehow, that if she touched the portrait, she could return to her own time and that the fire would be gone. She knew it with a certainty that stunned her. This was her moment of reckoning.

Modern plumbing, movies, fast food, women's rights, her salon, Great-Aunt Pearl . . . Compared to love, none of that mattered.

She'd made her choice. Giving Cole's arm a squeeze, she turned to leave the Gold Mine Saloon with him one last time. She never wanted to see the place or Lolita's portrait again. But before they reached the door, it swung open and a masked man strolled through, gun drawn.

Cole pulled Jackie back into the shadows along with Chief Byron and Todd. The masked man's movements were smooth and graceful, his dark eyes familiar.

Blade.

His gaze met hers and she shook her head. With a shrug, he moved toward the stage and leaped onto it. A gasp rippled through the crowd, and Lolita stopped singing. Jackie sure hoped he didn't have any bullets in that gun, because she had a hunch he didn't know how to use it.

Blade grabbed the buxom singer around the waist and threw her over his shoulder, staggering beneath her substantial weight. Jackie knew what would happen next.

"It's in the script," she whispered. "But I have to guess about the ending. And we know she won't be harmed, because she's too valuable to Merriweather and Goodfellow. Right?"

"I reckon," Cole said, rubbing his chin thoughtfully.

"We wouldn't want to interfere with history. Would we?" She smiled. "Maybe Lolita will fall in love with her kidnapper—just like I did—and they'll live happily ever after."

Cole chuckled. "That's nice, but I only care about us living happily ever after."

"Bank on it, big guy." Jackie looped her arm through his as soon as Blade and Lolita were gone. "Let's go to church."

The patrons in the saloon booed and shouted in outrage. Goodfellow climbed onto the stage and offered a reward for Lolita Belle's safe return. Several men raced after Blade and Lolita with dollar signs in their eyes.

Jackie laughed. "I'm really free now," she said.

"Only until you say 'I do.' "

"I can hardly wait."

They walked down the street of Devil's Gulch, ignoring the crazed men galloping through town after Lolita. None of it mattered now. Only the man on her arm and her new family mattered. "Where's that church?"

"Right there." Cole pointed to a small building constructed of logs and stone right at the edge of town. He held the door open and they all stepped inside.

"I'll fetch the preacher from the parsonage next door," Cole said. "You wait here."

"Wait, Pa. I forgot something." Todd pulled an envelope from his pocket and passed it to his father. "This came for you today."

Cole opened the envelope and scanned its contents. "Well, I'll be."

"What is it?" Jackie asked.

Cole smiled at her, then turned his attention to Chief Byron. "You remember those stories I wrote about you, Chief?"

"I do."

"They want to publish them." Cole's smile revealed his pleasure at this news.

"You're a writer?" Jackie asked, amazed all over again by this man she loved. "That's wonderful, Cole."

"The publisher bought the whole series, and they want to see anything else I write." He pulled a check from the envelope and his eyes glittered. Glancing from Todd to Jackie, he said, "*Now* we're going to Oregon."

Todd and Jackie danced around in a circle, and Chief Byron joined them. Cole laughed and put the check and letter back in the envelope.

"Chief, how would you like to come with us to

Oregon?" Cole asked, and they all stopped dancing to stare at the chief.

The old Indian appeared thoughtful, then he said, "I remained here after my people left because my pride would not permit me to leave my homeland. Pride does not keep a man from being lonely." He drew a deep breath. "When you came here, I had family again. When you leave, I will be old and alone. Yes, I will go with my white family."

Todd and Jackie both hugged Chief Byron, and Cole shook the old Indian's gnarled hand. "I'm glad," he said. "Real glad."

"We all are," Jackie said. "So let's get married, big guy."

"I'll let the preacher know we're here." Cole stopped in the doorway and smiled. "I'll bet I could write a whole book about Lolita Belle and the people here. Maybe I'll call it *The Legend of Devil's Gulch.*"

A wave of dizziness washed through Jackie.

Cole held the envelope out to her. "Hold on to this for me?"

"Sure." She took the envelope and scanned the address.

C. R. Morrison
General Delivery
Devil's Gulch, Colorado

A few incredible minutes later, Jackie walked down the aisle of the small church on Chief Byron's arm. She exchanged vows with Cole as if living a dream, though she had to laugh when her promise never to sing again was part of the vows. Finally the minister said, "You may kiss the bride."

Yes, a dream. A wondrous, delicious dream.

Cole pulled her into his arms and covered her mouth with his. She kissed him with all the love burning in her heart and soul.

"Are you happy?" he asked as their lips parted.

She nodded and smiled up at him. "Yes, more than I ever believed possible."

"Can you wait until after we're in Oregon for a proper honeymoon?"

Todd said, "Ewwwwww."

Chief Byron chuckled.

Jackie sighed and said, "Every day will be a honeymoon with you, big guy, but forget that 'proper' business."

Cole's eyes glittered. "I guarantee it."

"Good," she said, heading down the aisle with her husband and new family. As they stepped into the evening together, she sighed.

"I hope that's a happy sound," Cole said, squeezing her hand. "As long as it isn't singing."

"I promise. I have everything now—a man who loves me, a son." She smiled at a blushing Todd, then looked at Chief Byron. "And, if you're willing, maybe you can be the father I've never known."

Chief Byron's eyes widened. "You honor me, Miss Jackie."

"Thank you, and no more of that squaw business, Chief."

Chief Byron, Cole, and Todd all laughed, and Jackie sighed, meeting her husband's loving gaze.

"Yes, I have it all," she said. "And now I even know how that script ends."

ABOUT THE AUTHOR

Deb Stover's novels have appeared on bestseller lists, and she's received several awards for her unique work, including both the 1999 and 1997 Pikes Peak Author of the Year, a 1998 Heart of Romance Readers' Choice Award, three *Romantic Times* nominations, several *Affaire de Coeur* Readers' Choice Awards—including 1996's Romance Novel of the Year and 1997's Best Time Travel. Four of her first six novels received *Romantic Times* magazine's coveted "Top Pick" rating, and *Publishers Weekly* called her "clever, original, and quick-witted." Her first eight novels are time-travel, historical, and contemporary romances for Kensington Publishing Company.

For more information, visit her home page at:

http://www.debstover.com/